THE
IRONCLAD ALIBI

The Harrison Raines Civil War Mysteries
by Michael Kilian

MURDER AT MANASSAS
A KILLING AT BALL'S BLUFF
THE IRONCLAD ALIBI

THE
IRONCLAD ALIBI

A HARRISON RAINES CIVIL WAR MYSTERY

Michael Kilian

BERKLEY PRIME CRIME, NEW YORK

THE IRONCLAD ALIBI

A Berkley Prime Crime Book
Published by The Berkley Publishing Group,
a division of Penguin Putnam Inc.,
375 Hudson Street, New York, New York 10014.

Visit our website at
www.penguinputnam.com

First edition: January 2002

Library of Congress Cataloging-in-Publication Data

Kilian, Michael, 1939–
    The ironclad alibi / Michael Kilian.
        p. cm.
    ISBN 0-425-18325-4 (alk. paper)
    1. Raines, Harrison (Fictitious character)—Fiction.   2.
United States—History—Civil War, 1861–1865—Fiction.
    3. Richmond (Va.)—History—Civil War, 1861–1865—Fiction.
I. Title.

PS3561.I368 I76 2002
813'.54—dc21

                                                    2001036854

PRINTED IN THE UNITED STATES OF AMERICA

10   9   8   7   6   5   4   3   2   1

Acknowledgments

My thanks to Ann McMillan, Ernie Cox, John S. D. Eisenhower, William Seale, and Marc Pachter for their help and/or encouragement in the creation of these books. My deep appreciation to Gail Fortune and Dominick Abel for their splendid guidance and assistance. I am grateful to my wife, Pamela, and my sons, Eric and Colin, as only they can know.

FOR ROMA DOWNEY

And a lovely Richmond day

Author's Note

THIS is a work of fiction. Harrison Raines, Louise Devereux, Palmer and Arabella Mills, Caesar Augustus, and Joseph Leahy, among others, are fictional characters. The goal here, though, is to present their story as part of a significant chapter in Civil War history—the battle of the Ironclads *Virginia* and *Monitor*—and to do so as authentically and accurately as possible. Elizabeth Van Lew was a very real and heroic person. Nestor Maccubbin, Captain Godwin, and their Plug Uglies were just as real. As best as I can determine— from Davis's inauguration to the destruction of the USS *Cumberland* and USS *Congress*—events unfolded as depicted here.

Michael Kilian
McLean, Virginia

Chapter 1

As they turned their rain-wet, road-weary horses into Richmond's Main Street near the center of the Confederate capital that cold and miserable February morning, Harry Raines's black manservant Caesar Augustus of a sudden commenced singing "Dixie."

He had an excellent baritone and sang the tune with great brio, causing several of the many pedestrians on the sidewalk to stare. And, prompting his companion, a Virginia planter's son and now Union federal agent, to wonder if the emotional and mental strain of being back in this city had proved too much for the former slave.

"Den I wish I was in Dixie, Hoo-ray, Hoo-ray!

"In Dixie land I'll take my stand, to lib and die in Dixie.

"Away, away, away down South in Dixie. Away, away, away down South in Dixie!"

Harry smiled at the onlookers politely, feeling foolish, hoping these Richmond folk would think that in Caesar Augustus he was blessed with an example of that very rare slave who found happiness and contentment in the bondage that the South was fighting to uphold in this awful war, now in its second year.

But few seemed so persuaded. More than one eyed Caesar Augustus with apprehension, as though he might be a loon, and dangerous. What black man could be so cheerful in such a time?

Cheerful or no, Caesar Augustus was quite sane—and no slave. Harry had seen to that—in this very city—several years before, well in advance of the guns at Sumter.

Very dark in color, the black man had been born into servitude at Belle Haven, the sprawling James River plantation that had been in Harry's family for four generations. He'd been one of more than a hundred Negroes belonging to Harry's father, now a Confederate colonel serving with General James Longstreet.

Only a few months apart in age, and lacking any other companions on the large plantation save Harry's older brother, the two had been friends since early childhood. Acknowledging the relationship, Colonel Raines had spared the young African the life of a field hand, to which his large size and unusual strength had commended him. Instead, upon Harry's twenty-first birthday, the Colonel had given his youngest son Caesar Augustus as a present, to do with as he might, thinking this a kind and magnanimous gesture.

The very next day, Harry had hurried Caesar Augustus into Richmond and secured the emancipation papers required for his freedom. For this, Harry and his father had nearly come to blows, and might have done, if Harry had not then and there left the family and taken up residence in Richmond, signifying his profound dislike of "the Peculiar Institution" on which his family's wealth had for so long depended.

Eventually, he crossed the Potomac and settled in Washington City. Caesar Augustus did the same.

Now, they were returning, in a good cause but in probable folly. This had become a war of vicious, consuming passions, especially in the Confederate capital. They could forfeit their lives for this homecoming. The Rebel government had taken to hanging captured spies publicly at the Richmond fairgrounds on the western edge of town, and it hadn't been particular about the evidence used to convict them.

Harry was well qualified for the noose. He was on a mission for the Secret Service recently organized by the former railroad detective Allen Pinkerton, a mission requested by President Abraham Lincoln himself.

The Confederates were at work on a monstrous weapon—an iron-sided ship believed to be invulnerable to enemy shell and shot. Little was known about it, but much was rumored. It was feared the vessel would be able to destroy or push aside the Union's blockading squadron on Chesapeake Bay—and then steam all the way up to the Potomac and pummel Washington at its leisure. With the North's defeats at Bull Run and Ball's Bluff the year before, spirits were at a low ebb. This sailing fort could spark a panic of disastrous proportions.

Help was said to be on the way, though Harry had no idea what that could possibly be. In the meantime, Lincoln and Pinkerton wanted to know how close the Confederate vessel was to ready, how well it was armed and worked, its strengths and weaknesses, and what the Confederate government intended to do with it.

This was a lamentably tall order. Harry knew a lot about boats; little about ships. He was going to need some significant help, and this his black companion was not now providing.

Caesar Augustus had volunteered to accompany Harry, in the guise of slave and servant. He was well aware of the dangers attendant upon this adventure. His behavior now was mystifying.

Harry pulled up his coat collar and down his broad-brimmed hat, slouching forward in his saddle and pretending at first not to hear as Caesar Augustus returned to the refrain. "Away, away, away down South in Dixie . . ."

This had to stop. Harry turned to evidence his displeasure with what he hoped would be taken for a steely glare. This was not easily managed, as he was near of sight and was not wearing his spectacles.

He could see well enough, though, to note that Caesar Augustus was grinning broadly at him in response.

"Have you abandoned all sense, Sir?" Harry said.

"Ise jist tryin' to be a good darkie, Marse Harry. Show ma deep and abidin' loyalty to de glorious South and its noble cause."

The servile dialect was a further irritant. In serious contravention of Virginia law, Harry had over the years educated Caesar Augustus to a level of literacy approximating his own. The man could quote whole passages from Shakespeare. This "darkie" talk was mockery.

"You are already in Dixie, Sir," Harry said. "You needn't sing about wishing to be here. You've no more wish to be here than do I."

"Yet here we be."

"Then let's get on with this, so that our departure may come the sooner. You risk more than our lives with your tomfoolery, Caesar Augustus. I would remind you of our purpose here."

The grin disappeared. "I'm sorry, Marse Harry."

"An apology is not necessary. A little more caution here is."

"Yessir, Marse Harry. From now on, you won't hardly know I'm here."

Harry looked back to the thoroughfare before them, noting crowds of people crossing it in the far distance. They seemed to be heading for the hill on which stood the neoclassical capitol building, once solely Virginia's but now the Confederacy's. Even in this soggy drizzle, it loomed majestically over this scrubby little industrial city. They had started construction of a new dome for the hilltop U.S. Capitol in Washington City, but until its completion, the Southern ediface would seem the grander thing. Thomas Jefferson had been a poor president, in Harry's judgment, but was a splendid architect.

He wondered at the great numbers of people accumulating there in such a cold and wet inclemency. Perhaps there was some momentous news being announced. A Union general out west named Grant had been advancing on the Confederate bastions of Fort Henry and Fort Donelson in Tennessee, last Harry had heard. Other Union forces had invaded the coast of North Carolina. He feared the Federals might have suffered some reverse or disaster and that all these people had come forth to publicly rejoice.

But then, the disaster might just as easily have been one befalling the South. He thought of asking someone on the street, then thought better of it, not wanting to draw that much attention to himself.

A squadron of resplendent Confederate cavalry, wearing better uniforms than Harry had seen on a Southern back in months—or a Northern one, for that matter—came trotting out of a side street of a sudden, turning so closely they almost drew Harry and Caesar Augustus into their formation. A few of the horsemen glanced at them as they passed by, mostly in appreciation of Harry's horse, but the troop continued without pause, spurs and sabers jangling. One rider at the rear looked Harry's way again, with some curiosity, receiving a quick and deferential nod in response.

The troop moved on.

As they neared Ninth Street, the crowd became even thicker, the people all in a general press toward the capital grounds. Someone among them—it was a woman's voice—of a sudden called out Harry's name.

He snapped his head in that direction, but could see no one he knew—no one, at least, whose features he could make out without his spectacles. There was the blur of a woman's face turned his way. A blue bonnet and cloak. Riding on a few paces further, Harry pulled forth his spectacles and quickly set them in place. By the time he looked again, the lady had vanished.

"Did you see who that was?" he asked Caesar Augustus.

"Yes," said Caesar Augustus.

Band music could be heard ahead.

"Well, who was it?"

"A woman."

"That much I could tell. What woman?"

"A woman with a Confederate officer. I stopped lookin' when I noticed that."

Harry reined his horse to a halt, looking carefully among the throng this time but recognizing no one. He idly ran his hand over his jaw. He wore no beard, only a longish, cavalier's moustache, which was now soaked with rain. He feared he must look more like some saddle tramp than a Virginia gentleman.

"Where are they?" he asked, quietly.

"Guess they've gone." Caesar Augustus moved his horse ahead of Harry's. "Hope they've gone."

Filling the street, the crowd had fully blocked the way. Harry could see people swarming up over the capitol's wide, sloping lawn.

He'd been happily anticipating the warm comforts of Richmond's Exchange Hotel—the cheery fire that would be blazing in the main lobby, the reviving whiskey to be had in the hotel's pleasant bar—for nearly all the days they'd been on the road. But now he decided that would have to wait.

Abruptly turning his horse left, he proceeded back one block, then started up Eighth Street toward Broad and the top of the hill. When they were clear of the crowd, Caesar Augustus came alongside him.

"Thought you wanted to go straight to our hotel, Marse Harry."

"I think it best we establish our bonafides now, without delay," Harry said. "We'll go directly to the president's house and call upon Mr. Davis. That should preclude a great many questions people might have."

"Still think that's a damn fool idea."

"President Davis is my father's friend."

"Maybe so, but are you? And what are they going to think about your horse?"

The mount, a bay gelding, had a military saddle set upon a U.S. Army blanket bearing a major general's stars. Harry's coat covered much of this suspicious tack, but when he dismounted, it would occasion some notice.

"Only a few blocks more," he said.

Away from Main, the streets were largely deserted. At the next intersection up the hill, they stopped for a rumbling farm wagon, remaining in place as they took note of a carriage approaching behind it, the driver hunched over his knees with an oilskin draped about his shoulders. A woman peered at Harry from behind the leather window curtain.

This face he knew. It had been a few years since he'd looked upon her, but he recognized her at once.

She was pale and drawn, and blonde of hair beneath her bonnet. Her eyes, which fixed on him, were an extraordinary bright blue. The curtain dropped back in place as the coach went by.

"Miss Van Lew!" he cried.

The carriage rolled on along the street a few feet more, then stopped. The pale face reappeared.

"Harrison? Harrison Raines?"

He quickly moved his horse to the carriage's side. She was a pretty lady for her years, but wan, and very serious. Her voice was as musical as he remembered, but had lost its joy. She seemed to speak from a deep well of melancholy.

"Harrison Raines I am, Miss Van Lew," he said, bowing in the saddle with a sweep of his dripping hat. "At your service."

She came from one of Richmond's wealthiest and most socially prominent families, though her mother was from Philadelphia and her late hardware merchant father came originally from New York. With the war, the Van Lews were doubtless now considered pariahs. Elizabeth had never married, and was now over forty—about the same age as the notorious Rose Greenhow, the Confederate spymaster in Washington who'd been found out and jailed.

"Why are you in Richmond?" Miss Van Lew asked, as though amazed by his presence. "You went North. Why would you come back here?"

Harry had prepared an elaborate, all-purpose answer to that query, but it would be of little use with this lady. She knew where his true sympathies lay in this war.

"Personal business, Miss Van Lew."

She studied him a moment. She was extremely intelligent, he recalled, and seemed to be making some assessment about him. Nervous suddenly, she glanced quickly up and down the street.

"How did you get through the lines?"

"With difficulty."

"I would speak further with you, Mr. Raines. And soon. But this is not the place or circumstance. I've just come from my farm and must get home." She paused. "Can you call upon me this evening? You remember the house?"

"Yes, of course. On Church Hill. Grace Street. Across

from St. John's, where Patrick Henry made his speech."

"He demanded liberty," she said, derisively. "But he offered none to his slaves."

"He was my father's hero. Not mine."

She smiled, looking oddly a little daft.

"Later, then, Mr. Raines. I shall be most happy to see you. Supper will be at eight o'clock."

He tipped his hat. "That's most kind of you."

"The invitation extends to the gentleman traveling with you," she said. "Come to the rear of the house. I don't know the nature of your 'personal business,' but it will do you no good to have people suspect we are friends."

The window curtain fell, and the carriage moved on, attaining some speed.

He would be discreet, but he expected she would prove a useful friend. He had scant other in this city of his youth.

"Who is that woman?" asked Caesar Augustus, pulling his horse close to Harry's.

"You never met her, but she knows about you. Her name is Elizabeth Van Lew, and I daresay at this moment she is the only publicly avowed Abolitionist to be found in Richmond."

The black man stared after the moving coach. "Then she's a mighty dangerous person to be around," he said.

"Everybody's dangerous here," was Harry's reply.

THE Confederate President's House on Twelfth Street sat atop a hill as high as the one supporting the capitol. Unlike Mr. Lincoln's grand official residence in Washington, it was not a very imposing structure—four stories tall, but otherwise an ordinary house fronting a gravel court, with adjoining stable and standing very close to the street.

Two Confederate soldiers loitered on the gravel, while

another pair stood more ceremoniously to either side of
the steps leading to the high, first floor main entrance.
Three civilians, all dressed in black and smoking cigars
on the steps, eyed Harry and Caesar Augustus with some
curiosity.

But Harry was not challenged until he reached the door.

"I'm calling on the president," he said to the soldier
who stepped in his path. "I'm Colonel Raines's son, Harrison Raines."

The soldier grinned. "You want to see President Davis?
Don't you know what day this is?"

Harry stood stupidly for a moment, then shook his
head.

"It's Inauguration Day," the soldier said, as though to
a child. "He's down there at the Capitol, taking his oath
of office."

Harry felt immeasurably stupid. He was, according to
an oath he had sworn in Washington, a captain in the U.S.
Secret Service—a scout, for want of a better term for what
he did. Yet somehow it had escaped his notice that the
very head of the Confederacy was being formally invested
in that office on what was likely the most public occasion
Richmond had ever staged. "Major Allen," as Allan Pinkerton clandestinely styled himself, would not be amused
at this incompetence. He might wonder if Harry ought not
be reassigned to a task more in keeping with his abilities—such as cleaning stables.

"I've only just arrived in Richmond," Harry said, at
length. "Been on the road a long while, and haven't read
any newspapers."

That was true. They'd taken a circuitous route, avoiding
population centers and troop encampments, arriving at the
Southern capital from the west, not the road south from
Fredericksburg.

"Where'd you come from?" the soldier asked.

"Western Virginia." That was also the truth—if not all of it.

"They ain't got newspapers in Western Virginia?"

Harry decided it was time to fall back on his dignity. This was the South. Harry was, by birth at any rate, a member of what so pretentiously called itself the "Tidewater chivalry."

He stepped back a half pace, drew himself up fully, and presented the soldier with one of the elegant visiting cards he had prepared for this mission.

"My respects to His Excellency," he said, trying to muster sufficient pomposity. "Please inform him that Mr. Harrison Raines has arrived in the capital and will be staying at the Exchange Hotel, where I await his pleasure. In the meantime, I am leaving him this gift."

"Gift?"

Harry indicated the horse he had arrived upon, with a grand sweep of his arm. "This excellent mount, sir—late in the possession of Major General Joseph Hooker."

"Hooker, the Yankee general?" The man's expression reflected equal measures of amazement and dark suspicion.

"Indeed. The very one. I borrowed the mount. I now contribute him to the Confederate cause."

Without further word, he went to where Caesar Augustus stood with the two horses, asking him to remove his saddle bags from Hooker's bay and deliver the animal into the hands of the soldier. The private took the reins uncertainly.

"My thanks to you, sir," Harry said, swinging into the saddle of Caesar Augustus's mount. "My compliments."

"But . . ."

Harry gave the man no opportunity for further comment, spurring the animal he'd borrowed from his manservant into a quick trot out of the courtyard. The black man followed, trotting along unhappily, glowering at Harry with no small displeasure when he finally reined to a stop at the next corner.

Slipping out of the saddle, Harry dropped to the dirt street. They were on a prominence that looked down upon the Capitol and the masses of people spread over the lawn and square below it. Davis's words, if he was on the rostrum speaking them, did not carry to Harry's ears, but the crowd was being held in thrall by something.

"I think we have established our bonafides," said Harry.

"Marse Harry? Sometimes I think you are the craziest man there is."

"I would ask you to suspend that judgment until we're done here." He reached into a pocket of his coat, removing a leather bag and, from it, five $20 gold pieces.

"If you would, sir," Harry continued, "go to Sloane's stable, if it's still there, and buy me a replacement horse and saddle. Then bring it and this animal to the Exchange, secure my rooms, and wait for me there."

"You gonna start now on what we came down here for?"

"Presently, Caesar Augustus. Presently."

Happy to be stretching his legs, despite the rotten weather, Harry turned and started walking toward Seventh and Broad Streets and the Marshall Theatre—in hopes of finding there an actress he'd last looked upon sleeping prettily on a counterpane in this city in the heat of the preceding summer.

Chapter 2

HARRY knew very well that, as one of the Confederacy's leading espionage agents, Louise Devereux probably had it in her power to have him arrested and, for all he knew, shot or hanged on the spot. In extremis, he supposed, he could seek the intervention of his well-born, Confederate colonel father, and upon his family's long-standing friendship with President Davis. But even that might not suffice to overcome the connections and influence to be wielded by a woman of such abundant wiles, attractions, and local celebrity.

Still, theirs had been an amicable and, for a time, even intimate relationship while she was residing in the Federal capital, and there was a chance she might be willing to resume their friendship. It was he who had brought her through the Union lines to Richmond when there was a price upon her head in Washington. Even spies were occasionally grateful.

However she was inclined toward him, he doubted he could accomplish much without her. He'd made a list of people it was imperative for him to meet during this visit, and Louise's name was at the top of the list.

She was not as accomplished an actress as her erstwhile

friend, the British-born Caitlin Howard, long the object of Harry's unrequited adoration. But, in her time upon the Washington stage—before she'd been publicly accused as a Confederate spy—the raven-haired, New Orleans-born Miss Devereux had been universally held to be the most beautiful lady to grace the theater in the Federal City. It was an attribute that had served her extremely well in both her careers.

With Louise, though, one could never count upon much of anything—except charm, quick wit, and devilishly clever deceit. And a willingness, when necessary, to kill her fellow human beings. She'd murdered a politically well-connected Union officer when he'd threatened to reveal her true wartime occupation.

Harry had been told by Caitlin Howard that Louise was working at the Southern capital's Marshall Theatre, but hurrying to that fondly remembered establishment now, he was stunned to find a burned out ruin. An inquiry made of an old vagrant near the premises produced the explanation that the management had staged a melodrama called *The Old Log Fort* that featured a realistic battle scene complete to the firing of a cannon. On a cold January night a few weeks before, the presentation had become entirely too authentic when some gunpowder had accidentally ignited. No serious injuries were reported from the fire and explosions that had resulted, but they'd left the place largely rubble.

The vagrant directed him to the city's Richmond Varieties Theatre, at Franklin and Fourteenth, where he said Louise had quickly been hired and the February bill rescheduled to permit the staging of a play that would accommodate her—a popular Irish-set drama by Dion Boucicault called *Colleen Bawn.*

As he walked to his new destination, following a route that led him through the main commercial district, Harry was struck by the high prices proclaimed by the window signs. Coffee had risen to $1.50 a pound—ten times what it had been when he'd been living here. Apples were $20 a barrel!

The North was being victimized by unscrupulous manufacturers and wholesalers who sold shoddy goods to the military to reap enormous profits. The South was at the mercy of profiteers and smugglers—and vile, greedy merchants who charged a fortune for basic necessities.

Of course, the North would be blamed for all that. The Union blockade was proving to be Mr. Lincoln's most effective counter to the rebellion. The Federal navy now controlled virtually all of Chesapeake Bay, including the approaches to the Virginia capes and the estuaries of the James and York Rivers. Though Confederates had seized the U.S. Navy's big Gosport base at Norfolk at the start of the war, the Union still held mighty Fortress Monroe across Hampton Roads from it. A Yankee fleet had just penetrated the barrier reefs of North Carolina's Outer Banks and was moving against the nests of blockage runners operating from the sheltered waters of Pamlico and Albermarle Sounds, with Roanoke Island the principal target. The Union stranglehold on this part of the Confederacy was unbreakable.

For now.

The streets Harry followed gave glimpses of Richmond's wide James River. It was scarcely navigable this far upstream, and the fall line was visible in a series of rapids between the city's main bridges. But downstream, somewhere beyond the mists of the rainy February gloom, lurked a monster thought to be capable of brushing the blockade aside as one might crumbs from a tabletop, a monster that had already begun to unnerve the more timid residents of Washington City, though they knew few if any facts about it.

Harry's job was to discover those facts—and soon. He quickened his step.

"I know you," said the drunken actor who greeted him just within the theater's stage door. "You're Harry Raines. What the devil are you doing here? I thought you turned Yankee and went North."

The poor old fellow's better days were not only long behind him, but hadn't amounted to that much in his prime. His specialty was pathos. He was a popular Polonius, if only because audiences were so pleased to have Hamlet run him through. Then, rather than simply expire behind the arras, he'd stagger forth, clutching his belly and bulging his eyes, moaning and wailing, tottering about the stage, and, given his usual state of inebriation, nearly toppling off it. Once Caitlin Howard, playing Gertrude in that scene, had lost patience and tripped him with that end in mind.

The South was likely now short of actors, as it was everything else, so the drunken man was likely enjoying unusual favor among theater managers, if not audiences. Certainly he seemed able to afford drinking a better grade of whiskey—Old Overholtz '58, Harry's favorite tipple. How this got through the Atlantic blockade or the Union lines to the North was an interesting question.

Harry had always enjoyed the company of theater folk. When he'd lived in Richmond before the war, he'd bought this man countless numbers of drinks in recompense for his amusing backstage stories.

Inviting Harry further within, the actor moved to the throne that was the centerpiece of the set occupying the stage, wielding his whiskey bottle as though it was a scepter.

"I've not gone Yankee," said Harry, after declining a

sip. "I've come home. The prodigal son—with his slave."

"Then I'm disappointed in you, Raines. I've got no love for the darkies, but by God I cannot abide this abominable institution which regards them as mindless beasts." He drank, straight from the bottle, then fixed Harry with his bleary gaze, and smiled. "How fares the fair Caitlin?"

Harry was often reminded in this rude fashion that he was not the only man bearing affection for Miss Howard. Her own passions, alas, were directed at a man Harry thoroughly despised.

"Haven't seen her for a while," Harry said. "She's traveling with John Wilkes Booth, who's on a grand tour of sorts. Last I heard, they were in Cincinnati."

"Have no respect for that man," said the actor. "Nothing but a gymnast. Never be the actor his father was."

Indeed, no one on an American stage had yet shown himself the equal of the late and very great Junius Brutus Booth, though his son Edwin, John Wilkes's brother, showed considerable promise.

And was a Lincoln man.

"Where is Louise Devereux?" Harry asked.

"Ah, Louise. Many a man asks that question these days." He drank. "But as she is not with me, I cannot answer your query with any certainty."

"Would you tell her I have returned to Richmond and would be pleased to call upon her? And, if it's agreeable to her, would she be so kind as to send word to the Exchange Hotel, where I am staying?"

"Swounds, Raines. You do put on airs. At all events, I don't know when I can get your message to her, as there is no performance tonight—on account of the great presidential occasion."

"The Exchange Hotel," Harry said, and quickly took his leave.

* * *

He had intended to go to his rooms, presuming Caesar Augustus had attended to their arrangement. But every turning in this once familiar city produced something well remembered, or something foreign and new, and so distracted him. Harry found himself stunned by the proliferation of brothels along Cary Street, extending almost to Capitol Square—their inhabitants perched in windows or lounging in doorways despite the rain. There was a whorehouse established even opposite the hospital at Tenth and Main, with a few of its inmates bold enough to open windows and call to him tauntingly. The great occasion on the capitol lawn had doubtless deprived them of customers for the day—though Harry assumed the lack would be made up for that night.

Washington City was suffering from the same explosion of corruption, moral and fiduciary, but the provost marshal's office there was at least containing it—confining such activity largely to the area south of Pennsylvania Avenue. Richmond, which had prided itself so much on its refinement and respectability, seemed hardly to care.

Win or lose, this war was going to bring the South something more than independence. In the end, it might not recognize itself at all.

He had always been fond of this old Southern City, despite the hateful institution it fostered. Before the war, Richmond had been a much more substantial city than the Federal capital. The outbreak of hostilities and Richmond's new prominence as center of the Rebel government had made it a more busy and lively place, but beyond all the earnest bustle, there was an unsettling, almost morbid grimness to it. He wondered if he should want ever to live here again.

It seemed curious that, six months after her escape from

Washington, Louise Devereux was still residing in this town—as a Southern spy would have little useful work to do in these environs. She might more logically have been sent West to do her mischief, where she was less well known.

Harry, however, was precisely where he ought to be.

Avoiding the capitol grounds, Harry decided to take the opportunity to range further and take note of where the Confederate government had situated various of its departments and military facilities. He needed to make contact with someone involved with the Confederate Navy, but he could recall no one among his old friends and acquaintances so situated.

Perhaps Miss Van Lew would have some ideas.

THERE was a crowd of citizenry, mostly men in both military and civilian dress, gathered outside the Exchange when Harry finally reached the hotel. The rain was drizzle now, and they paid it little mind. The formal ceremonies at the capitol lawn had concluded, giving way to more boisterous celebration. One imposing fellow, leaning against the entranceway with arms folded across his chest, looked not at all merry, however. He reminded Harry quite a bit of a colleague in Mr. Pinkerton's U.S. Secret Service named Boston Leahy.

"Are you Harrison Raines?"

"I am, Sir." Harry didn't recognize the man.

"What's your business here?"

"I'm staying at the hotel."

"You had your Negro register."

"No, I had him bring my bags here. I'm going to register now."

"He put your name in the registry. Where'd he learn to write?"

"He was a house servant on my father's plantation." Harry pulled himself up very straight again. "The Belle Haven Plantation. Whom am I addressing, may I ask."

The man leaned close. "Mark my name well, for you will not want to run afoul of me. It's Nestor Maccubbin and I am with both the State Guard and the municipal police. I work for Captain A. C. Godwin, the assistant Provost Marshal. On his orders, we have arrested six men this day."

"Spies?"

"Lincolnites. You didn't answer my question. Your business in Richmond."

"It was my home, and now I've returned to it."

"The registry says you are from Washington City."

"It was my home, and now I've fled from it."

"Fled?"

"I am wanted by the military authorities there."

"Anyone here who can vouch for you?"

"Yes."

"Who?"

"President Jefferson Davis."

Harry gave a quick, curt nod and moved on past the man into the hotel. The smoky lobby was crowded, but none there moved to impede him. When he looked back to the doorway, the Maccubbin man had vanished.

The desk clerk eyed him curiously, but treated him with courtesy. The rooms he'd been given included a large corner one, with windows looking out both over the street and toward the river. His luggage was there. Caesar Augustus was not.

HIS former slave was one of the most resourceful men Harry knew, so he decided to forego any serious concern and attend to his numerous grooming needs, starting with a hot bath and shave and concluding with clean clothes and a fresh cravat. This consumed the better part of an hour, during which Caesar Augustus persisted in his absence.

Standing before the mirror in his room, he decided he still looked the wealthy plantation owner's son he'd been when last resident of this city—an image that might serve him well. The Southern caste system was so deeply entrenched that "gentlemen" privates in the Confederate army often refused orders from officers of "common" origin. The spacious, elegant corner room he'd been given by the hotel management was testament that he continued to merit this kind of respect.

Harry didn't much cotton to these snobbish notions. The man he admired most in the United States of America—the country's president, Abraham Lincoln—was as "common" as they came, yet uncommon in all respects.

Pulling out his pocket watch, Harry at last began to fret about his missing friend. He knew how unhappy Miss Van Lew would be if he appeared without Caesar Augustus in tow. He supposed he'd soon have to go searching for him. The black man had numerous friends in Richmond—all slaves but for one freedman. They were largely quartered in the back lanes and alleys behind their masters' grand houses. It would be dark soon. Not the best time to go a wandering in the shadows.

He turned the gaslights up against the gathering gloom. The room boasted an elaborate chandelier. Its brightness was cheering.

Harry felt in need of more cheer than that. His traveling flask was still half full of whiskey. He went to where it stood upon the dresser and took a happy swig. He was contemplating another when there came a knocking at the door. Wondering if Caesar Augustus had forgotten to take a key—a most uncharacteristic lapse—he went to it.

"Where in blazes have you been?" he said, as he pulled the door open.

Caesar Augustus was not there. Instead, he found himself looking into the beautiful face of a very expensively dressed young woman with copper-colored curls and bright green eyes, who smiled radiantly and then flung herself into his arms.

It was not Louise.

Chapter 3

HARRY stepped abruptly back, stood helplessly flustered a moment, then moved quickly to shut the door behind her as she entered in a great flurry of hoop skirt and cape.

"Bella, are you mad?"

She came up against him again, lifting her chin in an assertive invitation to a kiss. When he did not respond, she at last turned away.

Her full name was Arabella Armstrong Mills. When they both were all of seventeen years of age, and she the belle of Charles City County, he had loved her with a passion that had consumed his every waking moment. Now he could respond to her only with alarm. She was married to his erstwhile rival, Palmer Mills, a young Tidewater aristocrat whose qualities included a ferocious tendency to jealousy and an ill-kept temper.

"You think I'm crazy, Harrison Raines? I was crazy to let you ride out of Richmond when you did, you foolish, foolish man."

She came toward him again, but he retreated farther, to the window that fronted the street, hoping she'd not be so brazen as to follow him there. Her behavior was not simply brazen, it was unthinkable—even lunatic. A respectable married woman did not call upon a man not her husband at his hotel room unless she wished immediately to shed both the "respectable" and the "married," even though in the Commonwealth of Virginia the latter required an act of the legislature.

"You had reason enough to let me go," he said. "Just as I had mine to leave."

"False reasons. Dumb reasons. No reasons, really." She looked about the room, her eyes lingering on the bed. "But all that's vanished now."

"It has?"

She came up to him again in a rush, close enough to take his hand and clasp it to the bodice of her dress. "You've come back to Richmond, and you do so in the service of the Cause. You've seen the light at last, Harry, and come back to me. And I am overjoyed."

"Bella, you presume . . ."

"My word, Harrison. You stole General Hooker's horse! You brought it to our president as an inauguration gift. What I presume, Sir, is that you have at last cast aside your foolish notions on the 'peculiar institution,' and have joined us in the struggle for our rights."

The reference was to slavery. Harry caught himself before indulging in an honest reply. It was his hatred of the institution that had driven him first from his father's home and then from Virginia. Bella's family owned nearly as many Negroes as did the Raines, and she had believed in slavery as passionately as Harry did not. "I've not expressed myself on that question."

Bella kept hold of his hand. "You need not, Harry. Your man Caesar Augustus himself proclaims that he has returned to a state of bondage, which he accepts as the price of remainin' your servant."

He could feel her breast rise and fall with her breathing. Her face was flushed.

"And how do you know that?" he asked.

"Because he came by my house and spoke those words to my face."

Still the Southern coquette Harry too well remembered, she dropped his hand and twirled away from the window, dropping herself into a red velvet armchair with a billow of skirt and petticoat. She affected a stern demeanor, but seemed to be enjoying the moment as might a little girl.

"He came to your house?" Harry said.

"He was sniffin' around my Estelle, like he was always doin' in the old days in such pesky fashion. I've come here to ask you to make him desist. To demand it. We're havin' enough trouble with our darkies as it is."

"Whatever your reason for coming here," Harry said, as gently as possible. "You should not have. A married woman, alone with another man in a hotel? Has the war changed Richmond that much?"

"It has changed me—and my marriage. Palmer is never home. Always at the Ironworks. Or at Norfolk. Feeding the Monster."

"What monster?"

"They haven't talked of it up in Yankeeland? They soon shall, if they haven't. It's that ironclad ship our Navy has built from the burned hulk of the *Merrimack* they refloated at Gosport. I am surprised that you don't know of it. Folks are sayin' the whole northern coast is terrified and that even Washington City is atremble."

"They greatly exaggerate." That could be said of any of Richmond's newspapers, and Washington's, too. "What has Palmer to do with it?"

"Why, he's the most important lieutenant in the Confederate States Navy right now. He has responsibility for producing the iron plate for the Monster. President Davis is truly pleased with his accomplishment, for the job is nearly done."

Mills's family were investors in the Tredegar Iron-works, the largest industrial complex in the Confederacy. Palmer was very knowledgeable about heavy metal. It was perhaps his only talent.

"Monster." Ironclad ship. Harry had come to the Confederate capital so uninformed he'd been ignorant of the fact that it was Jefferson Davis's inauguration day. Now, amazingly, here he was acquiring knowledge of precisely what he had come to learn all about, brought to him with a rustle of skirt.

But Bella could be a prattler, willing to say almost anything that might keep attention fixed on her.

"You should be more discreet, Madam," he said, knowing that any remonstration would only goad her to be more contrary.

"When have I ever been that, Harrison Raines? And don't call me 'Madam.' "

"You are a married woman. You should be with your husband."

"I'm never with him. And he's never with me. Anyway, Harry, I wasn't supposed to be with him in the first place. I was to marry you, as memory serves."

"We were younger then."

She rose, standing before him defiantly. "Are you saying I'm an old crone?"

"You definitely are not that."

"I saw you in the crowd today."

She'd been the one who called out his name. "Was that Palmer you were with? I couldn't see clearly."

"I'm not tellin' you who I was with."

"But it wasn't your husband?"

"I told you. He's busy all the time with the ironclad."

Harry would have to be leaving soon for Elizabeth Van Lew's.

"What do want of me, Bella? If you want me to chastise Caesar Augustus for importuning you, I shall. It was very bad manners to intrude upon your household like that. I will talk to him."

"I don't expect manners from Negroes, Harry. I do expect better manners from you—a gentleman belongin' to one of the First Families of Virginia."

He sighed. "I will call upon you, Bella, if you wish. At your house, in appropriate fashion."

She didn't budge from the chair. "If you think a rendezvous in a hotel is inappropriate, why would you be wantin' one in my home? What if Palmer was to return?"

"I would enjoy seeing him again."

"That, Sir, is a ridiculous lie!"

Sighing again, loudly, Harry went to the door and opened it. This was a rude and ungentlemanly gesture, but he had to gain control of the situation. "I will call upon you both, Bella."

She glared at him, bright fires gathering in her green eyes. He noticed someone waiting out in the corridor—a large, muscular black man, carrying a carpet bag. Harry thought at first it was Caesar Augustus, but, looking again, he saw that it was Arabella's coachman—an excellent horseman, whom he remembered from plantation days. Back then, the man had only been a groom.

There was someone behind him—a young black woman, Arabella's maid.

"I'm not going to leave it like this, Harrison."

"For now, you must."

Her eyes were very moist. "Please, Harry. Don't send me away."

"As I said, I'll come by. Where do you now reside?"

"Across the river in Manchester."

He bowed, keeping a hand on the knob of the open door. "As you wish."

At long last, she rose with a swirl of skirt, then marched past him, halting on the landing just outside the door. "When you do come, Harry, please leave that Caesar Augustus of yours behind."

"Bella. You've known him half your life. Why deride him so?"

"Because he's impudent. And a rascal. And I don't want him foulin' our stock."

"Stock?"

"My house servants."

"Last I looked, your Estelle was a human being. So is this gentleman in the corridor who's been so patiently waiting for you."

At last she was ready to retreat. "You're a fool, Harry."

He started to close the door. "Good day, Madam."

Her eyes were now ablaze.

"The damn Negroes, once again!" she said, loudly enough to be heard in the lobby downstairs. "Always the Negroes. All you care about, Harrison Raines, the damn Negroes. It's, it's unnatural!"

Another swirl of skirts, and she swept on down to the stairs, the heels of her pretty blue shoes thudding on the carpet as she descended. Her coachman gave Harry a quick look, his expression revealing nothing. Then he turned to follow.

Harry closed the door and bolted it, as though that futile act could make any difference. He'd handled this badly, ineptly. But had he been more receptive to her, he feared the encounter would have ended dangerously indeed.

He went to where he'd left his flask and took a calming swallow. Then he gathered up his coat and left his quarters, fearing he was late.

*   *   *

ASCENDING Church Hill by way of Broad Street, Harry walked past the imposing Van Lew house and continued on until he came to the end of the street. Pausing to light a cheroot, he stood there smoking a while, pretending to look down at the gas-lit city below while actually trying to ascertain if he'd been followed. Nestor Maccubbin, the Virginia State Guard agent, might prove a considerable nuisance—especially with all the attention Bella Mills's visit must have attracted.

But no one stirred. Not even a dog's bark disturbed the decorum of this geographical and social height. Dropping the little cigar and crushing it out, Harry retraced his steps. A wrought iron gate at the side of the Van Lew property opened onto a narrow lane that led to the rear. Harry took that path, crossing through the garden and announcing himself at the kitchen door.

He was greeted by two familiar faces. One was the dark, friendly countenance belonging to Mary Elizabeth Bowser, Miss Van Lew's maid, a comely and remarkably well mannered young lady.

The other face belonged to Caesar Augustus.

"Good evening, Sir," Harry said, as he stepped inside. "What a pleasant surprise to find you here. What a pleasant surprise to find you anywhere, as I'd no idea where you'd gone."

"I'se a free man, Marse Harry."

"You won't be for long if you insist on roaming around this city where your fancy takes you."

Miss Van Lew appeared in the far doorway, her expression a mixture of concern and confusion. "Mr. Raines, welcome. Is something wrong?"

Harry bowed, then stood very straight. "Hello Miss Van Lew. What's wrong is that my friend here went visiting where he shouldn't have—calling at the house of Palmer Mills."

"I don't need your permission, Marse Harry."

"That's not the point. They're a dangerous clan—and you riled his wife. She sought me out at the hotel to complain—after you told her where I was staying."

"Do you mean the Palmer Mills whose been put in charge of the ironclad project at Tredegar?" Miss Van Lew asked.

"Yes. They've made him a lieutenant in the Confederate Navy. He and I never liked each other much, but his wife and I are, uh, old friends."

His hostess seemed to flush a little. "Why don't we all go in to supper?" she asked.

THE dining room was large, with space enough at the table to seat twenty guests comfortably. Miss Van Lew took her place at the head, motioning Harry to sit at her right. He was surprised, though he realized he should not have been, when she then gestured to Caesar Augustus to take the chair on her left.

The black man hesitated, then did as bidden, treating the invitation as a command. With the exception of when he and Harry dined alone, Caesar Augustus was seldom a guest at a white man's table.

Miss Bowser took the chair next to him. An elderly Negro servant, however, remained standing—then moved on Miss Van Lew's signal to the sideboard to commence serving the first course.

Miss Van Lew nodded and smiled to Caesar Augustus, then turned to Harry. "Just how angry was Mrs. Mills—and why?"

It was Caesar Augustus, however, who made the reply. "I was visiting with her maid Estelle," he said, "She's an old friend. Mrs. Mills took exception to it. We had some harsh words."

"You're not her slave," Miss Van Lew said. "She has no right to be harsh with you."

Harry recalled that every African person in Miss Van Lew's household was free and paid generous wages—a Richmond anomaly that had sorely displeased the local society.

"Yes'm," said Caesar Augustus. "Mrs. Mills carried on like I was bent on doing something sinful with Estelle—but that wasn't why I went there. Anyways, it wasn't why I stayed there. Estelle told me about what Mr. Mills is doing for the Secesh navy. I thought I might learn something."

He was addressing these remarks directly to Harry, who glared at him sharply across the table. He'd sung "Dixie" in Richmond's most public street. He was blabbering aloud about their mission—to a woman he'd only just met. What next?

"Why did you come here to Miss Van Lew's house instead of to the hotel?" Harry asked.

"Mrs. Mills was so agitated, I feared the worst. Didn't want to go back to the hotel—thinking I might bring trouble with me. So I took some shortcuts I remembered, and here I be."

He'd been nervous and stiff after taking his seat, but now he relaxed a little.

Miss Van Lew, her blue eyes very bright even in the candlelight, remained serious, her gaze studious and fixed upon Harry. He returned the stare, until she at last broke the silence.

"Why are you in Richmond, Harrison Raines?" she asked.

He coughed, politely. "As I told you, some personal reasons. Family."

"Your mother has gone to her reward, and your father and brother are horse soldiering above the Rappahannock—with Longstreet, as I recall."

"That's true."

She took a spoonful of soup, pondering a thought. "Does this visit involve a woman?"

"In part." He was going to go looking for Louise Devereux the next morning.

"Mrs. Mills?"

"No, Ma'am. That encounter was entirely unexpected—and unwanted."

Another spoonful. "Shouldn't be. That woman can be a great help to us."

"Did you say 'us,' Miss Van Lew?"

She sat back, smiling sweetly. "After dinner, Harry, I should like to take a turn with you through the garden."

IT was very chilly in that place. Miss Van Lew had added only a woolen shawl to her ensemble, and was hatless. She was bone thin, and Harry worried for her health. Yet she gave the wretched weather no mind. Harry caught himself shivering and compelled himself to stop it.

They walked the path from one end to the other, Miss Van Lew chattering about life in Richmond before the war. Then, as she raised a finger to her lips, they fell silent, and remained that way, listening.

In this drizzle, not even night birds called out.

"I have a question for you, Harry. Before you left Washington, were you given certain times of day and place you might repair to here in Richmond if you had an urgent need for help from someone you could trust?"

Harry returned her stare, but, uncertain, could not bring himself to speak.

"Was the place not the Church Hill burying ground at St. John's and the times noon and midnight?" she continued.

There was no point in evading this any further. "Yes." He watched her carefully. "Were you the person I was to meet?"

"Me, or if necessary, someone to represent me."

"But for you to be in such a place after dark . . ."

She moved closer to him now, glancing about the shrubbery. "I was told they would be sending someone," she said, her voice only slightly above a whisper, "I'm so pleased it's you—and yet I fear for you. They're arresting people now on the slightest hint of treason. There's talk of hangings."

"I don't think I'm in much danger. I've been accused in the Northern papers of being a Southern sympathizer— and worse. I stole General Hooker's horse and made a gift of him to Davis. I'm home, as it were, and know a few who will vouch for me. I think I'll be all right as long as we stay in Richmond. It's getting out of here that may prove the problem."

"Yes. Always." She looked about them again, fixing her eyes finally on the lane that led to the street. "I need to know why they've sent you."

A sudden wariness came over him. He had learned at the near cost of his life that confiding in people outside of Mr. Pinkerton's immediate circle was a dangerous practice. But Miss Van Lew had been despised in Richmond for her Abolitionist sentiments for as long as he had known her. If he couldn't trust her, there was no one. "I'm here about the 'the Monster.' "

She looked about the shadowy trees as though such a creature might lurk there. "Monster? You mean the armored vessel?"

"It's what Mrs. Mills calls it," Harry said. "The ironclad

ship the Confederate Navy has constructed from the remains of the *Merrimack.*"

"Now called the *Virginia.*"

"Yes. I need to find out how close they are to completing her—and what their plans for her are."

She drew closer still. He wondered now if she were feeling the cold. "Harry. You are not alone in this pursuit."

"I don't doubt it. Washington is powerfully worried about this infernal machine. I think even Mr. Lincoln believes some of the wild tales going on about it. How it might steam up the Potomac and destroy everything in its path."

"They're all true," she said. "But it's said to have weaknesses as well."

It occurred to Harry they must look like two lovers in a bower, but for the drizzle—and the disparity of their ages.

"Whatever I am able to learn, I need to get the information to Fortress Monroe by the most direct means possible, so that it might be telegraphed to Washington and New York. Do you know a way?"

"Yes," she said. "Of course. But it's less easy than before."

"I'm uncertain how to proceed," he said. "I am yet unaware of any means at hand to accomplish what's required of me."

"You said you had this encounter with the wife of Palmer Mills."

"Yes."

"Did you once enjoy a close friendship with this lady?"

He saw where this turn of talk was leading and wished he could turn it back. " 'Friendship' is perhaps not the most appropriate term for it," he said. "Matters ended badly. I fear she accepted Mr. Mills's proposal of marriage for the wrong reason. And now . . ."

Miss Van Lew beamed. "And now the means you seek are at hand."

"No, no, Miss Van Lew. You don't understand. It's impossible. Mills is a bad tempered and jealous sort of man. What you're suggesting, I fear, would only increase the danger for us all. Besides, she and I quarreled in parting. She's a racialist—irredeemable."

"Harry, it's a heaven-sent opportunity. Her husband knows all there is to know about 'the Monster.' You must ingratiate yourself with them both as much as you can."

"No. I'd rather no further encounters with her. And anyway, Miss Van Lew, I doubt he'd receive me."

"But you must try. Lives, I think, will depend on it. Lives, and the cause of Father Abraham."

HARRY and Caesar Augustus walked back to the Exchange, taking a circuitous route that led down by the river. In marked contrast to his demeanor upon their arrival in Richmond, the black man mostly stayed silent, despite several attempts at conversation on Harry's part.

"Do you trust her?" Harry asked finally—and bluntly.

"Who?"

"Miss Van Lew."

"Only just met her."

Harry could see the lights of the Exchange ahead. The other buildings along the street were dark.

"I suppose what I'm asking is, do you trust her judgment?"

"Well, now, Marse Harry. Most of the time I don't trust yours. And I *know* you."

"This is not helpful."

They stopped. Caesar Augustus looked over his shoulder, then at Harry, then to the hotel, which was now looming up the sloping street. To the west, the increasing clatter of a carriage could be heard.

"I think I done all I can to help you today, Marse Harry. I'll be back in the morning to help you more."

The coach appeared, pulling to a stop in front of the hotel. It was military, with a small cavalry escort.

"You have your own quarters?" he asked.

The black man nodded. Both watched as an officer descended from the conveyance. Harry gathered he was of high rank, as he had several aides.

"Where?"

"With a friend."

Harry hesitated. "Caesar Augustus, we don't need more trouble."

"Sure don't. Got a whole city brim full of it all around us." He paused, then grinned. "Goodnight, Marse Harry. I'll be back at first light."

The weight of the hour was becoming heavy. Harry yawned. "Goodnight then."

THE loiterers and layabouts in front of the hotel happily did not include the menacing Nestor Maccubbin at this hour. Neither was he to be found inside, though there were a few in the crowded lobby Harry took to be police agents. Ignoring them, he went to the bar, ordered an Old Overholtz, finished it quickly, then returned to the lobby, starting for the stairs.

"Mr. Raines! Harrison Raines!"

Harry froze, half expecting someone bearing manacles, or a drawn revolver. He feared his mission was concluded. All his missions.

He turned slowly, to find the hotel manager hurrying toward him in a state of high excitement. He had something in his hand, which Harry hoped was not a weapon. "This came for you, sir," said the manager, handing Harry an envelope. "Not an hour ago."

"Thank you."

The man stood there. Harry ignored him, breaking the seal and removing the letter within.

After reading it twice—holding it close, as he'd neglected to put on his spectacles—he looked to see that the manager hadn't budged an inch.

"It's an invitation—to dinner," Harry said. The man simply stared. "Tomorrow night."

"Think of that," the other said. "The day after his inauguration. You must be somebody special."

Harry slid the envelope and invitation into the breast pocket of his coat, hard by his .44 caliber Derringer pocket pistol. "He's an old family friend," Harry said, turning back toward the stairs.

"So I see, Mr. Raines. Are your accommodations comfortable?"

"Yes. Thank you."

"I think you will find them quite comfortable tonight, sir. Quite comfortable indeed."

THE scent of perfume came to him the instant he opened the door to his suite of rooms. He thought at first the aroma must have lingered from Arabella's visit that afternoon.

But that seemed doubtful in the extreme.

Instead of turning on the gaslight in the sitting room, he went to the door of the bedroom, which was open. Taking his Derringer from his coat pocket, he paused, then put it back again. He had enough difficulties without adding accidental gunshots.

He had to get this annoying woman from this place at once—from his rooms and from the hotel. Harry sensed the worst possible scandal and the wreckage of his mission and plans, the whole imminent disaster waiting right there for him. Palmer Mills was the sort of man who would make the worst of any situation.

Why was Arabella so obsessed with him? They had parted, in no way amicably, years before. He'd not had a word from her since—until . . .

Stepping quietly into the bedroom, he went to the gas valve and struck a match, turning the light to its brightest and blinking in consequence.

The woman on the bed, murmured, stirred, then rolled over to look at him, her long, dark hair spread out upon the pillow. She smiled, and extended her arm in invitation. "Hello, Harry."

"Louise."

Chapter 4

"WHY do you look so stricken, Harry? Are you not glad to see me?"

Louise smiled, as prettily as when he'd last seen her perform in *Much Ado About Nothing*.

"Of course I am, but I would prefer a more seemly circumstance," he said.

She sat up, revealingly. "You? Embarrassed?"

He flushed, but it was not from embarrassment. "Let us say, distressed," he said.

Strands of her long, wild dark hair had fallen over her right eye. She tossed them back with a shake of her head, then leaned back slightly, invitingly.

"I do not know why you should be, Harry. You will recall that the last time we looked upon one another, it was in this very room, and I was in this very bed."

And in almost the very same position.

"I haven't forgotten, Louise. But, do believe me, the circumstance now is quite changed."

She put hand to brow and looked away, as though toward an audience. " 'Take, O take those lips away, that so sweetly were foresworn,' " she recited, " 'And those eyes, the break of day, Light that do mislead the morn;

But my kisses bring again, bring again; Seals of love, but seal'd in vain, seal'd in vain.' "

"What play is that from?"

"*Measure for Measure*, you clod. Was your mind elsewhere all those nights you've spent in the theater?"

"When you're on stage, Louise, I'm always much distracted."

He sank into the room's only chair. He'd put his flask in a coat pocket and now retrieved it for a welcome draught. The whiskey cheered him, but was no help as far as Louise was concerned. Her presence was dizzying.

"You say the circumstance has changed, do you mean you are no longer a Yankee spy?" she said, with mock theatrical anger. "That you no longer need to go around seducing innocent young Southern girls for the evil purposes of the despotic federal government?" she asked. Her smile became a wicked grin.

"Louise, you are a lady of surpassing beauty and many admirable talents, but 'innocent' is perhaps something of an exaggeration."

There was a sudden commotion outside on the street below—shouts, a horse whinnying, and the improbable sound of a baby crying. Then came the unmistakable unison thumps of soldiers in formation, marching away. Harry held back from rushing to the window. These days, odd noises in the street could mean absolutely anything, and little of it good. People were being dragged off to prison here in Richmond just as rudely as they were in the North. It would do no good to add his staring face to this tragic tableau, whatever it might be about.

"Harry, I asked if you were still a Yankee spy?"

He smiled, though not so wonderfully as had she. "I was never that, Louise."

"Oh? I have seen you with that dastard, Allen Pinkerton, have I not?"

"I have friends in the federal government is all. As did you—when you resided in the federal city. Caitlin Howard asked me to look after you, and so I did. It was necessary to make use of those friends. You might be dead now—certainly still in jail—if I hadn't."

"I'll grant you that is true. And I am grateful." She lay back upon the pillow. "But do you think the likes of Nestor Maccubbin and the Richmond Municipal Police would believe your long, many, and frequent associations with the Yankee Secret Service were just to help little old me?"

"I don't think that gentleman would believe anything I had to say."

"He's a disagreeable fellow, and I think would judge you a traitor, Harry, needing only the slightest crumb of proof to fetch the rope. I am grateful to you and won't betray you, but this makes you far more obliged to me than I to you."

"It's an honor and a pleasure to be obliged to you, Louise," he said, lying.

"Then tell me under who's auspices you return to Richmond."

"Auspices?"

"Why in hell are you here, in this increasingly desperate city?"

"I'm here under my own auspices, Louise. I'm homesick is all. And sick of the war. Life has been hard for me in Washington lately, as it has been for many Southerners. I've been accused of several crimes. The authorities do not trust me. Here, at least, I am among friends. Including you, I hope."

"You came prowling 'round the theater after me. What do you want?"

"Just to see you again—now I'm back in town."

"I do not know if I believe you."

"You can believe me. I wanted to see you."

"See me." She spread her arms wide, and then laughed, as loudly as though on the stage. The hotel was full, and she would be heard.

"Well, here I am for you to see, but with your eyesight, you'd best come closer."

Allen Pinkerton had picked the wrongest possible man in the U.S. Secret Service for this mission.

He rose, but came no nearer the bed.

Louise snuggled into the covers. "Turn out the lamp and come 'see' me in proper fashion, Harry."

"Louise . . ."

"It's a cold and miserable night, sir. You don't want to spend it in a chair."

He had to admit that he did not.

SHE did not leave his room until after sunrise—an indiscretion flagrant enough to have caused her to be run out of town or fired from the theater before the war. Now, it was as though she'd been issued a license to behave as she wished.

He lay in bed, thinking upon how much help or hindrance she might be to the accomplishment of his task. Before long, he was simply, dreamily, happily thinking of her.

Finally, he stirred himself to face the day, prodded to do so mostly by his annoyance over Caesar Augustus's tardiness. His continuing absences were poor service to the Union cause.

Unless he'd gotten himself into trouble—of which there was more than fair chance in this city.

Harry breakfasted, then went out onto the hotel's gallery, finding an empty chair and settling himself into it, glad of the warm, sunshiny day.

Years before, when barely fifteen, Harry had accom-

panied his father on a trip to Mississippi, where the elder
Raines was acquiring a part interest in a cotton plantation.

Harry's memories of that adventurous journey were
most vividly of smoky, cinder-spewing railroad trains,
magnificent white steamboats, and the great, broad rivers
of the West that dwarfed the Potomac and the James. He
remembered as well the vast plantation they'd gone to
see, an endless expanse of steamy green fields with an
army of slaves moving through them like so many in-
sects. The backs of those poor folk had looked so bent
and broken with their ceaseless labor one wondered if
they might ever straighten again. Yet on they had moved,
filling the long, canvas sacks they dragged behind them
through the long, hot day, receiving not a penny for their
effort.

Complementing that recollection was one of the main
street of Natchez, still something of a wild frontier town
back then, but for the foppish finery of the city's young
men of "society." These proud fellows were arrogant in
their idleness, lazing and loitering about the sidewalks and
verandas, each bearing his walking stick as though it were
a badge of high office. But for recurring visits to the taverns, they passed the entirety of their days in this manner,
swatting flies and yawning. Work was fit only for beasts
and Negroes. Exalting their indolence as proof of their
aristocracy, they were the most useless human beings
Harry had ever encountered.

But now, at ease in a chair on the gallery of the
Exchange here in Richmond, Harry emulated them in
every regard, complete to the affectation of a walking
stick, and a very genuine series of yawns.

Like their own George Washington, who was in the
saddle working his Mount Vernon farms from morn to
dusk even into the illness that killed him, Virginians were
a more industrious people than those of the deeper South.

Harry's father and brother had been just as busy about their place along the shore of the James.

But there were still slackers enough to be found here in the Confederate capital, despite the war and the government's impassioned call to arms for every able bodied man.

By joining these laggards, Harry hoped to make a self-defining statement. He'd been considered something of a wastrel himself upon first coming of age. When not gambling or racing horses, he was at the theater or reading books or strolling along the river with a pretty girl, if one would have him. Never had he taken a hand in the business affairs of the family plantation—though of course a far more compelling reason than laziness accounted for that.

But indolent is what he now wished to appear, and thus provide the curious with an explanation for aimless-seeming wanderings about the town. He wanted people to believe he had tired of having to support himself in the North and now wished only to live again off the Raines family fortune. Lies were often more readily accepted if they gave people a reason to think ill of a person.

The absurdly fanciful accounts of the battles of Manassas and Ball's Bluff Harry had read in newspapers both North and South had diminished his confidence in any of their reporting, and he considered them now a poor tool indeed for espionage. It amused him to think that the federal government had made it a crime to mail Northern newspapers to the Secessionist state. The information reported therein could only subvert the Southern cause with its wild exaggeration and inaccuracy.

But he sat reading the *Richmond Enquirer* now as a means of passing the time until Caesar Augustus's return, contenting himself with the knowledge that half-truths were preferable to none.

The very first story he read, however, seemed true enough—and alarming. He'd heard that Richmond had been put under some formal pronouncement of martial law, but hadn't realized it had gotten as bad as the dictatorship the Union Army was running in Baltimore. Here, too, anyone could be dragged off to prison on the slightest pretext.

"Yankee Spies," the headline read.

"Two Lincoln spies," the story began, "giving the names of John Scully and Pryce Lewis, were arrested at the Monument Hotel on Friday last, and are now in prison. The proof of their connection with the secret service of the enemy is most positive. They were recognized on the street by a young lady, whose baggage they searched in Baltimore, while she was on her way to the South. Suspecting that they were detective officers sent by the Yankee Government to Richmond, she communicated her suspicions to a young man, who gave information of the presence of the strangers at General Winder's office. The officers in pay of our Government were immediately put upon the track, and discovered them in a private house. Here the young man was introduced to their presence, much to the discomfort and chagrin of the guilty parties. They became so much confused that they hastened away to the Hotel, leaving their overcoats behind. They were followed and captured by the detectives. Both of them claim to be English subjects, and they are in reality native born Englishmen, and have claimed the protection of that Government. But this will avail them little, since it is clearly shown by evidence not prudent to detail in this place, that they are paid hirelings of the enemy."

Harry had been warmed by the sun but now felt quite chilled. He and his fellow Secret Service operative Joseph "Boston" Leahy had done some work in Baltimore, but

Harry could not recall a pair of Englishmen assigned as agents there. Of course, his master, Allen Pinkerton, preferred to keep his people as ignorant of each other as possible, lest a single arrest bring down an entire network.

He read on. Another story proclaimed: "Arrest of Honorable John Botts and Other Suspected Unionists!"

Now his flesh began to crawl in earnest. Was this some sort of sweep? Was no one safe—in particular, recently arrived gambling gentlemen from Yankeeland with a local history of antislavery sensibilities?

"The Honorable John Minor Botts was arrested at his residence on Broad Street near the city limits yesterday at the early hour of six a.m. by a detachment under command of Captain Godwin, assisted by detective Cashmeyer. Mr. Botts was very indignant when, after his house had been surrounded, he found himself called upon by the officers to accompany them to prison. The household of the prisoner appeared very much alarmed at the 'intrusion,' and his son became so much excited that he lost all consciousness and fainted. Immediately after his capture, Mr. Botts was carried in a buggy to the private jail of McDaniel's on Franklin Street, near Sixteenth, where he now remains."

Private jails? Of course, federal Detective Lafayette Baker of the Washington provost guard was operating much the same thing in the basement of the U.S. Treasury.

Harry continued.

"Frank Stearns, a wealthy distiller of Northern birth, was arrested at about three o'clock a.m. at 'Tree Hill,' his country residence on the banks of the James River, some three miles distant from the city. The house of this prisoner has been suspected to be a rendezvous for Lincoln sympathizers during the past one or two months. Its occupant is believed to have been in communication with the enemy and is known to have expressed sympathy for their cause. When captured he remarked, 'I suppose you take me because I am a Union man.' The officers replied that that was the reason, and added that they intended to arrest all of the same stripe in the city of Richmond, to which Mr. Stearns responded, 'Well, you'll have your hands full.'

"The distillery owned by the prisoner is located on Fifteenth between Main and Cary Streets. It, together with all its appurtenances, have been seized by order of the Government, and placed under guard."

Dropping the paper to the veranda floor, Harry abruptly stood up, overwhelmed by a sudden panic, looking up and down Pearl Street as if a squad of Confederate dragoons were about to ride up and snatch him.

There was only a brewer's cart, with horses laboring uphill, and a few pedestrians. His companions on the sunny porch hadn't even seemed to notice his sudden start.

He calmed himself and sat down, finishing the article.

"The arrest of Stearns was accomplished through the instrumentality of a detachment under Captain Porter, assisted by detectives Maccubbin and Clackner."

No wonder he hadn't been bothered or shadowed by Maccubbin that night. The gentleman was well occupied elsewhere.

There was more.

"In addition to the parties above-named, the following well-known residents of Richmond were also arrested: Valentine Heckler, a butcher; John M. Higgins, grocer; Burnham Wardwell, dealer in ice; Lewis Dove and Charles J. Mueller. These, too, were arrested at their residences, and confined with those first named in McDaniels's private jail."

Harry turned the page, pretending to read of other matters, but his mind was elsewhere. Pinkerton and Leahy had told him to repair to "Tree Hill" and seek the assistance of distiller Stearns if anything went awry. Oddly, they'd told him nothing of Elizabeth Van Lew, nor she of him.

Had they told Stearns to expect him?

Caesar Augustus at last appeared just shy of eleven a.m., dragging himself up the hill in the manner of someone ending a long journey. His head hung down a little, which was rare. Caesar Augustus was normally given to walking proudly and demonstrably erect, especially when in the company of white folk.

Lamentably, Harry would now be required to diminish that pride even more.

He waited until the black man had drawn near, then leapt to his feet.

"You damned wretch!" he shouted, for half of Richmond to hear. "Do you know the hour? Where in hell have you been?"

Caesar Augustus held back from a reflexive anger, but only barely. He was about to shout back at Harry—certainly not the first occasion he would have done so—but then hesitated; doubt and confusion clouding his gaze.

"Damn you!" said Harry, raising his walking stick in threatening fashion. "I asked you where you've been?"

The black man carefully mouthed his reply, so that it could be heard by no one but clearly understood by Harry, nearsightedness notwithstanding: "Don't go too far, Marse Harry."

With that, Harry lowered the stick to his side, looked carefully about them, then stepped forward and grabbed his servant by the arm. "Come with me, you layabout," he said. "There's something I want you to see to with my horse."

In this manner, they crossed the street, descended the hill a little, then turned down an alley toward the livery where Caesar Augustus had quartered their mounts.

Harry dropped his hand from the other's arm. "And just where were you last night, if you don't mind?" he said, pleasantly.

"All that shoutin' was just for show?"

"Of course. But where were you?"

"Visitin' folks."

"Anyone of my acquaintance?"

"I came back around sunup but they told me not to bother you because you were entertaining a guest."

"Who told you that?"

"Man on the stairs. Seemed like he worked for the hotel."

Or the Confederate government.

They stopped before the stable door. "If you were back at sunrise," Harry asked, "where have you been since?"

"Down along the waterfront by Rocket's Landing. Tryin' to learn somethin.' "

"About the ironclad?"

"Yessir. Darkies down there say they loaded the last iron plates on a boat for Norfolk some days ago. They figure to be seeing the ironclad soon."

"Not likely. She'll be of small use up here. If that thing is anything like it's been described, she'll be headed for federal shipping. Bust the blockade. Head up the Potomac for Washington."

"You say so, Marse Harry." He glanced at the stable. "What you want me to do for you with your horse?"

"Nothing. That was to get us to where we could talk."

He could see a stable boy eyeing them from within; so attentive he'd stopped raking straw. Harry moved nearer to Caesar Augustus. "We need to find out more," he said. "Go where you think best. I don't want to linger in this city a minute longer than we have to, but we have to be certain. Be back by this evening, as I will need you to attend upon me."

"And what will you be doin' the rest of the day? Entertaining guests some more?"

"I'm going to try to find myself a poker game—one with some Rebel officers in it. People get amazingly talkative sometimes, when the cards are running well."

The black man turned to go, then halted. "Why you need me this evenin'?"

"I have a most important dinner invitation. It came last night. I'll need you to accompany me and hold our horses, but I'm afraid you can't join me at table as you did at Miss Van Lew's."

"Why not?" Caesar Augustus said, mockingly, as though it was a commonplace in Richmond for black slaves to take dinner with white masters.

"Because it's at the residence of Jefferson Davis, President of the Confederate States of America."

HARRY found a game going in the barroom of one of the city's seedier hotels, a place below Main Street, near the river. The day was bright, but this chamber was dark and foul with cigar smoke and the smell of burnt grease.

There were two army officers at the table, one a captain, the other a lieutenant. Neither they or the three civilians in the game were known to Harry. All seemed to be well practiced at cards.

Harry was ahead five dollars before any of them got curious about him.

"You new in Richmond?" asked one of the civilians, a beery-faced, squinty-eyed man with bushy sidewhiskers and a wool vest so thick it seemed made of bristles.

"Newly returned," Harry said, raking in a small pot. "I lived here until a few years ago."

"Where you been since?"

Harry gave a quick glance over the group, then told the truth—partially. "I have a horse farm up near Martinsburg."

"That's behind Yankee lines," said the captain.

"Sometimes," Harry said. "Maybe General Jackson has turned the tables on them again."

"You don't look like a farmer to me."

This voice, full of suspicion, belonged to the other officer—a man about Harry's age whose lieutenant's insignia appeared quite new.

"I own the farm," Harry said. "I don't work it. Have hired help for that."

"Hired? You have no slaves?" asked the captain, an older man with spectacles and a professorial mean.

"One," Harry replied, after a pause. "He's with me here in Richmond."

"You'd better keep him out of trouble," said the lieutenant. "They're grabbin' loose Negroes and puttin' them in labor battalions."

"The country needs every man—black or white," said the captain.

He stared at Harry's expensive civilian clothes. Harry kept his eyes lowered, watching his cards as a new deal commenced. "Maybe we won't need so many once we sic the 'Monster' on them," he said, picking up his hand.

"What 'Monster?' " asked the captain.

"The ironclad vessel down in Norfolk."

"What do you know about that?" the lieutenant asked.

"Only what I read in the newspapers."

He'd read nothing about it in the newspapers.

"And which would these be?" the Captain asked.

"Yankee papers. Frederick, Maryland, for one."

"They know about the ironclad?" the lieutenant interjected.

"Rumors. I'm told Washington City is full of them."

Both officers were looking at him hard, but one of the civilians, a grumpy-looking fellow who'd been chewing on a cigar, came to his rescue.

"Don't matter no how," he said. "That damn thing's just going to sink with all that metal they're hangin' on it. Come on. Let's play cards."

Harry looked at his hand. There were three aces. He discarded one, along with a deuce, and drew two cards. He lost the hand after three raises. Within the next fifteen minutes, his winnings vanished and he was ten dollars down, most of it going to the captain. When he'd lost twenty—not long after—he quit the game. On his way out, he bought a round of whiskey for the table. He hoped at least to leave some friendly memory of himself.

When he had resided in this city, such happy weather often prompted him to a walk along the James. It did so again. Proceeding down the street, he remembered another alley that led past some wood yards down the hill toward the river. Turning into it, he walked perhaps fifty feet, then halted, reaching to light a cheroot. He was not really interested in a smoke. Upon leaving the saloon, he had noted someone rising from the far end of the bar to exit behind him. Whoever it was, Harry sensed that he'd turned into the alley as well.

Harry was not wearing his eyeglasses, but didn't want to take the time to fetch them out from his pocket and put them on. He was a poor shot at all events, and armed with nothing more dangerous than his pocket Derringer, which had an effective range of about six feet with his aim.

Taking the little pistol firmly in one hand, he shook out his match with the other, tossing it with a swift, sweeping gesture to the side. As he did so, he spun to his right, pulling the Derringer forth and thrusting it in the direction of where he sensed his pursuer to be—hoping all the while that it wasn't Nestor Maccubbin, who doubtless was a crack shot.

Indeed not. He found himself aiming his pistol at a small mouse of a man with a bushy moustache and lumpy suit who was pointing a very heavy military-looking revolver at him.

They stood there, neither of them shooting or even moving, looking like participants in some daft, cowardly duel.

"Give me your valuables, and you won't get hurt," the smaller man said, his voice a little high and nervous, and German accented.

The gunman was short, his moustache too large for his face, and he had lank, greasy hair hanging messily over his ears. With his small, darting eyes, he altogether resembled a muskrat. A nervous one at that. There was something about the loose, gingerly way he held his large pistol that gave Harry encouragement.

Keeping his Derringer to the fore, Harry took a step toward the man, and then another.

"There's no sense both of us getting killed," Harry said, trying to sound steadier than he felt. "Or even one of us. Not on such a lovely day."

The small man hunched down a little, the revolver wavering in his hand. He seemed to be wrestling with himself.

"No need at all," said Harry, taking more long steps, and stopping with the Derringer just a few inches from muskrat's large nose. With his left hand, Harry grasped the revolver and yanked it loose.

He stepped back and examined it. There was rust everywhere. He rotated the cylinder, noting with some amusement that the chambers were empty.

The man began to run. The very last thing Harry wished to do was fire a gunshot or cause a commotion by chasing after the would-be robber, but he wanted to talk to him. Taking up the old pistol in his right hand, he threw it hard. His eyesight was poor but his aim was true. Spinning through the air, the gun hit the man at the top of his back.

It caused him no great apparent injury, but possibly some pain. He halted where he'd been struck, a few paces from the end of the alley, and stood there, quivering.

Harry strode up to him, grabbed him by the collar, and spun him around, shoving him against a wooden fence and bringing up the Derringer again. "You're name, sir!" he demanded.

"Atzerodt," he said. "George Atzerodt."

"Are you a professional cutpurse, or have you some honest livelihood?"

"I'm a boatman. From Port Tobacco, Maryland."

The town was on the Potomac, not far from Chesapeake Bay.

"That's Union territory. What are you doing here?"

"The Yankees may claim it, but we are with the South."

"You come down here to enlist?"

The very mention of that word seemed to make the fellow shake all the more.

"No, no. Because of the blockade—the Yankee patrols on the river—I can make no money. I come down here but it is all the same. I saw you in the bar, playing cards. You looked rich—free with your money."

"So you decided to take some?"

He nodded, so sheepishly he seemed about to weep.

"You have a family?"

Atzerodt nodded, perhaps with too much vigor.

Harry released him, and stepped back, returning the Derringer to his pocket. From another, he pulled out a five dollar gold piece and gave it to the man.

"Feed your family," he said. "If I should ever be in need of a boatman and encounter you again, just remember that I was generous to you when I could have blown out your brains."

"Yes sir. Thank you sir."

"Now go. And remember that an unloaded pistol is far more dangerous than none at all."

The wretch scurried off, very much the rodent. Harry retrieved the rusty pistol and tossed it over the fence.

He felt certain of two things—that the man would eventually turn smuggler, and that he'd never hear of him again.

RICHMOND'S wharves were downriver from the center of town, running alongside the terminal and tracks of the York River Railroad. It was a place Harry had avoided when he'd lived in the city, as it was considered dangerous, though it was not far from the wealthy precincts of Church Hill.

Walking the wharves now, he saw no one he recognized, and encountered few willing to talk with him. Those who did were of small help. Harry asked how far down the river was clear of Yankee gunboats, explaining he came from a Charles City County plantation and wanted to return home by boat. He was told, variously, that the James was Yankee-free all the way to Norfolk, that the Union blockade had moved on upstream past Jamestown, and that there were Federal troops moving up from North Carolina who might well have reached the

James, that the Union Army could be in Richmond in days.

None of them seemed to know or care much about the fearsome Confederate ironclad, though one dock worker offered the opinion that if there was such a vessel on the river, it would have a hard time with the shoals.

Feeling futile, Harry wandered away, hoping he'd not asked too many questions. If Nestor Maccubbin was even half as diligent as Allen Pinkerton, he'd have a man on Harry's trail at all times.

None such seemed much evident. Ascending the embankment by the York River Railroad depot, he followed the shoreline toward the other end of town, passing first the long horse- and footbridge across the James and then the covered bridge that carried the tracks of the Lynchburg rail line. A bit further along, where the river tumbled down steps of rapids through a watery field of rocks, was a pretty, partially wooded place that harbored some happy memories for Harry.

Most involved pretty ladies, now one in particular. It was here he had first kissed Arabella, when both were in their teens—having arranged a secret rendezvous during a trip she had made to Richmond with her parents. It was here he had gone with her to say farewell before he had left for the North, an interlude of truce in their quarreling.

There had been more to that evening than mere truce.

Harry stood on that spot now, looking across the wide, wind-ruffled river, remembering how he had held her tightly in his arms, feeling the warmth of her cheek against his neck.

The future had seemed so absurdly simple in that youthful time of first kisses—simple, and absurdly wonderful. Any prophesy back then of the vast calamity that now gripped the nation, but most particularly the South, would only have seemed the most insane fantasy.

She was indulging in fantasy with him now—ignoring the reality of the enormous chasm of circumstance and sensibility that now divided them. How well, if at all, did she really know him?

Of course, she might not be concerned at all with what and who he had become. She might only be using the fact of him as a tool in dealing with some other problem in her life. He never thought her marriage to Palmer Mills would turn out to be a happy one. Palmer was a man who acquired women, rather than loved them. He was full of the airs of the "Virginia chivalry," but he could be a disagreeable fellow.

In her girlhood, despite the primitive notions of racial superiority she'd learned from her parents, Arabella had been playful and sweet, at times even poetic. Her eyes always shone when Harry came round.

It was so long ago.

A short distance later he came to the mouth of the Kanawha Canal that bypassed the worst of the James rapids and extended more than a hundred miles west to Lynchburg. Walking along its towpath, he eventually reached a point where the narrow waterway intersected with the wide mouth of a creek. There was a bridge across the canal here that carried the Petersburg Railroad tracks, and then another, smaller span, wide enough only for a large wagon to pass. It led onto a large island formed by the canal and the James.

Crossing it, his boots loud upon its wooden planks, he ultimately reached the top of a rise with a view of the river and the sprawling jumble of brick buildings, spewing smokestacks, mill races and iron waterwheels, railway cars, stacks of cannon, and piles of shot and ball. The Tredegar Ironworks had been the largest industrial complex of its kind in the South before the war. Now it was the virtual heart of the Confederate war machine, turning out cannon, rifles and muskets, railroad rolling stock, bridge trusses, even swords and pikes.

And armored siding for a warship called "the Monster."

The great, dark, heap of buildings rose above the river as might the fortress castle of some evil prince in a storybook, the effect heightened by the smokestacks fouling the clear, late winter air with sulfurous black billows.

Harry stood contemplating the establishment. It was said to employ more than eight hundred workers, many of them free blacks. Women were employed there as well, mostly as office clerks. There was enormous activity about the place—including comings and goings through the main gate. He noted four cars and an engine on one railroad siding, but the cars were carrying coal, not iron plate.

He supposed it might be possible to stroll up to the gate and ask for Palmer Mills, and so he did just that.

A civilian watchman and two soldiers were lounging at the gate.

"I am calling on Mr. Palmer Mills," Harry said. "He is supposed to have a position here."

"Ain't on the premises."

Harry's suspicions about the readiness of "the Monster" required confirmation. There was no one better qualified to provide that than Mills.

"My name is Harrison Raines. My father owns a plantation down the James. Mr. Mills is an old friend. I have just now returned to Richmond and would like very much to speak with him. Sir."

"I tole you he ain't on the premises. When he is, we know it, but he ain't, and we know that, too."

There was the sound of boots on the gravel. A sergeant

and two privates, looking much better uniformed than the
soldiers Harry had seen out in the field, came up and
arranged themselves around Harry.

"Who're you?" the sergeant asked.

"I live here—downriver, at the Belle Haven Plantation."

"What's your business here?"

"No 'business.' I'm calling on a friend. Lieutenant
Mills, of the Confederate States Navy."

Harry produced one of his *cartes de visite* with a flourish. The sergeant eyed the card with grumpy suspicion,
then shoved it into a pocket of his unbuttoned tunic.

"How'd you get across the canal bridge?"

"I walked."

Wrong answer. The man glowered. "How'd you get
past the sentry there?"

"There was no sentry there."

The sergeant fidgeted in frustration. He appeared about
to become very angry over something—the absent sentry,
the present Harry, or both.

"Mr. Mills don't want no visitors—unless they're from
the government. You from the government?"

"No."

"Well, be off then."

"Is he here? I'll wait on the other side of the canal, if
you'll just send word—his old friend, Harrison Raines."

"I said be off!"

"Perhaps I'll come back at another time," Harry said,
"or call on Lieutenant Mills at his home."

Harry turned and started walking quickly away, half
fearing one of the soldiers might rush up and grab him.
He wished he was a better actor.

Apparently his performance sufficed, however. No one
came after him. At the bridge, the absent sentry, a youth

too small for his uniform and musket, was back in his place. He let Harry pass unbothered.

If the war had utterly transformed Richmond, so much still seemed the same. As Harry went up Twentieth Street, he glanced at the familiar landmark that was Libby's warehouse as he had done countless times in the past, then abruptly halted. The drab, multistoried, utilitarian structure was in no way altered in appearance, but it had of course become something altogether different—and frightful. Instead of tobacco, grain, and dry goods, it was now used to store living flesh. Coming up from the riverbank, he'd heard the sound of coughing. Some of those poor men had been behind these forbidding walls since Bull Run, nine months before.

He knew very well it was unwise for him to go near this place, to show any interest or concern for the Union Army. But he could not pull himself away. He wanted at least to look at some of these men, to reassure himself that they were surviving well enough.

There were a few locals standing around in front of the prison's main entrance, only two of them in uniform.

"Any chance of getting a look at a Yankee soldier?" Harry asked one of the men, a pleasant looking fellow in eyeglasses, who might have been a schoolteacher in civilian life.

The reply was as chilling as the rising wind.

"They bring out the dead ones first thing in the morning," he said. "You can look at them then."

"They do that every morning?"

"Yes sir. Pretty near."

Harry thanked him and turned away, then halted again. One of the civilians there was an elderly Negro Harry recognized as Miss Van Lew's servant, the man who had stood so stoically through dinner. He was standing in much the same stiff manner now, much like a toy who'd been put away on a shelf after use.

As Harry moved toward him, he shifted slightly, pretending not to notice Harry's approach.

"Is Miss Van Lew here?" Harry asked.

The man said nothing. His eyes flicked once toward Harry, but that was all.

"Did you hear? I asked if Miss Van Lew was here," Harry said, a bit more insistently.

"You best go away from here, sir," was the hushed reply. The fellow barely moved his lips.

"Why?"

The older man made no reply, but his eyes, which had been looking off at some vague point in the distance, now shifted and became sharply focused at something or someone over Harry's shoulder. Harry turned about and saw Miss Van Lew emerging from the warehouse door, greeted by some rude remarks from the soldiers.

Harry started to go to her assistance, but was held off by her sharp rebuke. "You there!" she cried. "Why are you bothering my man?"

He stood with mouth slightly agape. What was afoot? "Miss Van Lew . . ."

"You be quiet!"

She lifted her skirt slightly to come at him all the faster. He was struck by how shabby she looked, as though she'd been transformed overnight into some poor woman of the streets who got by selling flowers or begging—even to the large, empty basket she carried on her arm.

"You stay away from my servant, you horrible slaver!" she said, far more loudly than was necessary. "You'll not be selling him down the river."

She stood close to him now, her delicate blue eyes hooded, reminding him of a snake about to strike.

Harry lowered his own voice. "Miss Van Lew, I have things to tell you. Things . . ."

She grabbed at his shoulders, pushing him away, but at the same time holding on so that he could not move. "Not now," she said, softly, then quickly added, for all to hear, "I hate you. You and your kind brought on this awful war! It's penance of sin! Penance of sin!"

"Miss Van Lew. Tonight I dine with the president. I . . ."

Her eyes now widened, she pulled him very close, hissing, "You'll see the means before you, Harry. Look for them." Then she shook him. "Slaver!!!"

The old black man now at last intervened, touching his mistress gently on the shoulder. It was as though he'd pulled the lever of some mechanical switch. She abruptly pulled away, saying not another word as she walked off with her servant in tow, making for the street up the hill.

Harry shook his head, then went over to one of the soldiers. Everyone present had followed the encounter.

"What ails that woman?" he asked.

"That there's Crazy 'Bet,' " said the soldier. "Crazy old rich woman lives up on Church Hill. Goes around town in ragged clothes muttering to herself. Brings food and such to these damned Yankees. Pretty far outa her mind, but don't worry about her none. Harmless, far as we can tell."

Harry nodded his thanks, and started for his hotel a block distant.

He smiled to himself. Elizabeth Van Lew was about as harmless as three army corps.

Chapter 5

HARRY changed clothes, dressing in the expensive black suit he had brought with him, along with a clean white shirt and a black silk cravat. It was hours before he was due at the presidential mansion, but he didn't want to take a chance on being late in the event he was waylaid.

As it turned out, he waylaid himself, encountering two old friends in the bar of the Exchange who invited him to join them in a poker game over at the American Hotel on Main Street by the Capitol. They were amiable fellows—planters' sons, as he had been—with surprisingly small interest in the war, or knowledge of it. The other two players, whom Harry did not know, were much the same, only visitors from Charleston. This pair carried on as though the war had been won with the firing on Fort Sumter, awaiting now only the formal Yankee acceptance of the impossibility of ever defeating the Confederacy.

With minds such as this involved, the game turned quickly in Harry's favor. Having no suspicious officers at the table this time, Harry indulged himself, raking in a number of splendid pots. When the final round was dealt, he was sixty dollars ahead—precisely his monthly pay as a captain in Pinkerton's Secret Service.

Money was a poor substitute for genuine intelligence about the ironclad—which his card-playing companions lacked utterly—but Davis's table was a far more likely source for that at all events.

Out on the street, it was fully dark and the gaslights were lit. He was late, and there was no time to stop back at the Exchange to gather up Caesar Augustus and horses. Hurrying up the hill that led to the President's House on foot, Harry hoped he'd find the black man there waiting for him.

Harry had every expectation of learning something of real significance at this presidential gathering—an opportunity Allen Pinkerton could only dream about. With luck, Harry might come away with all that he'd come to Richmond to discover. He wanted Caesar Augustus standing by, ready to carry the information to Union ears as quickly as possible—a task Harry could not well perform himself without further arousing Maccubbin's suspicion. Caesar Augustus, however, could simply scamper off into Darktown—much like the rabbit who disappeared into his briar patch in the old Negro folk tale.

Miss Van Lew had made that odd, daft promise that a way to fulfill his mission would present itself. Did she suppose President Davis would offer him the use of a courier? Perhaps there was good reason to be calling her "Crazy Bet."

IT was much busier outside the presidential mansion this cold evening than when Harry had come by on inauguration day. A dozen or more soldiers now stood about the front steps and gallery. There was a carriage in the yard, and two others standing in Clay Street. But no saddle horse and no Caesar Augustus. Soldiers at the front door came to attention at Harry's approach, making a presumption, for they could not possibly have known who he was—or how unimportant he was in the Confederate scheme of things.

Just inside was an ornate foyer, where Harry removed his great coat and broad-brimmed hat. He was then ushered through two curved double doors into the warmth of a small parlor beyond. There, a butler stood with a brass tray that already held a half dozen *cartes de visite*. Placing his upon the rest, Harry proceeded into yet another parlor, and then to another beyond that of greater dimensions, a high-ceilinged room, lavishly draped and furnished. When he had first visited Mr. Lincoln in the presidential mansion, he had felt rather in awe. Here, he was merely curious.

Davis stood with his wife, Varina, near the door. He turned to greet Harry with a weak handshake and a slight nod of recognition. Harry's father and Davis had known each other from the Mexican War and Harry had met the great man once when he was a boy. But he'd had no personal encounters with him after that, even upon moving to Washington City, where Davis served as a U.S. senator from Mississippi in the days before Sumter.

The Rebel president seemed tired, just as Mr. Lincoln usually did, and perhaps a trifle ill. There seemed something wrong with one of his eyes. But there was some small cheerfulness to his smile when he thanked Harry for the gift of General Hooker's horse.

"I've given it over to the army," Davis said. "An officer in General Stuart's command now has it."

"Perhaps the animal will encounter his old master," Harry said.

"I believe that is a possibility—though I'd be happy for Hooker to have it back if he'd ride it straight home to Massachusetts and take all his soldiers with him."

Mrs. Davis was somewhat less amiable. She was a

pretty, oval-faced woman with straight, severe hair done in a fashionable coiled coif and sad, almond eyes—quietly full of the pride of her place and station. Harry recalled that she came from Natchez, where they indulged in such pride abundantly. "Good evening, Mr. Raines," she said, coolly. "Word of your exploits precedes you."

Her voice was soft but her accent broad—far different from the echo of Restoration England to be found in the speech of Harry and his fellow Tidewater Virginians. There was something mocking about the way she emphasized the word "exploits." Harry wondered if she had been informed in some way of the less respectable aspects of his comport and life in the Federal capital.

"Trifling matters all, Mrs. Davis," Harry said.

Her countenance darkened slightly. "I am told you are acquainted with Abraham Lincoln." The words came coldly, his name uttered as though it were a satanic reference.

"I have had a conversation with him," he replied, quite truthfully, "enroute to my imprisonment at Fort McHenry."

Her eyebrows lifted. "However did you escape that predicament?"

"I was brought back to Washington for further questioning," he said, then bent the truth. "An opportunity to escape presented itself. I took it—with the aid of General Hooker's horse."

"Yes. That was audacious of you. And we do thank you for the generous and patriotic gesture of the gift. The army is so desperate for mounts."

"It's kind of you to reward me so abundantly with your invitation this evening."

"The invitation is from my husband, but you are of course welcome." She smiled, with some effort, then took him by the arm to introduce him to the others in the room. Most were strangers to him.

It was a small group. Harry was presented first to an older man in civilian clothes who had an oddly military air. He proved to be Milledge Bonham, until recently governor of South Carolina and now a Confederate brigadier and a member of the Rebel Congress as well. As he was quick to mention, he'd fought at Bull Run.

Then there was James Chesnut, Davis's aide de camp, accompanied by his wife, Mary, an attractive, dark-haired, older woman who seemed very much at home in presidential company. Another South Carolinian and member of the Confederate Congress, her husband had once been a member of the U.S. Senate.

The only one present in uniform was a remarkably distinguished general with steel gray hair and beard and impeccable manners more correct than courtly. Harry recognized him from visits the man had made to his father's plantation. His name was Robert E. Lee, and he was serving as President Davis's principal military advisor. Harry's father had spoken highly of his military abilities in the Mexican War, but Lee had proved a failure in his first field command of this war, losing an engagement the previous September in western Virginia at a place called Cheat Mountain when he'd been serving as commander of the Virginia militia.

Harry felt sorry to find such a magnificent looking officer relegated to a desk and office, but he'd been thrilled by the news of Lee's defeat. The farm his mother had left him was in western Virginia, and there was a chance now that those counties might secede from the mother state and become a new Union one, free of slavery. He liked the idea of being a local citizen of such a place.

The general was with a somewhat younger woman, plain but pleasant, who was introduced as a Mrs. Judith

McGuire. She said she and Mrs. Lee had escaped from Arlington together and that she was standing in for the ailing Mrs. Lee at this dinner.

There was one more female present, a raven-haired young lady in an expensive black silk gown with low décolletage. She'd kept her fan fluttering about her face but Harry instantly recognized her, stunned as much by her presence as by her beauty.

"Miss Devereux," he said, as Louise casually offered her hand to be kissed. "I'm surprised you're not at the theater."

"It's early yet," she said, with more fan flutter. "I trust you've had a happy day, sir."

"It's happier now, mademoiselle."

Mrs. Davis was eyeing Louise coldly. When she noticed that Harry had caught her look, she turned to Lee, placing her arm on his. "If you would be so kind, General," she said. "I do believe it's time to go into dinner."

It was indeed remarkable that an actress would find herself in such august company, even one as celebrated in the South as Louise was. Though Andrew Jackson had happily brought the great British Shakespearean player Fanny Kemble to the presidential mansion in his time, Harry doubted Mary Todd Lincoln would be so welcoming—especially of an actress with Louise's reputation for amour. Mrs. Davis seemed of a similar mind, but was being circumspect about it.

Richmond's population had been about forty thousand before the war began. It was now twice that, and most of the newcomers were far, far less respectable than anyone in Louise Devereux's profession.

Harry hoped that he might be seated next to her, but instead found himself placed between Mrs. McGuire and Mrs. Chesnut. It was just as well. Louise, seated opposite, ignored him entirely as she chattered flirtatiously with Congressman Bonham.

"You have come to us from Washington City?" Mrs. Chesnut asked Harry, after they'd all settled into their chairs.

"Yes, Ma'am. Had to work my way around the Union lines."

"That was very intrepid of you."

"I simply wanted to come home."

She nodded. "Well, Sir. You are most welcome here in Richmond. Your family must be pleased to have you back."

In truth, he'd informed neither his father nor his brother he was coming. He assumed they were still up in Northern Virginia with Longstreet.

"It's been a while," he said.

"Are they enjoying our misfortunes in Washington City?"

"No, Ma'am. I'd say they're mostly anguishing over their own. No one expected the war to last so long. They're hoping now for another big battle to end it."

Mrs. Chesnut had a high forehead, a very fair complexion, and sad, dark eyes. She lowered her lashes, looking down at her plate.

"Confederate affairs are in a blue way," she said. "Roanoke Island's taken. Fort Henry on the Tennessee River is open to them. We fear the Mississippi, too. We have evacuated Romney—wherever that is. New armies, new fleets, swarming and threatening everywhere." She wiped at her eye, as though to deal with a small tear. He repressed an impulse to put a comforting hand on her shoulder.

"There is fear up there as well," he said.

"Of what?"

"You have better generals," he said, wishing he'd said

"we" instead of "you." "And then, there's 'the Monster.' "

Mrs. Chesnut tilted back her head. Her husband was following their conversation. "What 'Monster' is that?" she asked.

"The great ironclad in Norfolk. They talk of it most fearfully in the Federal City—as they might a dragon in a medieval fairy tale."

"How do they know of it?"

He shrugged. "Newspapers, rumors."

"Well, I know nothing of it."

The meal was excellent by Southern wartime winter standards: fresh roast pork, forty-five minute biscuits—the intense labor of beating the dough doubtless falling to some slave—pickled turnips, dried butter beans, sweet potatoes, custard pie, and real coffee.

Harry complimented Mrs. Davis profusely, all the while reminding himself that the servant girl who kept hovering behind him probably was due it more.

"So, Mr. Raines," said Bonham. "Have you returned to your native soil to put on the uniform of your country?"

Harry flushed. He should have expected this query. He'd gotten it enough in the North, where people wondered why he wasn't in Union blue. "I would like to make my contribution to ending this conflict," he said. "But I've not decided whether it should be shouldering a musket."

"I think your father would be happy to have you in his cavalry regiment," Davis said. "He's told me you're an excellent rider—which I suppose accounts for the ease with which you have fetched General Hooker's horse to us."

"I've been thinking on it," Harry said, uncomfortable to have all this attention on him.

He wished desperately for Louise to prove herself his friend by intervening at this point with some trifling, but distracting turn of conversation, but she simply sat, elbows on the table, following every word with great amusement, as though enjoying his discomfort.

"I'd think upon it hard, young man," said Congressman Bonham. "Month from now, you may not have any choice."

"Why is that, Sir?" Harry asked.

Bonham looked to Davis, who gave a slight nod.

"Conscription bill," Bonham said.

The words came as a jolt. No one in the North was talking seriously of a draft. Mr. Lincoln's calls for volunteers were still being readily met.

"Conscription?" Harry asked. "A draft?"

"Yes indeed," Bonham replied. "Passage is guaranteed. All able-bodied white men subject to military service for the duration of hostilities. Free blacks to be called up, too—that's in a separate measure—they're to be used for labor details." He looked to Chesnut. "I think that may apply to slaves in some circumstances."

"Too many slackers," Chesnut said. "Too many idle Negroes. Got to do it."

"It does seem harsh," said his wife, Mary. "Dragooning young men against their will and sending them off to be killed. But how is our cause to prevail otherwise?"

"Our cause will prevail—with or without conscription," Bonham said. "Because it is right."

"The South has already given up so much," interjected Mrs. Davis. "Virginia ceded the Northwest territory to the United States. The Missouri Compromise surrendered all the new territory except Missouri north of thirty-six degrees and thirty seconds. The compromise of 1850 gave up the northern part of Texas, and the North took, by vote of a majority, all the territories acquired by Mexico."

"And that war was won by soldiers from the South," said Bonham. "That's why they call Tennessee 'the Volunteer State.'"

"When you say 'gave up,' " Harry said, "you mean . . ."

"The North and West have made a determined and pre-concerted stand against the admission of any territory in the benefits of which the South had any participation, except by the sacrifice of its right of property in slaves," Mrs. Davis said, perhaps reciting from some official paper of her husband's.

Louise was fanning herself with great vigor, though the temperature in the presidential dining room was decidedly chill. Despite her considerable experience in the world, she was probably unused to women speaking out so forthrightly on politics in the company of men.

The president returned the subject to the draft. "We do need the men," Davis said, his voice very matter-of-fact. "With General Jackson in the Valley, McClellan could well outnumber our army here in Virginia by two to one."

Harry smiled to himself. McClellan had told Lincoln he needed another one hundred thousand men.

"Do you find this amusing, Mr. Raines?" asked Mrs. Davis.

He was stumbling into trouble with his every step. "No, Ma'am. It's just that I don't think McClellan would move against you—against us—with twice the number of men he has now. In the North, they say he has 'the slows,' which is a polite term for what ails him."

The president cleared his throat. "You understand, Mr. Raines, this discussion is not something we can have repeated in the newspapers."

"Of course," Harry said.

He stared at the table as a female black servant reached to ladle some soup into his bowl, keeping his eyes from her. Looking into the faces of slaves at their labors upset him. When he lifted his gaze, finally, he noticed General Lee observing him, intently.

"You say you find General McClellan reluctant to

move?" he said. "I'm curious, Sir, how you have come to that conclusion."

"It's something of a national joke," Harry said. He caught himself. "I mean, it is in Washington City. He drills and drills and drills, and in between the drills, he drills some more. People wonder if he's going to try to win the war with a parade."

There was some polite laughter, but not from Mrs. Chesnut.

"Not parades," she said. "Win or lose, it will be with the suffering of great masses of people. Poor and rich. North and South. Their suffering all the same."

Mrs. McGuire began to talk about her own suffering, recounting her flight from northern Virginia in the company of General Lee's wife. She concluded with an anguished recitation of all that the Lees had been compelled to leave behind when the Union army had confiscated their Arlington estate.

The general coughed, politely, but pointedly. "Our loss is small, compared to that of many," he said.

"They have taken your plantation at Arlington," Harry said.

The general nodded, somberly. "Houses in North Carolina have been put to the torch. People have lost all their possessions, their livelihoods. Thousands have died. Our loss is small, Sir."

"It will all be put right when this war is ended," said Varina. "The president will see to it."

She meant her husband. He said nothing.

Louise finally leapt into the conversation, retelling her own adventures escaping the clutches of Lincoln and his Yankees, not realizing—as Harry well knew—that the United States president had personally arranged for her escape to spare the Union the shame and foreign scorn attendant upon being the first American government to hang a woman for wartime crimes.

"I was rowed across the Potomac in the dead of night," Louise said. "Our little boat was almost run down by a Yankee gunboat, but we managed to elude it and horse patrols as well. A gallant young gentleman did this for me, at great risk to himself. He had no reason to do so except his own natural chivalry, but he brought me through all that—the Union lines, swamps and bogs, and all manner of terrors. I am eternally in his debt."

"Who was that gentleman?" asked Mrs. Chesnut.

Louise beamed, eyes straight at Harry. "Why, he sits at our table, here before you."

Harry heard a sharp intake of breath, not knowing whose.

"Is that true?" said Mrs. Davis. "You could move that easily from there to here?"

"It was by no means easy," said Louise.

"It was early in the war, is all," Harry said. "Shortly after Manassas. The situation was more amenable to movement back then. Miss Devereux exaggerates my role. The bravery was all hers."

"Then you were in Virginia last summer?" Davis asked.

"Yes, Sir, for a few days."

"You didn't stay? You went back?"

Louise had built him a bear trap and neatly put his foot into it. He had to yank it out.

"I had personal reasons, Mr. President."

"Involving the war?"

Yet now Louise came to his rescue.

"Involving love, Mr. President," she said, with a gush. "Harry is sweet on a friend of mine—the actress Caitlin Howard—who resides in Washington City."

Harry blushed, his mind devoid of any word to add.

"And now?" Mrs. Davis asked.

"She has decamped," said Louise. "And so my gallant has come to live in Richmond, and I rejoice."

She pushed back her chair. "I do beg your indulgence, Excellencies," she said. "This has been the loveliest of evenings, and I do thank you so much for it. But I fear I must now myself decamp. For an actress, all the world truly is a stage, and mine beckons."

The men rose, Harry, still a little dazed by the run of conversation, the last to do so. Louise turned to him. "If you would see me to my carriage, sir," she said, "I would again be in your debt."

After saying her goodnights around the room, she took Harry's arm and led him with a prancing step out through the succession of parlors to the foyer. He waited as she put on her cloak and bonnet and long black gloves.

"What were you trying to do, Louise?" he said, as they descended the front steps into the clammy cold, "Send me to the gallows?"

"On the contrary, Sir," she whispered, as they moved across the gravel to the coach, whose driver sat huddled in his high seat. "Tryin' to save you from it. You've been under suspicion. Now you are not."

"And how do you think you have managed that?" He opened the door to the coach, waiting for her to put her dainty foot upon the step.

"I arranged your invitation to this dinner tonight, Harry. Mr. Bonham is a good friend of mine. Your bonafides are now established. You will be viewed as a friend of the president's. You will have nothing to fear."

"Then I am obliged to you."

She rested her hand on his arm as she put foot to step and swung herself into the carriage, leaning out the open window of the door after he shut it. "You are very, very, very obliged to me, and don't forget it."

"I won't. May I presume you no longer now consider me a Yankee spy?"

"I'm still not sure."

"Why not?"

"You're a puzzle, Harrison Raines."

"And if I am a Yankee spy after all?"

"I've prepared for that, too." She leaned out to kiss him on the cheek.

"Good night—sweet prince." She laughed.

She rapped twice on the side of the coach. The driver stirred, flicked his whip, and the carriage clanked into motion, rolling out of the yard with its side lamps flickering in the mist.

When Harry returned, the remaining ladies had retired from the table. President Davis had invited the men into his library. Harry accepted a cigar and glass of French brandy, contenting himself with listening to the others in hopes they'd turn to the subject of "the Monster" without his prompting.

They did not. The talk was all of politics—and of the refusal of England and France to recognize the Confederacy as a sovereign nation. As Bonham noted, England had for more than half a century adhered to a North American policy aimed at preventing the United States from expanding into a transcontinental power. Britain had tried to keep Texas independent; had invaded Louisiana in the War of 1812 in hopes of prying that region loose from the United States' grip.

Yet now, with all they had then wished handed to them on a silver tray, they had shrunk from its prospect.

"Perhaps another victory," said Chesnut. "Smash up the Yankees good. Give them another thumping. Perhaps then."

General Lee seized this moment to beg his leave. Harry leapt at the opportunity to do the same. When the Davises did not beg either to remain, the others took it for a signal and rose to depart as well.

Harry walked with Lee as far as the latter's coach, which stood in the street.

"I am residing at the Spotswood," the General said to Harry, as he helped Mrs. McGuire into the conveyance. "May I offer you a ride?"

"I'm a short walk away," Harry said. "At the Exchange."

"I have an office at the War Department on Ninth Street," Lee said. "If you have a moment, Mr. Raines, I'd appreciate it if you might drop by and tell me what you know of the situation north of the Rappahannock."

"Certainly," said Harry, hoping he'd be gone from Richmond before Lee got too serious about that invitation.

Lee put a foot on the coach step. "The cavalry needs good officers," he said. "You have amply demonstrated your worth."

"Thank you, General. You are kind to say so."

Harry made no more commitment than that.

HE walked the few blocks downhill to the Exchange briskly, trying to ignore the cold. It was probably foolish to be out alone on so dark a night with the city so full of roughnecks, sharpers, and brigands. But he needed to think. Though none at the table had been willing to take up the subject in front of him, Harry was fully convinced now that the Southern ironclad would be launched very soon. The North needed to know, and know quickly.

He looked east over toward Church Hill, the height on which stood the very grand Van Lew house. If lamps were lit, they were not visible. Perhaps it wasn't worth the risk of visiting this night. He'd find a way to get a message to Miss Van Lew on the morrow.

Harry was just approaching the Exchange's main entrance when a realization of his inestimable folly suddenly occurred to him. The readiness of the Monster for combat was far from the most important news he had to deliver. He'd heard something of much more consequence, and completely ignored it.

Conscription. The South was so desperate for men it was going to initiate a draft—within a month. If the Union struck soon, it would catch the Confederacy at a decided disadvantage. McClellan had to march immediately. Harry had to get word to those in the Union who could make him do it.

But that was something more to sleep on. He was so weary he could barely think.

Pausing before his door, he took the key from his pocket, then hesitated, listening—a practiced habit for those in Mr. Pinkerton's line of work. Maccubbin might well be in his rooms waiting for him, or conducting a browse.

He opened the door slowly, hearing nothing. The light from the corridor penetrated the chamber beyond only enough for Harry to see the vague outline of a large dark shape partially obscuring the window.

He shrank back, hand going to his pocket pistol, trying to focus on the form. It seemed to move, but slowly, from side to side.

Stepping inside, he struck a match, stumbling backward a little before the awful sight that flickering light revealed. There above him, hanging from the chandelier like some lifeless doll, twisting slowly and completely naked, was Arabella Mills. What he could see of the tormented look upon her face made him glad the room was so dark.

Chapter 6

SHIVERING now from more than the cold and damp, Harry stood collecting his courage for a long moment, then drew a deep breath and stepped forward, striking another match. Something else had caught his eye—in the far corner. A dark face.

"I didn't do it, Marse Harry," Caesar Augustus said. "I just found her like that."

Harry wanted to turn on the gaslight, but the dead Arabella was hanging from its principal fixture. Before anything else, he had to get her down.

There was a candle on the table. Lighting it, waiting for the flickering flame to grow, he felt himself in some weird, macabre tale—one worthy of the great Poe. Calming himself, he took out the thin sheath knife he routinely carried inside his right boot. Gently pushing aside poor Bella's clothing from where it lay on the floor, he picked up the chair that had been overturned and placed it beneath her. Climbing upon it, he had to hold on to her cold body while he sawed at the rope. He'd rather be among all the dead of the Bull Run battlefield than endure this dreadful experience, but he had no choice.

At length the rope gave way, dropping Bella down and

against him. He wavered, then lost his balance. The chair tipped, falling to the side with a crash. He came down hard on his back, with Bella's body sprawled across him.

"Help me, damn it!" he hissed to Caesar Augustus.

Too slowly, the black man rose and approached, just as Harry pulled himself free, and, with jittery knees, got to his feet.

"Didn't do it," Caesar Augustus said. "Came in, and there she was. Hanging like a chicken."

"Why didn't you go for help?"

Caesar Augustus gave him a hurt look. "I'm a darky, Marse Harry. I do that, and they drag me off to jail 'fore I can say a word. Maybe shoot me right here. On the spot."

"So you just sat in the corner waiting for me?"

"Couldn't think of anything else to do."

"How long have you been here, Caesar Augustus?"

"Don't know. Half hour maybe."

"Where have you been tonight?"

"Scoutin' 'round, like you told me to do."

Harry shook his head, then knelt beside Bella, arranging her body in a more seemly manner, wondering if he should remove the rope, then deciding against it. The law would be unhappy with what he'd done as it was.

"Fetch me a blanket from my bed, so I can cover her."

"Yes, Marse Harry," said Caesar Augustus, rising. He returned quite quickly, and the two of them gently draped the counterpane over her body, pulling it high to cover her stricken face.

"Now what do we do?" Caesar Augustus asked.

"I've no idea."

There was a sudden pounding on the door. Reluctantly, Harry opened it, finding himself faced by two wild-eyed men. The one in front, as he should have expected, was

Nestor Maccubbin, looking righteous. Just behind, looking powerfully grim, was Palmer Mills.

Maccubbin pushed his way in, while Mills stood glowering at Harry. The detective took note of the severed rope hanging from the chandelier, then of the form beneath the blanket. He pulled it away.

As he caught sight of his wife, Mills's countenance drained of all comprehension. Then all at once he erupted in a mixture of anguish and fury, lunging toward Harry with stark murder in his eyes. Maccubbin caught him, the two of them spinning around and crashing into Harry and all tumbling to the floor. As Harry fell, he heard shouting in the hall and the heavy thumps of many running feet. Soldiers crowded into the room, with much cursing and shouting. Harry tried to get clear of them, but someone struck him a blow at the back of his head as he was rising, and he went down on the floor again hard, landing so that his face came within a few inches from Bella's dead eyes, as they stared out from beneath the cover. He rolled to the other side, hearing Mills call out his name several times. Then someone kicked him. He recalled seeing Caesar Augustus pressed against the wall, his eyes widened with fear as Harry had never before seen in all the years that the two of them had been friends. Then all became very blurry.

WHATEVER curiosity Harry had had about Mc-Daniels's private jail from reading about it in the newspapers was more than sufficiently alleviated by examining it firsthand—from within. It occupied what had been a large, long storeroom in the rear of Dickinson and Hill's auction house at Franklin and Sixteenth Streets, the interior now cut up into several small cubicles of varying dimensions.

Harry had been put into one of the larger chambers. It boasted a barred window that looked out onto the alley. This must have been a comfort in the heat of a Richmond summer, but it was February. Though the window was shuttered, there were cracks big enough to see through, and gusts of chill wind found their way through every one.

Caesar Augustus had been dragged into this dreadful place as well, shoved into accommodations with doubtless far fewer comforts than Harry's. When the furor accompanying their arrival had calmed down, Harry tried calling to Caesar Augustus, but the only response came from the guard outside his door, telling him to shut up.

Happily, he'd been in his great coat when taken. He curled up in it, seeking his own body heat, and tried to go to sleep, but seemingly every time he approached the edge of slumber, the horrible vision of Arabella hanging naked from her rope intruded, spurring him to wakefulness. Twice he found himself crying.

He felt so wrenchingly sorry for the woman. Arabella had never meant anyone harm, least of all him. All she had wanted was to marry him and live a life much like her mother's. Had it not been for her sharing her mother's racialist ideas as concerned slavery, that might well have come to pass.

Now, instead of her mother's life, she had none.

Whatever the cause of Bella's death, he shared some guilt in this. He had an obligation here, to his mind one that superseded his mission for Allen Pinkerton—not that he stood much chance of carrying that out now.

Sitting up, he moved to the warmest corner of his cell, huddling into it with his arms wrapped around his knees. For some reason, probably simple haste, they hadn't searched him for weapons. He still had his pocket pistol and the sheath knife. But these would be of small avail in the midst of so much soldiery. If he was to escape his plight, it would have to be by means of mind and tongue.

Slowly now, as he'd been unable to before, he went over the entire tragic occurrence as it had transpired from the instant he'd opened his hotel chamber door. He thought hard, this time keeping back the tears.

Arabella had been without a stitch of clothing. Many a good husband was not able to see his wife so exposed in the cold of winter, when bathing was done in parts. Her clothes had been in a pile on the carpet beneath her feet, next to the overturned chair.

All these things and the chair might indicate suicide, yet her clothes had been beneath her, as though she had divested herself of her garments one by one as she hung from the chandelier. That fixture, fueled by means of an extended pipe, barely held her weight. The snap of a rope with a human being on it should have brought it down. But it remained roughly in place.

Had she left a note? The notion crossed his mind that she might have intended this horrid act as some twisted means of revenge. If so, was the man to be so awfully punished himself—or her husband? She'd said herself that she no longer loved the man—if she ever had at all.

There was a rattling of keys, and his door banged open. Maccubbin came in with one of his Plug Uglies, both halting just inside the door.

"Your story has been verified," Maccubbin said. "You're free to go."

"Verified by who?"

"By General Robert E. Lee, Confederate States Army. He said you're telling the truth—that he and you left the president's house at the same time, which was barely enough time for you to walk from there to the Exchange. We had a doctor examine Mrs. Mills's remains. She'd been dead for a fair while. There was dried blood on her ear. She had a cut on her ear—and a bruise on her cheek. Sure didn't come from the rope. We think she was assaulted."

"You mean rape?"

"I do."

Harry shook his head, as though to clear it. "In my room?"

"That's where you found her. Now get out of here, Raines. We've other business this night, and we're going to need these chambers."

Harry got stiffly to his feet. He'd come in for a few blows in the earlier altercation.

Maccubbin stepped aside to let him pass.

"The Exchange Hotel doesn't want you for a guest anymore. We packed up your things. They're waiting there for you."

"Where am I to stay tonight?"

"That's your worry. Unless you want to stay here."

Harry shuddered. "No thank you."

He stood in the narrow hall, brushing off his coat. "Where's my man?" he said.

"Your man?"

"My servant. My, uh, slave. Caesar Augustus."

Maccubbin grinned. "He's been hauled off to 'Castle Godwin.' Best we can figure it, he attacked Mrs. Mills and then killed her, trying to make it look like a suicide."

"You're charging him with murder?"

"We're not charging him, Raines. He's a slave. Tomorrow, we're goin' to take him out and hang him. Just like he did her."

Chapter 7

Iᴛ was nearing dawn, but darkness still cloaked the city. On the strong chance of his being followed, Harry went through the charade of stopping by a few hotels to inquire after rooms, knowing they'd be full. Then, pausing by an alley and making certain no one was near, he ducked into the blackness, inching his way along the fences to the other end. Keeping out of the lamplight, he went uphill from there, following Grace Street up Church Hill to the mansion that looked to be his best refuge under the circumstances.

Responding to Harry's repeated knockings—as well as the barking of some nearby dog—the elderly Negro man finally opened the back door. Harry pushed past him, apologizing, then looked to the further doorway, where Miss Van Lew stood in a long dressing gown, wraithlike and ghostly.

"What's afoot, Harry?" she asked. "What brings you to my door at such an hour?"

He gave forth his story in a rush, halted finally by Miss Van Lew, who put finger to lips and led him to the kitchen, where a fire had been kept in advance of the morning's breakfast cooking.

"Now, tell me all this again carefully," she said, pulling two chairs close to the hearth and its glowing coals. "Leave nothing out."

He did as commanded, including even the details of Bella's previous visit to his quarters and the unfortunate history of their truncated courtship.

"And they have arrested Caesar Augustus?"

"Yes. He offers no defense. He wouldn't tell me where he was."

"But you're his friend."

"I know. I don't understand."

She put her hand over her eyes. "It is a tragedy out of the classics," she said.

"I can't believe she'd take her own life."

Miss Van Lew got up to prepare tea. "Her behavior is said to have been peculiar these last few months. There are rumors of her having taken up with several young officers—though I daresay she's entitled to some riposte to her husband's dalliance with another woman."

"This is commonly known?"

"In Richmond, Harry, everything is commonly known."

"I think she was with such a young officer on Inauguration Day—at the capitol. But that's not a sign of suicidal intent."

"Certainly a flagrant display of marital infidelity. In normal times, she would have been shunned for that." She brought a small kettle to the fire. "With the war on, society begins to lose its moorings."

"I don't believe Arabella lost hers."

"What do you mean?"

"I don't believe she came to my room to kill herself."

"Then who . . . ?"

"Miss Van Lew, I do not know. But it was not Caesar Augustus. He's been my friend nearly all my life. He could not possibly do such a thing—murder an innocent woman. No matter what the provocation."

Her blue eyes searched his for the truth of this statement. "There was a provocation?"

"He is a friend of Mrs. Mills's maid. While calling on her, he was chased off the Mills property."

"You're sure your judgment is not clouded by your friendship."

"No, Ma'am."

She took a deep breath, her countenance for a moment resembling Lincoln's for the many matters on her mind.

"I'll help you, Harry—as much as I can—as long as there is no jeopardy to our cause. The Union comes first. It must."

"Yes, Ma'am."

He was not being fully truthful. As he could not bear an ultimate Confederate victory, neither could he abide being responsible for the death of his friend.

Harry hunched forward, paying no mind as the kettle crackled a splat of water onto the coals near him. "Forgive me, Miss Van Lew. I am woefully remiss. I have information we must get to Union forces at once. I believe the ironclad is very near to ready. The ironworks has stopped shipping plates. The construction must be complete. I could get no one at the president's dinner to speak on it, but their impassivity carried a message in itself. I think it is only a matter of days. When Bella spoke of it, she did so in terms of great immediacy. The 'Monster' is about to be unleashed."

"I have heard similar reports."

"There's more, Miss Van Lew. Conscription. The Confederate Congress next month is going to adopt a draft. Whites for the army; blacks for the labor battalions. The vote is assured. I have this from Congressman Bonham himself, with General Robert E. Lee concurring, right there at the president's dinner table."

She took a towel and wrapped it around the handle of the kettle, lifting it with surprising ease and taking it to the teapot on the table. "That I already know," she said.

"But I've only just this night learned of it."

"The same for me."

She poured the teapot full, then set down the kettle and went to a large tin box, removing from it several biscuits and putting them on a plate.

"I told you that a way would present itself to you," she continued, setting tea, biscuits, and cherry preserves on the table. "It was at your elbow throughout the evening."

He stared blankly. She smiled, a little playfully.

"Mr. Raines, have you the planter class's habit of paying no attention to servants?" She poured him a steaming cup of tea, which he accepted gratefully. "Do you heed them no more than the furniture? If you had been more observant, you would have noticed that one of the president's serving maids was my very own Betty."

"Betty?"

"Mary Elizabeth Bowser. The young lady with whom you and Caesar Augustus shared my table the other evening. Securing her employment at the 'Gray House' was one of my more felicitous accomplishments. She hears all. And, yes, she fully comprehends what she hears. When my father died, ten years ago, my mother and I freed all his slaves. Most stayed with us, for honest wages. Betty I sent to Philadelphia for her education. She's as smart as you, Harrison Raines. Smart as a whip."

He stared down at the floor. "So, too, my Caesar Augustus."

"If you think so highly of him, why hasn't he a last name?"

"His choosing. He says he wants to wait until he finds one of sufficient merit."

"Not Raines?"

"No."

She sipped from her cup. "And now he's in the hands of that vile Captain A. C. Godwin, who serves his spurious nation as provost marshal and commandant of prisons."

"Maccubbin said Caesar Augustus is to be hanged."

"As a freeman he'd get a trial, though the result would be much the same."

Harry began spreading preserves on a biscuit, feeling guilty as he did so. They'd no doubt given Caesar Augustus nothing to eat.

"Miss Van Lew, I mean to spare him that fate or die trying. I also mean to discover the villains who killed Arabella."

Her mind was turning elsewhere. "We must get our news to Fortress Monroe," she said. "They have a telegraph there direct to Washington. I have no trouble acquiring information here. More than I can keep track of, frankly. The rub is in getting it to where it needs to go. That becomes more and more difficult."

"Madam, I am followed."

"Sir, I am followed constantly. Three days ago, on Main Street, I turned and found a detective at my elbow! He seemed about to pounce on my market basket! They have men outside this house at all hours. With all your banging out back, I fear they are well apprised of your presence."

She brought her cup to her thin, small lips once more. Harry had devoured his biscuit, and reached for another.

"They're turning the screw, Harry," she continued. "They've taken Frank Stearns, closed our refuge there on the James. Martial law, midnight arrests. We poor Virgi-

nians might as well be under the thumb of Napoleon."
She paused, then grinned. "But we who labor in the Good
Cause are more numerous than they think."

"There is one person I might ask to help us," he said.
"She has no love for the institution of slavery, but she is
a loyal Virginian. Still . . ."

"I am a loyal Virginian," said Miss Van Lew, sternly.
"That is why I am with the Union."

"It's my sister," he said.

"Harrison. You have not spoken to her in years."

"We've written . . ."

"There's too much at risk to take a chance on her. No,
Harry. I've just thought of someone—a Lincoln man, a
civilian, who now works in General Winder's office as a
telegraph clerk. I told him I would not use him except in
extremis, but we are in extremis now, are we not, Harrison?"

In the rosy firelight, he could see how she must once
have been very pretty. She was the same age as Rose
Greenhow, the Confederate spymaster in Washington City
who had retained her allure so perfectly it had become
the principal tool of her craft.

Yet Rose now languished in Washington's Old Capitol
Prison, where Pinkerton had her under constant watch. If
a drab spinster, Miss Van Lew was by far the more successful at her trade.

She rose with a rustle and went to the window. "It's
nearing sunrise. You must leave, Harry, while you still
might be invisible. I'll give you the name of a man who
keeps a boardinghouse not far from here on Cary Street.
I pay him to keep a room free in the event I have unexpected guests. You are that, sir, and I will send you there.
It's near the waterfront."

He stood up. His fatigue was dizzying, and he had not
an ounce of desire to rejoin the cold outdoors.

"Come with me," she said, reaching for a lantern. "There's a short tunnel from my cellar to the smokehouse. I do not know why my father had it dug, but it has proved very useful."

"You are an amazement, Miss Van Lew."

"We all must live by our wits, these days. Return to me tonight, after midnight, by means of this same smokehouse."

She took his hand. He felt almost like a small child in her company.

DESPITE her demonstrable competence, Harry was disinclined to throw himself on the hospitality of one of Miss Van Lew's operatives. For all he knew, the boardinghouse keeper might be on Maccubbin's list of prospective detainees. If not, with so many detectives keeping watch on him, Harry might himself put the fellow on such a list by turning up at his premises.

He headed toward the other end of town, near the theater. Louise had told him where she was staying—in an old mansion turned boardinghouse, noted for both its elegance and discretion.

It was fully sunrise when he reached it. A Negro manservant in worn black coat was on the porch, holding an armful of firewood and attempting to open the front door without dropping any of his burden. Harry rushed to his assistance, causing the other some surprise—and wariness.

"I'm calling on Miss Devereux," Harry said.

The black man hesitated just inside the door. "Ah don' think de lady is home. Wait here, sir." He kicked the door closed behind him.

Harry moved to a corner of the porch, near a hanging pot full of winter-dead plants. A trash wagon was making its laborious way up the street. In the other direction, two drunkards were weaving along arm in arm, either returning from revels or seeking more.

"And who be you, sir?"

Harry turned to find himself confronted by a large, gray-haired woman wearing a thick overcoat over her nightdress and enormous slippers.

He thought of declaring himself Louise's husband, or brother. Truth was something that served her convenience, and for all he knew she had several of both.

But it was a maxim in the U.S. Secret Service that lies were always best held to a minimum, and so he refrained from telling yet another one. "My name is Harrison Raines. I am from the Belle Haven Plantation on the James, and a very good friend of Miss Devereux."

The woman folded her arms. "She has many very good friends."

"Yes, but I am the only one standing here."

"At an ungodly hour of the day, sir."

"On the contrary, Madam. 'Tis now when you find God-fearing folk arisen and at their labors—as I intend to be, after speaking with Miss Devereux."

He imagined the soft warmth of her bed. And then a bath and shave and a good breakfast.

"Well, she is not here."

"Please, Madam. If you would just tell her Harrison Raines from the Belle Haven Plantation is here, and that it is important."

"It don't matter how important it is, because she isn't here. Hasn't been since yesterday morning."

"You're sure? She didn't come home after the theater?"

"You deaf?"

Listening to her, he wished he was. Harry took out one of his *cartes de visite* and handed it to her. She glanced at it, then without another word, withdrew into her house.

*   *   *

DESPITE the early hour, there were already three others in the anteroom waiting to see the general—two of them fancy officers, and one a well-dressed civilian. Each had in turn looked disapprovingly on Harry's disheveled evening clothes and stubble.

A polite and industrious young major stood guard at the desk that dominated one end of the room, dealing with an immensity of paper that was recurringly augmented by couriers.

To Harry's surprise, he was the first one called, though the others had been there before him. The two officers were visibly affronted.

General Lee's office was surprisingly small, and extremely quiet. The gentleman sat at a much larger desk than his aide's, and it was heaped with an even greater abundance of papers. The general might have been a clerk himself, were it not for his magnificent, immaculate uniform and his station as one of the highest-ranking officers in the Confederacy.

He stood, shaking Harry's hand more as an obligatory courtesy than a gesture of friendship, then indicated a chair. He sat back carefully in his own. His eyes were dark and soulful, and it bothered Harry to look at them, for they seemed to see so much.

"I am distressed by the circumstance that brings you here, sir," Lee said. "I have shared the news with the president, and he is sorry for it as well."

"It is the sorriest thing that has ever happened to me, General," Harry said, "but for my mother's own death."

Lee ran his hand over his mouth, looked over Harry's unkempt and decidedly civilian appearance, then resumed his steady gaze at Harry's eyes. "Both Mrs. Mills and her husband are of excellent families, and he, I am told, is a very valuable young officer. The government desires as little public attention brought to this matter as possible."

"I understand, sir. But they have taken my slave."

The general's brows lifted slightly. "Your slave?"

"My manservant, Caesar Augustus. They have decided he is responsible for Mrs. Mills's death—for no other reason than that he found her body hanging in my hotel room. They have taken him to be killed this morning. No trial, just a rope."

Lee frowned, deeply. Harry recalled that he had been one of Virginia's foremost proponents of manumission— freeing the slaves and returning them to Africa.

"I do not believe such an act has sanction in law," he said, finally.

Harry felt like screaming that there was no such thing as law anymore in Virginia, that it was all military rule, with the rights of citizenry replaced by the whims of the likes of Nestor Maccubbin or the wrath of lynch mobs and drumhead justice.

But the same was true of the North—in significant parts of it, at all events. Certainly Baltimore had become one large federal prison camp.

"Nevertheless, he is taken," Harry said. "He is worth fifteen hundred dollars, and they strip me of him like cut-purses in the night."

The dark eyes took on a sterner cast. "You have come here to argue over a loss of property?" The general's quick glance at the piles of paperwork indicated how great an intrusion Harry had made.

There was something more on the general's mind. Harry reminded himself that Lincoln had thought so much of this man that he had offered him command of the Union armies. Had Virginia not seceded, he might now be sitting in an office in Washington.

"General, I'll confess it. This man is my friend. I trust

and value him as much as you must that bright young major outside. I know that he could not have committed this crime. He is a good man, a decent person, yet they've accorded him no rights. He's no more than an insect to be squashed on the wall."

Such talk on a public street, Harry knew, would be enough to get him locked up himself.

"Mr. Raines. I have always valued your father's friendship and am disposed to look kindly upon your complaint. But I should not intrude upon civil matters concerning the police. I serve as President Davis's military advisor." He waved at the stacks of paper, pulling one forth. "A request for an officer's commission. This is my jurisdiction here." He cleared his throat and pulled more papers to the fore. "I must return to my duties, Sir. I am sorry, Mr. Raines."

Harry stood, nodding sadly, then leaned forward, hands on the general's desk. "Then let me do it," he said.

"Do what, Sir?"

"Find the man who killed Arabella Mills, and so spare my slave an unjust fate."

Lee looked a little pale. He was so obviously overworked. "It is my understanding that Mrs. Mills may have taken her own life," he said, quietly.

"Provost Maccubbin will tell you otherwise, sir. And so will I. What I need to prove is that my servant did not do it."

"But what can you do?"

"Give me a week, and a letter of marque."

"Letter of marque? You are to become a privateer?"

"No, Sir. I mean a pass—a letter authorizing me to make inquiries in this matter. Something very official. If I do not resolve this in a week's time, then Maccubbin can do with Caesar Augustus what he will."

Lee leaned back in his chair, then swiveled it to one side, looking out his windows toward the east, and the rising sun. "I'm afraid this is not a matter for me to decide. The president . . ."

"All the better, sir. A letter signed by President Davis. And I promise you, General Lee, one way or the other, if you do this for me, at the end of this week you will find me fully in the service of my country."

The general pondered this, and Harry's anxious, earnest face. He sighed, much as Miss Van Lew had. "I will order Mr. Maccubbin to leave your manservant unharmed but imprisoned—until His Excellency decides what is to be done. I'm sorry, but I can do no more."

"I am grateful, sir." He started toward the door.

"If you wish to be assigned to your father's regiment, I can arrange that instantly."

Harry gulped. "Thank you, sir."

"A moment more," the general said.

"Sir?"

"You have lived in Washington City through all these months of war. Do you have much knowledge of General McClellan?"

"I do, sir. Were he an enlisted man, he would be regarded as a shirker."

"We talked of this a little last night. Do you really think he will soon move against us? What do they say in Washington City?"

"They say he had better move. The politicians are giving him no choice. He will move reluctantly, but he will move—or lose his position. He could not bear that."

"But move where? I am not interested in rumor. You have been in Washington society, I'm told. In Mrs. Greenhow's circle. I believe we had a brief encounter at a reception there—before the war. What are they saying? What is your best guess?"

Harry had no specific knowledge of the Union Army's plans, but Pinkerton had voiced his own opinion to him, and Pinkerton was a man at Lincoln's right hand. Pinkerton had said the Union Army would have to cover Washington as it advanced. It could not leave the road open to the capital. That meant a march along the western shores of the Potomac—a flanking move around Fredericksburg.

Harry hated lying to this excellent man—a friend of his father's, but truth was an easy casualty in this conflict.

He seized upon what struck him as the least likely eventuality—offering it has an uninformed guess, so the betrayal of honor between gentlemen would be less. "I believe he will try a flanking move, sir. But he will bring up his entire army for it, and the pace will be slow."

"Flank us how? To the left, or right?"

"To the rear, sir. It's just a guess, but think he'll come up the river."

"The James?"

"The James. Perhaps the York. But from that direction."

"Why?"

Harry tried to think like a soldier. "Surprise. It would relieve the pressure on Washington. The Confederate forces would have to pull back far."

"But we have batteries on the Potomac. McClellan could not easily move transports down the river."

Another guess. "Annapolis, sir. A day's march from the Union camps."

The general rocked gently in his chair a moment, his eyes again to the window. "Thank you, Mr. Raines." He bent to scratch something in the margin of the request for a commission. Harry could doubtless find himself transformed into a serving officer just as readily.

"Thank you, sir."

"Where are you staying?" Lee asked, as Harry turned the knob. "I assume you wish to be informed as directly as possible of Mr. Davis's thoughts upon this matter."

"Yes, sir," Harry said. He gave Lee the name of the landlord Miss Van Lew had urged upon him. It occasioned no unusual interest from the general.

Chapter 8

AT the mention of Miss Van Lew's name, the landlord turned and, without a word, led Harry upstairs to a front room that overlooked the street and possessed a view of both the Capitol and the James River. When Harry asked the man if he would send someone to the Exchange for his luggage, he received only a nod in response. His thanks for the man's good offices produced only another nod as the landlord went out the door.

The room boasted a rope bed with a tick mattress and two feather-filled pillows. Had they been filled with nails, it would not have mattered. Harry lay back still dressed in his evening clothes and was asleep before he could turn his mind to a single thought.

He awoke to find that the sun had moved to the other side of the room and that the landlord was standing over him, holding an envelope, which he thrust into Harry's hand.

The mute had found his voice. "A colonel brought this," he said. "Better read it."

Not quite shed of sleep and ever mindful of the looming conscription bill, not to speak of his promise to General Lee, Harry half wondered if this might be an order to report for duty as a soldier.

"When did this come?" Harry asked.

"Minute ago. Maybe two. Better read it."

The man stood there, as though waiting to be informed of the letter's contents. Harry glared at him until he finally shrugged and walked away, annoyingly leaving the door open behind him. Harry examined the envelope noting the seal of the Confederate States of America. He opened it carefully.

There was a brief note from Lee:

Mr. Raines:

I trust this will prove sufficient for your purposes. It is all that can be managed in the present circumstance.

We look to honor to be well served here, in most particular as concerns the good lady's name.

> *Your svt.,*
> *Robert E. Lee, Lt. General*
> *C.S.A.*

Enclosed was a simple but all-powerful pass, signed by President Jefferson Davis, authorizing the bearer to enter any and all military jurisdictions.

The landlord reentered, bearing Harry's luggage from the hotel. "Is this everything you had?" he asked.

"I'll know when I open the bags. Thank you."

He gave the man a dollar, which was a mistake, for it only encouraged him to linger.

"Anything else you need?"

"A meal," said Harry.

The man left, promising to stir his wife to culinary preparations. Harry washed, shaved, and changed into clean clothes. Both his saddlebags and grip had been gone through, probably at the hotel, but nothing appeared to have been taken.

He needed desperately to visit Caesar Augustus in prison, if that could possibly be arranged, but there was another visit he needed to make with an even higher priority.

THE desk clerk at the Exchange took note of him, but made no attempt to bar his passage through the lobby, perhaps presuming that, if Harry was now at large, someone important must have commanded it. Richmond was no place to interfere with authority. Not with so many people being dragged off to jail on the slightest pretext.

Detective Cashmeyer, one of Maccubbin's police thugs, was in the lobby, but was in conversation with another man and failed to note Harry's entrance.

Up the stairs he went, then, with no one following.

An advantage of working in the U.S. Secret Service was the education one received from the endlessly resourceful Pinkerton agent Joseph "Boston" Leahy. The muscular Irishman had been a police detective in Massachusetts before joining the Federals and had acquired a vast knowledge of criminal tricks and methods. One of the most useful things Harry had learned from him was the art of picking locks. Using a slender-bladed pocketknife, he had the door to his former room open in a few seconds.

The bedding had been changed and the furniture put roughly back in place, but otherwise the chamber seemed little changed. Closing the door behind him, Harry stood thinking a moment, then set about on a quick but careful search of the premises, looking for things he or Caesar Augustus might have left behind—as well as what any third parties might have.

The pickings were slim. Whoever had tidied up after him had overlooked one drawer in the chest that stood against the wall, and thus Harry was able to retrieve a clean shirt of his as well as two pairs of socks. Otherwise, his search produced only a deck of playing cards, a tin of tooth powder, a rag that smelled of saddle oil, a brass uniform button that he supposed probably belonged to a previous tenant of the rooms, and a small African figurine that Caesar Augustus had carved for himself and carried about as some kind of totem.

If it brought luck, he surely needed it now.

Placing the little sculpture and the military button in his coat pocket, Harry used his shirt to make a bundle of the other items. He was tying the sleeves together to hold it fast, when the door behind him opened.

Harry paused, but did not turn.

"Make no move, Raines, for I have a revolver aimed at your back." The voice was high and quavering and slightly familiar.

Harry turned to face the man and smiled. "Now you have it aimed at my front."

The intruder was the manager of the hotel, a small balding man with a moustache far too large for his face. He did have a revolver—an out-of-date Colt from the look of it—but did not seem to be aiming it anywhere in particular.

"You're trespassing," he said. "I've sent for Detective Maccubbin."

"I merely came back to retrieve some things you people failed to pack," he said, lifting his bundle. "This nice shirt for one. I paid four dollars for it in Washington City."

"Why aren't you in jail? You're a murderer."

"The answer to your question is in the breast pocket of my coat, if you'll allow me to bring it forth." He reached, but halted, as the barrel of the pistol came up, aimed quite directly now.

"That's where you keep that gambler's pistol of yours, isn't it?"

"No. I keep that in the other pocket. Please, I wish to show you something."

He snatched out the envelope from General Lee quickly, in the event the fellow actually was contemplating firing off a shot.

"Read them both," Harry said. "And then return them."

The manager was incredulous, he read both letter and military pass twice, squinting at the signatures.

"You should be in Castle Godwin," he said, "with that murderin' Negro of yours."

"Those two pieces of paper say I should not," Harry said, taking a big step forward to retrieve them. The man frowned, then held them out, somewhat gingerly.

Harry took another big step. His long nap had restored him to the point of reckless overconfidence. He was becoming very tired of having people point revolvers at him.

He snatched away the letter and pass with one hand, then grabbed for the man's pistol, gripping the barrel and twisting sharply to the left.

The manager stepped back, holding and massaging his now empty gun hand. In twisting, Harry had caused pain.

"I mean you no harm, sir, and none to your hotel," Harry said. "In fact, I need to talk to you, as my services have been enlisted to assist in the inquiry into Mrs. Mills's lamentable passing."

"What inquiry?"

Harry waved the pistol barrel back and forth in front of the man's face. "This one." He turned the weapon over and handed it back with the butt to the fore. "I'd like to talk to you for a few minutes. If you'll be more civil, I'd like to make it over whatever passes for good whiskey in the bar of this establishment."

The bar was just off the lobby. As they entered, Harry heard a small commotion and glanced behind him in time to see Maccubbin go pounding up the main stairs from the lobby. The manager didn't notice this—or had decided he didn't want to.

As the bar had already depleted its stocks of Harry's favorite Old Overholtz, he settled for a Tennessee sour mash.

"The deprivations of war," he said, as they both sipped. The bar was noisy and smoky and full of soldiers. But for the uniform color, it reminded Harry of Washington City.

"What do you want of me?" the manager asked, sounding as though Harry had not returned the revolver and was instead holding it to his head.

"Were you here when Mrs. Mills came to this hotel?"

"Yes. Of course. I must have been. I'm the manager."

"Did she come here alone?"

"I believe she came in her coach."

"When she entered this hotel, was she alone?"

"No one knows."

"No one knows? Your lobby's about the most public place in Richmond."

The man finished his drink. Harry gestured to the bartender to pour another.

"I expect she used the back stairs—what the maids and the other servants use. Nobody saw her come through the lobby."

"You wouldn't find a woman of Mrs. Mills's social station using back stairs."

"Yes you would, if she was calling on a gentleman who wasn't her husband. And she wouldn't be the only one. Your actress friend used them to visit you, at least for her arrival. With this war, it's a problem keeping a reputable establishment."

"Did anyone see her?"

"Your actress friend?"

"Mrs. Mills!"

"Seems not. The provost marshal's people asked pretty near everyone. None of 'em saw her, or was willing to say so."

"Who would have been on duty?"

"Cooks, maids, stable hand, baggage handler, pretty near everyone."

"Show me these stairs, please."

The staircase was at the rear of the building and served all of the hotel's floors. At the bottom, it opened onto a hallway that led in one direction to the kitchens and in another to the cellar and a storeroom. The corridor was much trafficked, what with comings and goings for fresh bedding and supplies.

There were three black women in the kitchen, all busy, none claiming to have remembered any white woman passing by their workplace. The same was true of a young black man loading cans of lard onto a shelf in the storeroom. "Nossuh. Ain't no white lady come by here."

He'd looked to the manager before speaking.

Harry examined the padlock hanging open on the storeroom door. It was clean and oiled and obviously had frequently been used. Going to the outside door just opposite the kitchen, he turned the knob. It was unlocked.

"Your hotel is noted for its discretion, is it not?" Harry asked.

"This hotel is noted for the excellence of its accommodations and genteel service to its guests," said the manager, full of his position once again.

"Catering to their every need," Harry said, opening the door and stepping outside.

The alley was narrow, barely wide enough for a cart or wagon, but led through to both side streets.

"Maccubbin said Mills came in here because he saw his wife's carriage waiting out in the street," Harry said. "Where would that have been?"

"This way," said the manager. He led Harry to the left, past several barrelsfull of malodorous trash and a skittering rat or two. At the street, he pointed left again, to where a coachee and a hansom cab now stood waiting, both doubtless eventually bound for one of Richmond's railroad stations.

"It was there," he said.

"How do you know?"

"One of the hack drivers complained that it had been there for a long time. I went outside and saw that it was the Mills's carriage, and so I let it be."

"Why is that?"

The manager now gave Harry a very knowing look, the whole effect supercilious and oily.

"More of your genteel service," said Harry. "What time was that?"

"I don't know. Late afternoon. Still light out."

Harry turned back toward the alley, only to see the looming form of Nestor Maccubbin approaching at a rapid pace.

"You there!" he shouted. "Stop!"

Harry was not about to disobey. The hotel manager disappeared back inside.

"I want a word with you," Maccubbin said, speaking more quietly as he came nearer.

Harry already had the military pass and General Lee's note out. He presented them to Maccubbin with a flourish.

The policeman read both over quickly. "I already know about these," he said, thrusting them back.

"I thought you'd best be reminded."

Maccubbin, who had a couple of inches on Harry, came even closer, pressing Harry back toward the alley wall.

"You had to go to 'old Granny,' did you? And make a mess of this whole business."

"Who's 'old Granny'?"

"That fussbudget General Lee. That's what they call the old priss. A meddlesome man. And so are you, Raines."

"I'm merely protecting my property. Caesar Augustus is probably the most valuable slave in Richmond."

Maccubbin stepped back. Harry suspected he might have a more amiable nature than his conduct as a police official indicated.

"Not now, he isn't," Maccubbin said. "A man bound to die in a week ain't worth a lot to no one."

"How is he faring?"

"I don't bother myself about the welfare of murderin' Negroes."

Something small ran over Harry's foot. He moved away from the wall.

"How would any man be faring at Castle Godwin, white or black?"

"Better than at the old City Jail. Hell of a lot better than in Libby Prison. God, you can smell that place from here."

Harry looked back to the street, thinking of Miss Van Lew and her daily visits. And her incomparable morality.

"I will see him free again," Harry said.

"Free?"

"Unshackled."

"Raines, I do not think you understand the situation here. If your man didn't do this, then the only explanation anyone's going to believe is that she took her own life. Think of it, man! A suicide! And the lady bare-assed naked! In the hotel room of her old beau, a notorious gambler and wastrel and a suspected Lincolnite to boot. From common report it's obvious you haven't a shred of shame or care for scandal. What with actresses crawling in and out of your chamber night and day. But Mrs. Mills comes from one of the most prominent families of Richmond. So does her husband—and he's involved in one of the most important enterprises of the war. We can't have this, sir. Not now. Nosir."

"So your solution is to execute a convenient Negro, even if he didn't do it."

"The rope goes where the evidence points, sir. And it points right at that man of yours."

Harry rubbed at his chin and moustache. The latter needed trimming; the former, a shave.

"What about me?" he asked. "I was Mills's rival. I was the one his wife was quarreling with."

"We've been over that. You've got an even better alibi than Mr. Mills has. You were dining with the president of the Confederate States of America."

There was a splash farther down the alley. Harry looked up to see that someone had just emptied a slop jar out the window.

"Let's move around to the front," he said.

Maccubbin nodded. At the corner, they paused as an army wagon came inching down the hill.

"What is Mr. Mills's alibi?" Harry asked.

"I told you. He's involved in an important enterprise. He was on his way home from the Ironworks when he saw his wife's carriage. That was after you got there, so you're both in the clear. Like I said, she'd been dead for some time."

"Hanged."

"Yes, sir. With a stout rope."

"And where did that come from?"

"From over by the window. There's a coil of rope in every room, in case of fire."

Harry felt an idiot. Why was he always overlooking the

obvious? They moved on back toward the hotel's main entrance. Eyeing the loungers on the gallery, Harry wondered what gossip they'd make of his promenade with Maccubbin.

"May I go back to the room again?" he said.

"Raines. You're just stirring up trouble."

Harry hefted his bundle. "Maybe I left more behind than this."

INSTEAD of in the neat coil that was its normal state, the fire escape rope lay in a jumble some distance from the window. Harry picked it up, examining one end, where it had been cut evenly through, as though with one quick slice of a sharp knife. A woman of Arabella's delicate strength would have had to saw it in twain.

But why cut it at all? Why not use the whole thing?

Maccubbin stood with arms folded. "See. A strong man cut that rope. Like your boy in Castle Godwin."

"He's strong all right."

The chair had been put back against the wall. Harry took it to below the chandelier, peered up at the fixture, then climbed up on the chair. It creaked a bit under his weight.

He pondered the distance from his head to the chandelier, guessing about a foot. He was six feet tall, and the ceiling was twelve feet high, the chair about two feet.

Arabella was some eight inches shorter than he, as he had good reason to know.

He went back to the fire rope, coiling it again.

"How long are these supposed to be?" he asked.

"This is a second floor room. Maybe about twenty feet. I think that's the regulation."

Harry ran the line through his hands all the way to the end. He guessed that about five feet had been cut from it.

Six at the most. With a knot around the chandelier pipe on one end and a noose made in the other, the length would have been even less.

He returned to the chair, looking up, recalling again the horrible sight of Arabella's dead face staring down at him. When he had stood on the chair to cut her down, her feet had not reached it.

He stood on the chair again, then got off and kicked it over.

"Easy, Raines! That's not yours."

Satisfied with what he'd discovered, he reached to right the chair, but halted at the sight of something white sticking out a fraction of an inch from beneath the bedcover. Going to it, he raised the cover and pulled out what appeared to be Bella's camisole, which was badly torn. "Your people aren't very thorough," he said, handing it to Maccubbin.

Harry got down on his knees, throwing back the bedcover to admit more light as he peered beneath. He found only one other item. A black woolen stocking, also torn. There was straw caught in it.

Sitting up on the edge of the bed, he stretched it out, then handed it to Maccubbin as well.

"This was pulled off her," Harry said. "With some force. She wouldn't have done that. A woman rolls her stocking down to remove it."

"You'd know that, surely, Raines."

He stood up, studying the chandelier again. "I know something else, Maccubbin."

"What? That you're wasting my valuable time?"

"No, that I think this was done by two people."

Chapter 9

THE theater was one Harry had frequented as a Richmond resident before the war, spending nearly as much time backstage as he had in the seats, most particularly when Caitlin Howard had been in the cast.

She was now in Chicago with the touring John Wilkes Booth, and, given his more pressing concerns, as far from his mind as she was from his person. Louise Devereux was his fixation now, though for reasons she could not possibly suspect.

He made his way unimpeded to her dressing room, halting before the door and hesitating. As he had never heard her do before, she was singing. It was a French tune, and she treated it sweetly. Despite himself—and his affections for Caitlin—he was becoming increasingly smitten with this Belle of New Orleans.

One day he would finally bring himself to accept the increasingly obvious fact that he had no future with Miss Howard—not so long as there was a Booth. One day this war would end, and Miss Devereux's loyalties would no longer be a concern.

He was perhaps too intimately familiar with the scope of her activities when she was operating as a Confederate agent in Washington, activities that included killing the Union Army major who'd been her lover. But he'd been about to expose her espionage role to federal authorities, and thus to the probability of a hangman's rope.

Belle Boyd, Harry's distantly related cousin out in Martinsburg, had shot and killed a Yankee sergeant the previous Fourth of July in her mother's parlor, and the Union commander there had let her go.

Harry needed no reminder of the fact that he had himself killed a Confederate sympathizer in Baltimore. The fatal occurrence was entirely unintentional and inadvertent. His shot had been fired in the dark. And the woman had not only been a Southern spy but an assassin. All that on the scale, he still awakened at night wet with cold sweat from having relived the experience in his dreams. He felt a kinship with Louise that few could understand.

Turning the knob, he gently pushed the door open. She was at her dressing table, faced away from him and wearing only undergarments. She was already in her theatrical wig, though the curtain was nearly an hour away. Stepping quietly within, Harry closed the door and went to her, placing his hands on her small shoulders.

She shrieked, turned to look at him, then shrieked again. With good reason. Whoever she was, she was not Louise, and she would have no idea who he was.

"I'm sorry," he said, with a slight stammer. "I thought you were Louise."

She got to her feet, covering her chest with her arms and backing toward her changing screen. "Who are you?"

"Harrison Raines, of the Belle Haven Plantation," he said, smiling to ease her quite evident fear. She seemed very young. "I'm a friend of Louise's. My apologies for the intrusion. I thought to surprise her."

"Well you surely surprised me." The girl reached for her dressing gown and hurriedly put it on.

"Where is she?" Harry asked.

"I am not at liberty to say."

"Why not?"

"Because she asked me not to."

"Are you her understudy?"

"She hasn't one. But I have stepped into the role."

"You performed it last night?"

"Yes. And received a good notice today in the *Dispatch*."

This would not please Louise, who had once put a hat pin into the backside of a rival actress who'd gotten better reviews.

"Congratulations," he said.

"You'd better leave."

He took a step back toward the door.

"When does she return?"

The girl shrugged. "When she wishes."

Harry took out a *carte de visite* and wrote his new address on it. "Would you give her this? I'd like very much to see her."

She took the card. "So it would seem."

"I'd like very much to see you, too. On the stage."

"There're still tickets for tonight."

"Perhaps another night."

THE wooden-sided tunnel from Miss Van Lew's smokehouse to her cellar had a lower ceiling than Harry had remembered from his last visit, and he banged his head on it twice in the dark. Once in the cellar, he stumbled against some barrels, making a great deal of noise and injuring his knee and ankle in the process.

Miss Van Lew and her elderly manservant, the latter holding a pistol, awaited him at the top of the stairs.

"I do believe you are in the wrong profession, Mr. Raines."

"I'm sorry. I should have carried a lantern."

"For the sake of my house, I am glad you did not. But do come into the parlor. Would you like some refreshment?"

"If it's not an imposition, and if you keep spirits in the house, I should be most appreciative of a bit of whiskey."

She frowned. "I do keep spirits, for necessary occasions. But why do you find it necessary now? We need our wits at their sharpest, Harrison."

"My nerves," he said.

"You've had an unsettling experience?"

"I'm about to. I mean tonight to visit the embalmers where they have Arabella."

"To what purpose?"

"I wish to examine her body. And take some time at it. I'd be greatly obliged if I might borrow one of your people to assist."

"You don't think that a little ghoulish?"

"More than a little. But I must do it."

"And you want one of my servants to be your lookout while you go about this macabre intrusion?"

"Yes. That would be most useful."

"Harrison, there is so much else before us that is pressing."

"I have only a week to save Caesar Augustus. Less, now this day is most gone."

Her frown deepened. "Come this way."

She took him into her library, opening an ornate cabinet of French design and removing a crystal decanter. "I have only brandy. I hope that will suffice."

"Yes, ma'am. Thank you very much."

To his surprise, she took a tot for herself as well, though in a glass half the size of the one she gave him.

He waited for her to seat herself in a high-backed chair, then took one near her. There was no fire in the fireplace.

"I need to speak to Caesar Augustus," Harry said. "I went by there earlier this evening, but that Captain Godwin would not admit me."

"No. You vex him. He wants the poor man dead."

"Could you manage to get word to Caesar Augustus?"

She sipped her brandy and thought a moment. "There may be a way. But it might take a while."

"Miss Van Lew, there is no 'while.' "

Another sip, the last. She set down her little glass. Harry thought he was about to be dismissed.

"Harry, we are at a desperate point here. My man in the war department has lost his courage and will not help. We must somehow get word through to the Union lines about the ironclad, and soon—if only to warn the warships on blockade station in the lower Chesapeake. We must do this, above all other things."

Rising, Harry finished his refreshment and set his glass down beside hers. He felt encouraged now to attend to his "ghoulish" task—if only to have it done and behind him.

Yet he could not abandon this kind and brave woman, who had certainly been friend to him—perhaps his only friend now in Richmond.

"Have you no other operatives in the city?" he asked.

"Mr. Pinkerton has four such in Richmond. I have made contact with one, and he's willing. But he has his own route to the North, by means of the west of Virginia, and it could take a week or more. He will take no other way, as he does not think them safe."

"And the others?"

Her voice quavered some. He wondered if she was reaching the end of her tether.

"They have not responded to me." She rubbed her forehead. "I have thought of using some of my 'people,' but they are rounding up Negroes found on the roads. Betty could do it, but her continued presence at the 'Gray House' is vital."

Harry looked about the room. The furnishings were expensive and elegant, but seemed oddly incomplete. There were no candlesticks on the mantel, and no painting above where there obviously had been.

"Could you spare me someone to help tonight?"

She grumbled to herself. "You may have John."

"John?"

"The gentleman who is always with me. But do not keep him long. I shall be very much alone without him."

"Yes, of course. Thank you."

"And do not expose him to danger. He has served me well and doesn't deserve such trouble."

"No, ma'am." He'd forgotten to ask her something important. "Miss Van Lew, these officers Arabella had taken up with—do you know any by name?"

"Carew. I think there was a Captain Carew, or Carreau. And the Pemberton boy. He's always getting himself involved with married women."

"He's a serving officer?"

She nodded. "Attached to the War Department, but in the Navy—not that they have much of one. His daddy's a member of Congress."

The cold was getting to Harry. He thought again of Louise's warm bed. Of anyone's warm bed.

"If I could impose on you for one more brandy, Miss Van Lew, then I'll be about my dark business. And, do believe me, I'm not going to neglect the matter of the ironclad. That's why I'm here in Richmond."

She smiled, sadly. "I do not doubt you, Harrison Raines. But remember, there is no 'while.' "

* * *

THE undertaker's was at the edge of Miss Van Lew's fashionable neighborhood, just at the bottom of Church Hill but on the other side, north of Broad Street. The embalming quarters were attached to a small house, presumably the residence of the proprietor. There was no alley, but a short lane ran from the street to the rear door of the establishment. As quietly as possible, Harry made for that, leaving old John near the street. He was to start coughing, loudly, if anyone approached.

Harry had difficulty with the lock, blaming it on the cold and the brandy. The inky darkness was no help. He'd brought a lantern, but dared not light it outside.

Finally, after dropping his penknife twice, he managed to click the door open. Stepping inside, he closed it again very gently, then set about lighting the lantern.

The flame illuminated two staring corpses lying shoulder-to-shoulder on a table in the center of the large room. The frightful scene caused Harry to shudder, though he'd observed far worse manifestations of death at Bull Run and Ball's Bluff without any such tremors. The powerful smell of formaldehyde added to his queasiness.

He needed to move on. Raising the lantern high, he turned slowly until at last his eyes fell on the sight he'd come to see. Arabella lay face up on a table in the corner, beneath a stiff cloth that appeared to be canvas. Taking a deep breath, regretting the smell of chemical that came with it, he moved carefully toward her.

Her expression had not changed, putting him in mind of a little girl's china doll. Setting the lantern carefully on the table next to her head, he put on his gold-rimmed spectacles and leaned close, gently pushing her hair away from her face.

The whites of her eyes were flecked with dark dots of blood, and a gray smudge of some kind darkened one cheek. As it didn't rub away, he took it for the bruise Maccubbin had mentioned. Lifting her hair, he found the clotted blood on her shell-like ear.

Her throat was much abused. The flesh was purple where the rope had been and torn in two places at the front. He moved the lantern a measure closer and lifted her carefully, examining the back of her neck. It was much the same.

Feeling slightly ashamed, he slowly pulled back the cloth, exposing her breasts, and then her belly. All seemed well and without injury, except for her hands, which bore abrasions on backs and fingers.

This was taking too much time. His army surgeon friend back in Washington City, Colonel Phineas Gregg, would have completed this grim examination much more quickly. Harry moved the lantern back to one side, then pulled the cloth off the body entirely.

Their youthful romance had been conducted in the shadows. The sight of her laid out without a shred of clothing in the bright lantern light was shocking, and fascinating. Thinking of her as an artist might, he was struck by what a remarkably beautiful woman she was.

But guilt and sadness began to creep over him. He chastised himself and set about finishing his task, taking her by the leg and shoulder and rolling her carefully onto her stomach.

There was a scratch along one calf, in keeping with his surmise that her stockings had been rudely pulled from her. The skin was torn along a line, but there was little blood. No other marks—no wounds or cuts or bullet holes—were evident.

Returning her to the state in which he had found her, he was pulling the cloth up over her body again when he froze at the sound of the door opening behind him.

It was old John.

"What's wrong?" Harry asked. "Is someone coming?"

"Ah just gettin' cold out dere, Mister Raines."

Harry blew out the lantern.

"Well, it's time to get cold again."

"You fine what you lookin' fo'?"

"I did. And something even worse."

A sudden regret came over Harry as he shut the door behind them. He hated leaving Arabella there like that, alone and dead and battered. He wished her into her peaceful grave, for her sake.

But he would not leave matters at that.

Chapter 10

ARMED with his military pass, Harry headed once more for the Tredegar Iron Works, taking a route through the town that sheltered him from the blustery morning wind off the river.

Images of Arabella kept him from sleep and deprived him of any appetite for breakfast. Cold and groggy, he rode his horse uncomfortably, wishing he had his faithful Rocket instead. That animal was so big and easy, Harry could sleep in the saddle—and had. He'd left him on his farm near Martinsburg, where he'd be reasonably safe from horse thieves looking for mounts to sell to the army. Pinkerton had promised he'd have Harry's horse trading business in Washington looked after, but Harry had small faith in that.

The beast beneath him would have been a difficult sale, even for sharpers practiced in cheating the Army. He stumbled frequently, had an annoying tic in the withers, and, when at a walk, kept trying to take a nip out of Harry's leg. Harry began to wish he'd kept General Hooker's horse for himself.

The mount Caesar Augustus had hired for his own transport was much smaller but more useful—an older mare with a long black tail and mane, and a far more agreeable disposition. Caesar Augustus had a much better eye for horse flesh than Harry.

A corporal and a private now stood guard at the canal bridge. Harry presented his pass to the corporal, who squinted at it, then handed it to the private, who read it carefully.

"It says President Davis sent him," he said. Both came to a slovenly approximation of attention.

Pocketing the paper, Harry nodded to them curtly and nudged his horse into a halting trot. The pass worked its magic at the gates of the Ironworks and at the entrance of the two-story office building that stood on the edge of the bluff. A clerk there told him the manager was on the floor of the big gun foundry just below.

HARRY had to raise his voice over the cacophonous din to be understood.

"Mills isn't here," the manager said, barely audible. "Wife died."

"I know," Harry shouted back. "That's why I'm here. Where is he?"

"Hasn't been here today. Not yesterday either."

"Has he gone to Norfolk?"

"Why would he? His wife died. Hasn't been a burying."

"But he was in Norfolk?"

"He's been there. Been back." The manager faced him. "What's your business here?"

"I'm investigating the circumstances of Mrs. Mills's death—at the request of President Davis."

"Seems to me Mr. Davis's got more to worry about than that. So do I, so if you'll excuse me."

He moved off to shout at a foreman, who was directing the replacement of a mill wheel belt. Harry decided it was time for retreat. On the way out, he passed through the huge armory rolling mill on the east end of the compound. There were no stocks of iron plates.

ONCE clear of the sentries and on the hard surface of Byrd Street, which ran parallel to the canal, he turned his horse toward the city center and urged him into a canter. Not half a mile later he reined him again, turning onto Pearl Street and following it across the James on the long Mayo Bridge.

The Mills house lay a short distance up the hill in Manchester across the river. He rode toward it steadily, wishing he were almost anywhere else.

THERE was a carriage in the drive, hitched to a team and waiting, though no driver was present. Harry tied his mount to the branch of a small tree at the side of the front gallery, then mounted the steps.

It took several loud raps of the brass knocker before there was any response. Harry recognized the African woman who finally answered as Arabella's maid Estelle. She apparently recognized Harry, too. Her eyes widened as she looked upon him, then she shrieked and ran away, pounding down the wooden floor of the hall. He heard a door slam, then all was silent.

Not for long. There were voices, and then the stomping of heavy boots on the wooden flooring, coming nearer. Palmer Mills was striding toward him in full Confederate naval officer regalia, sword clanking, hand going to a large leather holster.

Twice now during this vexatious misadventure, Harry had found himself compelled to stand down men pulling pistols on him. He was considerably less bold in this situation, though he had known Mills for most of his life and had once considered him a friend.

His apprehension had good cause. Still in full stride, Mills pulled his long revolver free of the holster's flap and without hesitation fired off a shot, the report so loud Harry barely noticed the bullet strike against the wooden door frame just to the side of his head. Had Palmer taken a second's more time to aim, Harry was sure he would have joined the many casualties of this war.

Having no wish to do that, he threw himself forward, landing painfully at Mills's feet before the other could recock his weapon. Palmer tried to back up, but Harry clutched him around the ankles, causing him to totter. The pistol, an expensive Le Mat revolver from the look of it, went off again, very near Harry's ear, but again he felt no pain. Rising on one knee, Harry took a higher hold on Mills's legs and shoved, causing the other man at last to go over. An outflung arm partially broke the man's fall, but there was a thud as his head hit the floor.

He sat up, holding his head with both hands.

"God damn you, Harry!"

The revolver was within reach. Harry kicked it farther down the hall, then pulled out his gambler's two-shot Derringer—a much more useful weapon at such short range.

"Are you all right?" Harry asked.

"No. Damnation."

Harry could smell whiskey. Though Mills was in full dress uniform, he looked otherwise unkempt—his eyes red and rheumy, his hair a tangle, his chin beneath his moustache unshaven. Curiously, he also had the slight scent about him of perfume.

"I didn't kill your wife."

"I know. Your Negro did."

"No, he didn't. And I think I can prove it."

Mills rubbed his eyes, then blinked. "It happened in your hotel room."

He pushed himself back a little. Harry kept a wary eye on the man's revolver, wishing he'd kicked it farther.

"Where it happened is beside the point. Caesar Augustus did not kill your wife."

"This is all your fault, Raines. Everything. Why in hell did you come back?"

Harry inched back a ways himself, but not too far. He rested the hand with the Derringer in it on his knee.

"I was on the wrong side."

"Some don't think you believe that."

"Palmer, I am truly sorry for what's happened. I thought Bella had put me out of mind when she married you. You were much the better man for her."

"We've had troubles." Mills rubbed the back of his head now, examining his hand afterward as though searching for blood. He glanced around him. "I want to stand up."

Still wary, Harry edged back a half foot, then got to his own feet. Keeping the Derringer in one hand, he extended his other to help Mills up. The man accepted, attempting no tricks. Standing, he rubbed his head some more.

"You want some whiskey?" he asked.

"Thank you, I will," said Harry. "Why did you shoot at me?"

Palmer started walking down the hall, not asking permission.

"Damned mad at you, Raines. I've been sick to heart over Bella. Can't eat. Only drink."

"You're supposed to be at work—at the Ironworks."

"I am at work at the Ironworks—most of the damn time. I've heard you've been snooping around there after me. Snooping around there nowadays can get a man locked up. Understand?"

"I guess I do."

Mills paused to retrieve his pistol. Harry kept his finger on his Derringer's trigger, relieved when Mills returned his revolver to its holster.

Continuing down the hall, he led Harry into a sitting room off to the right.

It was a handsomely furnished chamber, with velvet draperies and a horsehair sofa and chairs. Two decanters and several crystal glasses sat on a silver tray on a round oak table. One glass was half full of whiskey.

"So where do we stand?" Harry asked.

"We sit," Mills said, so wearily it seemed he could not have stood ten seconds longer. He put his hand over his brow for a long moment, then sat forward and poured whiskey full into two glasses, shoving one glass toward Harry.

Both drank. Mills said nothing further.

"I've been empowered to investigate Bella's death," Harry said.

"What?" Mills scrunched up his face in incredulity.

"I have a paper authorizing me, and it is signed by President Davis."

Mills still found this ludicrous. "You're no policeman. You're a goddamn horse trader—and a Yankee."

"I'm a Virginian, Palmer, as you damn well know."

"Why are you doing this? Why don't you just leave us all alone? Arabella's dead. What difference does anything else make?"

"They've locked up my man Caesar Augustus. They mean to kill him as soon as it is convenient."

Mills shook his head. "You always did love those darkies. Look where it's gotten you."

"He didn't do it, Palmer. And he's my property. I'm

not going to be deprived of it by some lynch mob in uniform."

More blinking. "I thought you gave him his freedom. Your daddy like to kill you for that."

"I did indeed. When I decided to return to Virginia, Caesar Augustus wanted to return with me. To do so, he agreed to abide by our local customs."

"I don't believe it. Never saw a darky didn't run for the bush like a rabbit given half a chance. Never heard of one come back into slavery on his own."

"Believe what you will, Palmer. Davis gave me a week to prove his innocence, and I mean to do it."

Mills took a large swallow of his whiskey, then set down the glass. "I'm leaving here, Harry."

"Where for? Norfolk?"

"What do you know about Norfolk?"

"They told me at the Ironworks that you go there a lot."

"I'm a naval officer, Raines. Norfolk's our biggest shipyard."

This was not the time to ask about the "Monster." Drunk or no, Mills would end the discourse fast. And might do worse.

"Maccubbin told me you came to my room because you passed by the Exchange Hotel and saw Bella's carriage parked outside," Harry said.

"Yes. That's true."

"Who was in the carriage?"

"In? No one. Bella was in your hotel room—as we came to see."

"There wasn't a driver?"

"Yes. Of course there was a driver. Our coachman, Samuel. Did you think Bella drove that rig herself?"

Despite his poor vision, Harry caught movement just outside the window, the motion of someone who had been there leaving.

"Did you talk to him?"

"Of course I talked to him. That's how I learned Bella went to your room."

"How long did he say she was there?"

"A long time. It didn't surprise me. What surprised me was that you weren't there. I expected to find you both—violating the oath she took as my wife."

"And then what? Dispatch us both with that Le Mat pistol of yours? Invoke the 'unwritten law'?"

Mills wiped his mouth and then started out of the room. "Have to go, Raines. I am late."

"To Norfolk?"

"It's time for you to leave, Raines. Get out of my house!" Mills moved on down the corridor. "Drop this, Harry. Go back North. The South neither needs you nor wants you."

"You have my sympathy—for everything."

"Just go."

THE coachman Samuel was now on the driver's seat of the carriage that still waited outside. He was a man perhaps thirty-five, and very muscular, reminding Harry in that regard of his fellow Secret Service operative Boston Leahy.

"Good day, Samuel," Harry said.

The black man simply glowered at him, his brow wrinkling beneath a rounded hat.

"I understand you drove Mrs. Mills to my hotel that night."

"Ain't talkin' to you."

"Can you at least tell me how long she was there?"

"Ain't talkin'."

Harry came close to the carriage, leaning on a front wheel. "I'm trying to save the life of my man Caesar

Augustus. They mean to hang him for Mrs. Mills's death—just because he's a black man."

"Ain't talkin'!" He brandished his horsewhip.

"Very well. Good day to you, sir."

He mounted his mad horse. As he settled into the saddle, he saw Mills come out onto the front gallery of the house, whiskey decanter in hand. Harry saluted him, then trotted down the lane.

RETURNING to the stable near the Exchange where Caesar Augustus had left his horse, Harry set about switching mounts, only to find that the other had vanished from its stall.

"Soldiers took it," said the stable hand.

"*Took* it?" Harry looked about the stable, counting at least eight animals.

"Yassuh. They had a paper. Said they was takin' it for a cavalry mount. Said it belonged to a Negro who had no right to it."

"It didn't belong to him. I hired it. Now I have to replace it."

"Well, it gone."

The man reached for Harry's horse's bridle. Harry stepped in the way.

"That won't be necessary," he said. "I won't be staying here."

He mounted, thinking how difficult his task would be on foot. It was looking to be nearly impossible as it was.

THE landlord at the boardinghouse, encouraged by a silver dollar, agreed to let Harry keep his animal in his barn, and to claim that it belonged to the landlord should anyone in authority come around and ask.

Harry then returned to the Exchange on foot, stopping in the bar for a beer and a midday meal. Munching on a slice of ham, he pondered the view out the window and found himself with an idea.

There were three hansoms waiting outside. The driver of the first said he'd been home sick the afternoon Bella had been murdered. The second allowed that he had been working, but when Harry started to question him, demanded that he be paid for his time.

Harry tossed him a dollar and got into the carriage—an open-sided coachee. Taking the seat just behind the driver, he told him to go down to the river and return.

"You don't want to stop somewheres?"

"No thank you. Just feel like a drive in this wonderful invigorating air."

Invigorating, indeed. Harry calculated it was well below freezing.

The driver, a grubby fellow with a patched hat, was happy to talk.

"I remember that coach," he said. "I made two hauls from the railroad depot, and it was still there each time I got back. Right where we're supposed to unload baggage. I went to complain to the driver, but he wasn't there."

"What about Mr. Mills?"

"Don't know who that is, but whoever he is, he weren't there, either. Nobody was. Finally, I took someone out to Hollywood Cemetery, and when I got back, the carriage was gone."

"Gone? You're sure?"

"Yup. Then it came back again, but it was just the driver aboard."

They rounded a corner, swinging by the wide road that led down to the wharves. Out on the river, a small Confederate gunboat was chuffing upstream toward the rapids.

"When did it come back?" Harry asked.

"After sundown. My passenger spent a long time in the cemetery, then had me drive her back."

"Sounds like you had a profitable day."

"It ain't easy work."

"But all you saw was the coachman? No white man with him?"

" 'Less he was inside. Didn't seem like it."

"Did you see a woman anywhere near the carriage?"

"Why are you asking me all these questions?"

Harry decided to keep his pass from Davis in reserve. "Official business. I'll compensate you for the bother."

"Good to hear."

"Did you see a woman?"

"Yes."

"Was she fair?"

"No. As I recollect. She had dark hair. Long dark hair, and no hat. She was talking to the driver. I waited for her to go afore I complained to him about taking our waiting space."

Harry thought upon this a long moment.

"Did you see anyone carry anything from the coach into the hotel? A large trunk, or a large bundle?"

"No, sir."

When they reached the Exchange, Harry gave the man twice the fare. "If you'd ask around, among the other drivers, I'd appreciate it."

"You don't want to tell me what this is all about?"

"Sorry."

Harry descended to the street, where he was set upon almost immediately by Maccubbin and Detective Cashmeyer.

"You've got to come with us, Raines. General John Henry Winder wants to see you."

Chapter 11

JOHN Henry Winder was as old as the century. Graduating from West Point in 1822, he'd fought Indians on the frontier, when that was still east of the Mississippi, and served in the Seminole War in Florida as well. He'd been in the Mexican fight and become acquainted with Jefferson Davis. Word was that he'd looked more kindly on Santa Anna and his green-jacketed legions than he did now his former comrades in the Union Army.

He was the all-powerful provost marshal for the entire capital region and was in charge of all its prisons, including Castle Godwin.

Harry was thrust into his office by Maccubbin and Cashmeyer, each contributing a forceful shove apparently intended to impress their master. The room already had Winder and Captain Godwin in it, and so became quite crowded. There was a spare chair, but Harry made no move toward it.

Winder consulted a sheet of paper with a few handwritten notations on it, then looked up at Harry with a look of disdain and suspicion so withering Harry felt himself as good as before a firing squad.

"Harrison Raines," Winder said. "Do I know you?"

"I'm from the Belle Haven Plantation. My father is a colonel in . . ."

Winder waved his hand dismissively. "I know all that. I mean, have we met before?"

"I don't think so, sir. I would have remembered."

Winder leaned back and lighted a cigar. "Godwin here says he got a report from our people in Washington that says Rose Greenhow says you're a Yankee spy and a traitor to Virginia."

"That's not true," Harry said. Godwin and Cashmeyer were eyeing him as snakes might their next meal. Maccubbin appeared less menacing, if not exactly amiable.

"She says the only reason she's in the Old Capitol Prison is that you betrayed her to Allen Pinkerton."

"She's in prison because of her own foolishness," Harry said.

"I'd mind well how you speak of that woman," Winder said, coming forward again. "She's a martyr to our cause. Her information helped us win the day at Manassas. She was the best we had in Washington City."

"And at times the worst. She used to meet with her agents in Lafayette Square, right across from the President's House. My role in this was to warn her, several times. And to help her escape—an enterprise she thwarted by running back into her house again. You can ask my cousin through marriage, Belle Boyd."

"That girl out in Martinsburg who killed a Yankee?"

"Yes, sir." Harry felt a little woozy, he was about to move to the chair, when Godwin abruptly went over and settled into it, looking very satisfied having done so.

"General Winder," Harry said. "I have myself been in three Yankee jails, including Fort McHenry. I have come home to rejoin my family and serve Virginia. I came here on a horse I stole from General Joseph Hooker, and . . ."

Winder gave another dismissive wave. "I'm aware of

all that. Stop worryin', Raines. You're vouched for by President Davis and General Lee. That's good enough for me. I was just twistin' your tail a little. Far as I'm concerned, you're free to leave and go about your business."

"Thank you, sir." Harry turned to go.

"Except for one thing," Winder said.

Harry turned back. "What's that?"

Winder's fist came down hard on his desktop. "That damned Negro of yours!"

"He's causin' bad trouble up at my jail," said Captain Godwin.

"The other inmates are raisin' a ruckus 'cause we put a darky in with them," Winder said. "All of them are, even those we know are Lincoln black Republicans. They claim it infringes or impinges or whatever on their rights. They want him out of there."

"What's that to do with me?" Harry asked. "You people put him there."

"Yes, well, we people want to take him down to the river and shoot him. That'll take care of everybody's problem."

Harry shuddered, hoping they didn't notice. He rubbed his arms, as though against the cold.

"You cannot do that, sir, not for another five days at least."

"We know about that, Raines. We're just askin' you to help us out."

"You'll be in uniform in a week," Godwin said. "Probably a captain or major, with your connections. You won't need that man."

"Yes I will, and I mean to have him." He looked to Maccubbin. "Your detective here and I have found evidence that Mrs. Mills may have been done in by two people—and maybe hanged after she was dead."

"That true, Maccubbin?"

The detective shrugged. "That's Raines's theory. I guess it's possible."

Winder puffed on his cigar a moment, till his face was obscured by its smoke.

"Any idea who they might be?" This was directed at Harry.

"It's what I'm spending every waking moment trying to find out. Her coachman was on the premises, and for a long time."

"What's surprising about that?" said Maccubbin. "He brought her there, didn't he? She didn't walk."

"One of Godwin's inmates said we should take your darky and move him to Libby Prison," Winder said.

Harry's thoughts, which had been a ramble, suddenly quickened. The prospect offered a number of possibilities.

"Those are mostly officers we've got in there," Godwin said. "I don't mean to show 'em any kindness, but you can't do that. Can't stick a Negro in with 'em."

Winder took another large puff from his cigar. "We'll put him in Libby. Those Yankee sonsofbitches got it comin'."

Godwin stared at the general, then nodded. "Whatever you say, sir."

Winder grinned. "Mr. Maccubbin—you see to it." He turned to Harry. "You go do what you think you must, Raines, but don't cause me any more trouble. If I have to, you know, I can have that rascal of yours shot tryin' to escape."

"Yes, sir."

"Five days?"

"Yes, sir. Plus what's left of today."

"Just stay out of our way. A pass from Davis doesn't mean you can do whatever you please. Not in Richmond City."

* * *

Returning like some stubborn, cast-off dog to the hotel where he was no longer welcome as a guest, Harry went through the alley to the rear entrance he had earlier explored, waiting until only black faces were evident through the kitchen window. Then he quietly moved inside.

They all turned toward him as he stood in the kitchen doorway. Eyes lifted as he took a silver coin from his pocket and tossed it in the air.

"I have a dollar here," he said, snatching it back from the air. "I'll give to whoever's willing to help me."

They all ceased their labors, and stood still, all eyes upon him.

"One of your own, my man Caesar Augustus, sits in Castle Godwin, wrongly accused of murder and waiting to die. I mean to save him. I'd like your help."

"What you need, sir?"

"I want you all to think hard upon this. Two days ago, at about this hour, or possibly earlier in the afternoon, did any of you see two men come through this back entrance and go upstairs, carrying something heavy? Might have been two black men, might have been two whites, might have been a white and a black. But there'd have to be two, and strong enough to carry a heavy burden between them."

"Two men, sir?"

"Yes."

"No, sir, I ain't seen 'em."

"Anybody else see anybody like that?"

There was a general shaking of heads.

"How about a woman—a white woman?" Harry tossed the coin again. "A silver dollar."

They began returning to their work. Harry lingered a

moment, to no avail, then made his way outside again, pausing there to give the rear of the hotel a more careful examination. He was poking behind some trash barrels when he felt a tug at the tail of his frock coat.

"Mister?"

Harry found himself confronted by a small, black face. The boy could not have been ten.

"Yes?" Harry asked.

"You say a silver dollar?"

Harry held it up, gripping it firmly. "Yes I did."

"I see a lady come in. She come in through this door."

"You work here?"

"I'se kitchen boy. I see a lady come in."

"Was she fair? Or did she have dark hair?"

"Don' know. She got her head all covered up."

"A hat?"

"Nosir. Cold outside. She got a hood pulled close over her head."

The boy was wearing ragged trousers, a soiled shirt, and cracked shoes, nothing more.

"Did you see anyone else?"

"Yessir, I see two men, like you ask."

"Two men? When did they come in?"

"They came in with her. One was feelin' poorly."

"What do you mean?"

"He was kinda hangin' on to the others."

"Did you see his face?"

"His head was hangin' down."

"What color was his beard?"

"Ain't got no beard."

"Did anyone else see them?" Harry asked.

"Don' think so. Only me. I was shinin' shoes in the pantry."

"Why didn't you tell me inside?"

"I'se 'fraid I git whupped fo' talkin' to a white man."

"Whupped by who?"

"Boss man come by yesterday and say not to talk to a white man if he come by. That be you?"

"That be me." Harry placed the silver dollar in the boy's hand, but held on to his shoulder. "What's your name?"

"Jimmy."

"Well, Jimmy, I may want to talk to you again. Maybe show you some pictures."

The boy grinned, but the expression abruptly vanished. "You won't git me whupped?"

"Won't get you whupped."

He released his hold. The boy darted through the door and vanished.

On his way back to his boarding house, Harry saw no fewer than three wagons idled in the streets with their traces empty and teams gone. The equine press gangs were out with a vengeance.

And soon, they'd be out after men.

Weary from his walk and day, he trudged up the stairs to his room, only to be halted on the landing by the voice of his landlord, calling from below.

"Say, Raines. Hold a moment."

"Yes?" Harry asked.

"Something for you in your room."

"From whom?"

"Don't know."

"Thank you."

Completing his climb, he saw light coming from the crack at the bottom of his door. It was unlocked. Swinging it open, he saw a wide-eyed black woman sitting on his bed.

Chapter 12

HARRY shut the door behind him.

"What are you doin' here, Estelle?" he said, "Last time you saw me, you took off running like a scared cat."

"I run away, Mister Raines."

"Estelle, you can't do that. They'll just hunt you down."

"Can't stay there. Mister Mills, he goin' crazy. Drinks all the time. Walks around with a gun. And Samuel, he been beatin' on me bad." She pointed to her cheek.

"But why do you come to me?"

"Caesar Augustus say he know a way to the Underground Railroad. Maybe you know it, too."

"Well, I'm sorry. I don't. And I am very preoccupied at the moment trying to get Caesar Augustus out of prison."

She looked down at the floor, sadly. He saw that she was wearing house slippers and black stockings.

"How did you get here?" he asked.

"I hear Mister Mills tell Samuel where you stayin'."

"Why did he do that?"

"I don't know. Maybe Samuel ask."

He took a step toward her. Startled, she hopped back a

little on the bed. She was a lovely woman, and he wondered if she had been presumed upon in her servitude—
possibly by Palmer Mills himself. Harry was feeling extremely uncomfortable with this situation.

"You and Caesar Augustus are, uh, friends?"

"Yes, sir. Long time."

"I mean to save him, Estelle, but it's a hard row. I have
to find the person who killed Mrs. Mills. And I could use
your help."

"My help?"

He sat down on the bed next to her. She kept her eyes
lowered.

"Were you in the carriage when Mrs. Mills came to see
me—on the day she died?"

"Nosir. I was at the house, all that day."

"But you accompanied her the first time she came visiting me. She took you everywhere."

"Yessir. But then she git real mad at me. Tol' me I
couldn't come. I weren't to leave the house."

"Why was she mad at you?"

" 'Cause I'se friends with Caesar Augustus. 'Cause he
come by the house. She won't let me go nowheres."

"What about Samuel, the coachman?"

"He the coachman. He goes where de coach go."

"Did she say anything about coming to see me that
afternoon? Did she say why?"

"She just tell me to stay home."

Harry rose from the bed. "Can you think of anyone who
was mad at Mrs. Mills? Mad enough to do this?"

She lifted her gaze to the window. The view was of the
back wall of a brick house across the yard.

"Don' know."

"Think. There must have been someone."

"Mister Mills, maybe. They always fightin'."

"What about?"

"Everythin'."

"She had gentlemen friends. I was given the names of Carreau and Pemberton. Do you know them?"

"Yessuh."

"Who are they?"

"Captain Carreau, he be in the Army. Lieutenant Pemberton, he a Navy man, like Mister Mills. There's 'nuther one—a major. I seen him at the house this week."

"His name?"

"Broward."

One of the idle dandies of Harry's time in Richmond had been named Broward—a bully known for his arrogance, though he was from a family of small distinction.

"George Broward?"

"Yessir."

"He's a major now? He actually joined the army? And Mrs. Mills—liked him?"

"Yessir. But he ain't done no fightin'. I think he's at the War Department."

Harry went to the window. The sky was lowering. The wind was whistling through a crack in the sash. "Have you eaten?" he asked.

"Not since mornin'."

"I'll have some food sent up. I'm going to leave you here until later this evening, then I'm going to get you to a place of safety. You can't stay with me. It'll only mean trouble for you."

"If I go back to Mister Mills, I git sold down the river."

"Palmer Mills is not my favorite person, but he wouldn't do that."

"Yessir. He say this mornin' he goin' to sell me and Samuel and move away from here."

"But he's in the Navy. He can't just go where he wants."

"Dat what he say."

He went to his saddlebag, which was lying on a chest beside the bed, and removed his favorite pistol, a .32 caliber Navy Colt, putting it in his belt. "I have to go out, Estelle. Don't go anywhere." He paused at the door to look at her.

"Caesar Augustus say you are a kind man," she said.

"It was kind of him to say that."

"Could you git me some mince pie?"

"Mince pie it is."

WARTIME had changed Richmond as profoundly as it had Washington. Establishments Harry remembered as genteel—or at least, respectable—had degenerated into rough places, what Pinkerton liked to call "the abodes of crime." Knowing nothing of Captain Carreau or Lieutenant Pemberton, Harry had no idea what sort of saloon they might patronize—if any.

Broward was an easier matter. He had been a regular of the Main Street bars near the Capitol, favored as they were by influential figures of Virginia politics and society.

After seeing to Estelle's supper, and his own, he set out, heading west on Main Street and turning in first at the double doors of the Bell Tavern, where he had done much of his apprenticeship as a gambler.

He was remembered.

"Heard you'd vanished into Yankeeland," said the bartender, setting down Harry's whiskey.

He drank. "Reappeared."

"How come? 'Tain't so merry in Richmond nowadays."

"Every prodigal returns."

"You lookin' for a game?"

There were two in progress already, one table loud with frequent laughter, the other grim and quiet.

"Later. Right now, I'm looking for George Broward. Do you remember him?"

"Doesn't give us much chance to forget. What do you want with him?"

"Have you heard about the death of Arabella Mills?"

The bartender leaned close, then slowly nodded. "Heard she took a Negro to bed, and he killed her."

"That's not the truth of it," Harry said. He produced his pass, flashed it before the bartender's eyes, then returned it to his pocket. "I know that because I'm investigating the matter. That's why I need to talk to Broward."

"What's he got to do with it?"

"Wasn't he keeping company with Mrs. Mills?"

The bartender shrugged. "Never brought her in here."

There were women in the saloon, but none of Arabella's caste. One rather oversized lady was sitting on a captain's lap. When Harry had last lived in Richmond, the municipal authorities would have closed the place down for such flagrant immorality. Now it barely was noticed.

"Does he come in regular?" Harry asked.

"Too regular."

"Do you know a Captain Carreau? Or a naval officer named Pemberton?"

Another shrug. "Not by name. Lot of whiskey shops in Richmond."

Harry finished his drink.

THERE was indeed an abundance of dram shops in the capital. Harry visited some twelve of them before abandoning his search for the night, including the Swan Tavern. In none of the establishments was there knowledge of any Carreau or Pemberton. Nearly all the saloons were familiar with Broward, but none had seen him within the last two days.

It occurred to Harry the man might actually have gone to find some fighting. There'd been skirmishes up in Fairfax County, though McClellan had not yet budged the main Union army.

Having had too many whiskeys in pursuit of his investigation, Harry decided to clear his head with an extended walk in the cold. His path took him past the Richmond Varieties Theatre, and, on impulse, happy for the warmth, he bought a ticket and stepped inside.

There was a policeman at the head of the aisle, a custom Harry had noted in Northern theaters, stationed there to keep painted ladies from entering the audience to ply their trade. The play, which was well under way, was a French farce with which Harry was unfamiliar: *Fanchon, the Cricket.* There were rowdies in the audience, most of them soldiers, so it was well the fare was comedic. Raucous laughter followed most every line.

The actress on stage was older, and somewhat fat. Harry, who'd taken a rearmost seat, watched uncomfortably, waiting in vain for a lady younger and lovelier to make an entrance, but Louise did not appear. There was a loose program on the floor. He retrieved it and, after putting on his spectacles, read over the names of the cast. "Devereux" wasn't there.

Despite the guffaws and other boisterous noise, sleep was creeping over him. He snapped his head to regain alertness, but, like fog from the sea, drowsiness returned, and overcame him.

When he awoke, it was to a nearly darkened theater. Someone was shaking him by the shoulder, someone with a sweet and familiar scent.

"Harry! Please! Wake up!"

He blinked. His eyeglasses had fallen askew. Taking

them off and placing them in a pocket, he turned in the direction of the lovely voice. "Louise?"

"You must leave, Harry. You shouldn't be here."

"You weren't in the play, Louise. Where have you been?"

Glancing apprehensively over her shoulder, she sat down beside him. "I can't stay," she said. "Please go, Harry. Go now."

"What's wrong?"

She leaned close, her perfume reviving him, though the world still seemed quite misty. Her eyes were wider than he remembered, worry creasing her brow, aging her while she held that expression. It occurred to him she was wearing theatrical makeup, though she hadn't been in the play.

Once again she shook him. "I'll come to you, Harry— but later."

"When?"

"As soon as I can, but not soon."

Louise was whispering now. She gave another look over her shoulder, toward the stage. There was the glow of a gaslight coming from an open door.

She was wearing a thick winter cloak, with fur trim.

"I missed you," he said.

"Good God, you're drunk."

"Sorry. I've been investigating. I need your help, Louise."

"I'll come to you, Harry. I promise." She rose with a great rustle of skirt.

"You don't know where I'm staying now."

"Yes I do." She hurried down the aisle, disappearing through the illuminated doorway. A man's head and shoulder appeared in the space after her, then the door was pulled shut.

*   *   *

HARRY managed to find his way through Miss Van Lew's smokehouse tunnel without banging head or limb, but he stumbled on the stairs leading from her cellar, scraping his shin. The injury served to restore his spark. He gave complaint in profane voice.

Miss Van Lew shrank back from him a little as he entered the house proper, as though he were some wild man.

"You reek of spirits, Harrison," she said, raising a handkerchief to her dainty nose.

"My apologies, Ma'am. I've been prowling the taverns in search of information—and Arabella Mills's several beaux."

Her handkerchief was scented, though less sweetly than Louise had been. She waved it in front of her face a few times, then seated herself in a parlor chair, one at some remove from that which Harry took.

"Did you find them?"

"No, Ma'am. Not any of them, but I learned a few things. A captain told me General Johnston is pulling back from Manassas and will likely settle at Gordonsville. That puts him on the railroad. He can get his army to Richmond damn quick if McClellan tries to outflank him."

"Harry . . ."

"And shipments of powder and shot have been rushed to Norfolk. Naval ordnance. The Monster is readying for a fight."

"Harry, something odd has happened."

"An hourly occurrence nowadays in Richmond."

"No. Listen. I managed finally to get word to Fortress Monroe. I used my brave Africans, bless them. One was stopped by a Rebel patrol, but they failed to discover that her basket had a false bottom. Our message got through."

"Well, then," said Harry, relaxing a little in the too comfortable chair. "Our work is done."

"Our work is never done. But, Harry, they'd already had word at Monroe of the ironclad. They knew. They have a direct telegraph line there to Washington. The government's been warned, thank Heavens. Help is on the way—or will be."

"That's splendid news."

"But it's disconcerting. The only message I sent was the one entrusted to my black folk. Pinkerton's people here have remained in the city. I am perplexed as to the identity of this mysterious benefactor. Surely it was not you?"

"No, Miss Van Lew. I've been here."

"Attending to another matter." She pulled her shawl closer around her.

"Yes, ma'am."

"Well, there's good news on that account. Caesar Augustus is now in Libby Prison."

Harry came forward, leaning in toward her. "Truly? With the Union officers?"

"I think in separate quarters, but there nonetheless. I may be able to visit him. I've been waiting up in hopes of your coming tonight—expecting you will have a message for him."

Harry pondered this. "Only that he should not give up hope—and that I will try to visit him."

She frowned. "I do believe that will be impossible."

"I will try."

There was a thump, from the floor below. Harry lifted his eyes in that direction. "What was that?"

She smiled. "We live in perilous times, Harrison. Soldiers came today and took my carriage horses."

"Your matched pair? Those splendid animals?"

"Indeed. A punishment I'd gladly bear, were it not for the evil work to which they'll be put in the Confederate Army."

"How will you . . ."

She put a finger to her lips, then rose, extending her hand. "Come with me."

Lighting a lantern, Miss Van Lew led him to a wide staircase that led downstairs from the main hall. At the bottom, she took him down a hall and then opened a door to a dark chamber that smelled oddly. Following her within, Harry saw straw on the floor, then, hearing a snort, turned quickly around to the right. There, calmly munching hay, was a Thoroughbred saddle horse.

"He's all I have left," she said, "but he's a good fugitive. The soldiers looked through the house, but he made no sound, and they failed to discover this place, for I place a chest in front of the door."

"What will you do with him?"

"I'll keep him here another day, in case they return— as is sometimes their way. Tomorrow night I'll move him to the stable of a friend who is not so suspect as am I."

"I can do that for you."

"No, Harry. It would do no good for us to be linked in that way should you be caught. And you have more important business before you." She put her hand to his arm. "You need sleep, sir. It's writ on your face like a curse. Go get some. You're no good to anyone in this state."

They descended as they had come. She gave him a cup of hot cider in the kitchen, then accompanied him to the tunnel.

"You're going to Libby tomorrow, then?" she asked.

"If I can. I must."

"If we encounter one another, we cannot speak, nor make any sign of recognition."

"I understand."

"Be on your guard tonight. The streets are unsafe. There's as much danger from the law as from the gangs of thugs out there."

Harry patted his coat pocket. "I have my Navy Colt."

THOUGH he heard odd noises behind him once or twice, Harry returned to the boardinghouse unmolested. He found his room empty. Estelle's dinner had been brought and thoroughly consumed, but she was gone.

He'd worry about that later. Without removing his clothes, he lay down on his bed and rolled himself into his blanket, then sank into sleep.

Chapter 13

A pounding at his door put an end to Harry's strangely blissful sleep. He shook his head until he could see and think clearly, then threw back his blanket and went to make the banging stop.

Standing before him in the hallway was a frightened and weary Estelle, her arm gripped by the forbidding figure of Nestor Maccubbin—a man who seemed to have no need of sleep.

"This one yours?" the detective asked.

"Mine?"

"She says she's yours. That you bought her."

Harry reached to take Estelle's other arm, pulling her gently away from her captor. "Yes. She's mine. Where did you find her?"

"Skulkin' around the streets east of the Capitol. Looked like she was half froze."

"Yes. Well, thank you, Mr. Maccubbin. I appreciate your taking the trouble."

"Almost took her down to Hopkins's auction house. That's the law on stray Negroes without freedom papers. Pretty one like this'd fetch a proud dollar."

"Well, thank you for not doing that." Harry took hold of the door, easing it toward the man.

"You oughta take better care of your Negroes, Raines."

"I will. I promise. Thank you, Maccubbin. Goodnight."

"It's near six a.m."

"So it is. Good morning, then." He shut the door.

Estelle scurried to a corner and huddled there, arms around her knees.

"Why did you go off like that?" he asked.

She sniffed. She had lost one of her slippers. "You never come back."

"Yes I did. You just didn't wait long enough."

"I'se sorry."

"And no doubt hungry again. It's too early to get a breakfast out of this landlord, but when I come back, I'll get you more to eat."

"Where you goin'?"

"Libby Prison—to see Caesar Augustus."

"I wants to come with you."

"Estelle, you've been up all night."

"I wants to."

He rubbed his eyes. "All right. We'll find you some shoes."

INSTRUCTING her to remain in the prison's open outer yard, Harry took out his military pass and strode toward the sentry at the main gate.

"I'm investigating a murder and need to talk to one of the prisoners," Harry said.

The signature of Jefferson Davis worked its magic. The young man pulled himself to attention. "Yes, sir. When you get inside, ask for the duty sergeant." He stepped aside.

"Don't let that girl go anywhere," Harry said. She was watching him. "Runaway."

"I'll watch her, sir."

Harry walked on, trying to look as confident as Maccubbin would be in this situation. Two other guards inside were also readily obedient to Harry's magic document, the last one escorting him to a small room at the end of the corridor. Inside was a sergeant, eating bread and gravy off a tin plate. His jacket was unbuttoned, and he'd been drinking, which Harry took as a good sign. A man whose soldiering was that slovenly ought to be amenable to a bribe.

"Who are you, and what do you want?"

Harry produced his paper. "I need to interview a prisoner."

The sergeant wiped his mouth and moustache with the back of his hand. "No regulation against that." He pulled a greasy ledger book before him and opened it to the first page. "Name?"

"Caesar Augustus."

"Augustus," he said, drawing his finger slowly down the page. "Nope."

He turned to the next page, and then the next. Soon he had gone through the *A*'s.

"Nope. No such man. You sure you got the right name?"

"He's a Negro."

The sergeant's expression darkened. "You mean, *the* Negro. You've come to talk to that black bastard that killed the Mills woman?"

"Yes. I'm authorized . . ."

"Not with me you ain't."

Harry waved the military pass. The sergeant shook his head.

"Nothin' on that piece of paper says you can talk to the Negro. Sorry. Get out of here." He paused. "Sir."

"I'll be back," Harry said.

*   *   *

Iᴛ was a long, cold walk to the War Department, but Harry had no wish to risk confiscation of his hired horse, knowing he'd have need of it when the time came to escape this city.

He reached the War Department well after it was open for business, finding a substantial crowd milling outside, including civilians he took for contractors hard after a share of the Confederate treasury—though the new "republic's" money was losing value day by day.

To the anger and consternation of many, Harry pushed his way past them into the building, then through more of them within as he sought the stairs. General Lee's anteroom was filled as well. Harry went directly to the young major serving as aide de camp.

"I won't be bothering the general," Harry began, but was cut short by the young officer.

"Indeed you won't," said the major. "He has not yet arrived, and, when he does, he has many with more vital matters than yours awaiting him."

He gestured to the full chairs behind Harry.

Harry declined to look. "I am at a point of impasse. The authorities at Libby refuse to let me speak to my slave, and I cannot resolve this issue without doing so."

"They put your Negro in Libby?"

"Yes, sir. It was General Winder's doing."

"That's unfortunate."

"Perhaps. What will be more unfortunate is that I may be compelled to go to the *Richmond Whig* or some other paper to relate the full details of this sorry episode and make the public aware of the injustice being done to me."

The major flushed a little. "I am sure that General Lee would view that as most regrettable—as would President Davis. But if you think the general would be persuaded to assent to your demand or change his views in any way because of your threat, you are seriously misinformed as to his character."

The words stung.

"You are right," said Harry, more gently. "I regret the rashness of my remarks. But they are an indication of my desperation. I needn't bother the general. All I need is a simple scrap of paper authorizing me to talk to the man, which is only fair. He belongs to me."

Shaking his head, the major reached for a small sheet of letter paper and then a pen. He scratched out something hurriedly, then affixed his signature, adding a "for" and the name of Gen. Robt. E. Lee.

"There."

"Thank you," Harry said, pocketing the paper before it could be snatched back.

"I would remind you that the general remains mindful of your promise to him," the major said. "Concerning your military service."

"I am mindful of it as well." He hesitated, realizing he must avail himself of every opportunity. "There's something else I need."

The major threw up his hands.

"I need to know the units and locations of three officers, all of whom have a bearing on this case—a Captain Carreau, a Lieutenant Pemberton, and a Major Broward."

Now the major lost all patience. "It may come as a surprise to you, sir, but this sort of thing is not among General Lee's many responsibilities."

"Might you direct me to whoever's it is?"

Another note was hastily scribbled and pushed across the desk toward Harry. The major then turned to other work without further word.

"Obliged," said Harry.

Harry turned, thrusting both prized scraps of paper into

a coat pocket and started toward the door. It was then that he saw the tall officer sitting stiffly in a wood chair at the other end of the room. He had a kingly beard, going from black to gray, and, behind a pair of gold spectacles, hard, dark-brown eyes that stared past Harry as though he were invisible.

Harry stood his ground, waiting for recognition. When none came, he walked over to the man, standing uncomfortably before him.

"Father?"

There was no response. Harry did not exist.

Sensing the stares of everyone in the antechamber now, Harry twitched, uncertain as to what to do.

"I've come home, Father," he said.

Finally, the cold eyes shifted to take him in. To Harry, it was much the same as being run through with a bayonet. After a long, painful moment, the officer looked away.

Harry faced away, shaking his head, and started toward the door—achieving no more than a single step when he was nailed to the place by the first words he had heard from that gentleman in nearly four years.

"I will speak to you," his father said, "when I see you in the uniform of your country."

Harry knew better than to look back.

THE clerk in the War Department's paymaster section seemed dubious about the freshly written authorization Harry presented him, but agreed to the request. Unfortunately, he said, it would take all day, and he instructed Harry to come back at four o'clock that afternoon, or better, the next day.

Harry's impatience was beginning to frazzle him. "If it

were President Davis asking this, would you tell him to come back tomorrow?"

"Are you President Davis?"

"No, but . . ."

"Come back tomorrow, sir."

Libby, much like Willard's Hotel in Washington City, was a series of three connected buildings. Set on the flats near the river at the bottom of Church Hill and served by a railroad spur, the thickly walled and floored structures had been warehouses used for grain, tobacco, and manufactured goods before the war. Now they held men, crowded into pen-like enclosures on each floor.

Some of the officer residents were high-ranking, and for a time, their inmates included Congressman Albert Ely of New York, captured at Bull Run when he'd pressed forward too adventurously during the fighting for the Stone Bridge. He'd been paroled and exchanged the preceding fall.

The interior was dark, dank, stagnant of air, and malodorous. There were stoves, largely for the benefit of the jailers, but most of what heat there was came from the sheer volume of closely packed human flesh.

It was also a noisy place, a steady drone of conversation punctuated by continual coughing and occasional angry oaths and wails.

With marked disgust and reluctance, a sergeant led Harry down wooden stairs to the basement of the central building. Pushing through the prisoners with pistol out at the ready, carrying a lantern in his left hand, the man growled and snarled his way to a small wooden door set in the masonry wall at the rear. Harry and two Confederate privates with muskets followed closely behind.

It was the prisoners' eyes that most unsettled Harry.

Never before in his life had he felt himself the focus of such intense, collected hatred. One set of very blue eyes seemed the most hateful of all, oddly belied by a slight curl of lip. The man was taller even than Harry's six feet, and extremely muscular, standing out considerably in that regard from his fellow prisoners. Otherwise, he was much like them, his white cotton shirt soiled and torn, his uniform tunic bearing captain's bars on the shoulder straps but missing buttons.

Startled by the man's appearance, Harry gave a slight nod and then hurried on to catch up with the sergeant, who waited at the door unhappily. "How long you need?" he asked.

Harry had no idea. Presuming his presence would be a comfort to Caesar Augustus, he would want to stay with him as long as he could.

"I don't know," he said. "I'll let you know when I'm ready to leave."

"Fifteen minutes," said the sergeant, unlocking and then swinging open the door.

Caesar Augustus had been kept in total darkness. Harry could see him curled up on the floor of this ridiculously small chamber, a vague figure in the shadows.

"I'll need more than that," Harry said.

"Fifteen minutes."

"Give me the lantern," Harry said, taking it from the other's hands. At that instant, he saw advantages to becoming a Confederate officer, if only to have the chance to discipline the likes of these prison guards.

Lowering his head, he crawled into the small space. The door was slammed, and, from the sound of it, locked behind him.

Caesar Augustus sat up. The smell in here was the least pleasant of all.

"Where you been, Marse Harry?"

"Doing my damnedest to get here. It's taken the help of General Lee and President Davis himself to do it."

The black man shifted, with a heavy clank of chain and manacle, moving to lean back against the wall. Harry took his flask from a coat pocket and handed it to his friend, who readily accepted it.

They hadn't searched him for weapons or asked him to surrender any. He still carried his two-shot Derringer pistol. For a passing moment, he considered leaving it with the prisoner.

But that could prove a deadly mistake. They'd have provocation for killing him.

"Thanks," said Caesar Augustus, handing back the whiskey after a second swallow.

"Keep it. If nothing else, you may be able to trade it for easier treatment."

"Marse Harry, they keep sayin' they're goin' to hang me. But then the next day, they don't."

"I'm trying to make sure they never do."

"And what chance we got?"

"I'm making progress. And we have friends."

He took a sip of whiskey himself.

"I believe two people killed Arabella. And at least one may have been a white man."

"How do you know that?"

"Found a witness."

No Confederate court or police official would much credit what the boy had to say, but he had satisfied Harry's with his veracity.

"This witness saw them do it?"

"No. He only saw them enter the hotel—using the back door by the kitchen."

Caesar Augustus looked away. "That don't do me much good, Marse Harry."

Harry put his hand to the man's shoulder. "Well, it helps me."

Time was passing. The sergeant would be back. Harry wished he'd had the foresight to bribe the man beforehand.

If nothing else, he might arrange for his friend to get better food. Harry had noted a plate with a half eaten piece of wormy bread on it, soaked in grease. There was a cup, doubtless containing only water.

"Caesar Augustus, I have only a few days more. You've got to help me. You have to tell me where you were that night. I need to establish an alibi for you."

"I already said I can't do that."

"It could mean your life, sir."

"Marse Harry, the folks I was with, they're all black. Nothin' they say is going to count. Forget that."

"We have to try everything."

"No we don't. Like you say, there's no time."

Harry sat back on his heels. The sergeant would return directly, yet his mind was an utter void.

"Can you tell me anything? Anything at all?"

"I already told you everything. I was somewhere else. When I came back, there she was. I'm sorry, Marse Harry, but that be all I know. I didn't kill her. I didn't do anything to harm her."

"She said you quarreled with her."

"She did?"

"When you visited Estelle. Are you sweet on the girl, Caesar Augustus?"

"Was once." His eyes had become wary, unfriendly. Harry was prying—but he had to.

"She's with me."

"Who, Estelle?"

"Yes. She's outside. She ran away from Mills. I'm pretending I bought her."

"God Almighty, Marse Harry. She's done for now. And I am done for. I come down here with you, and now I'm in the clutches of the devil. That's what he is, that Jeff Davis. That's what they all are. Maybe you, too."

"I'll get you out of this," Harry said.

"No. I'm a dead man. Save yourself. Save Estelle."

"Damn it all, you could help, you know! Tell me where you were. Tell me what you know."

Caesar Augustus folded his arms around his knees and put his head down.

"Get Estelle out of this hellhole, Marse Harry."

There was a loud rapping at the door, metal on wood. The sergeant.

Harry turned to leave, then hesitated. Reaching into his pocket, he pulled out the carved African figure he'd retrieved from his room at the Exchange.

"This is yours," Harry said. "Maybe it'll bring you luck."

Caesar Augustus took the object, eyeing it almost with wonder.

"They took everything of mine," he said. "Everything I had."

"You must have dropped it," Harry said. "In the hotel room."

"In the hotel room." Caesar Augustus put it in a pocket of his trousers.

"Raines!" shouted the sergeant. "Your time's up!"

Harry put his hand on the black man's arm, then moved toward the door.

"Marse Harry!" It was a loud whisper.

"Raines!"

Harry leaned back. "What?"

"Trust the lady on the hill. No one else."

*   *   *

THE door clanked shut behind him. Standing up fully straight, Harry followed the sergeant out through the crowd of prisoners who had gathered around. Passing through them and heading for the stairs, Harry suddenly halted. "I need to use the sinks," he said.

"Got an outhouse behind the office."

"No. I can't wait."

He'd noticed the long, running urinal on the opposite wall when he'd entered this section. Turning, he pushed his way through the prisoners. The tall, red-haired, muscular man in shirtsleeves pressed in beside him.

"What in hell are you doing here?" Harry asked.

"Got taken prisoner," said U.S. Secret Service Agent Joseph "Boston" Leahy. "Quickest way to get into Richmond."

"The ways out are slower."

"Not planning to stay long." He lowered his head. "Talk to me through Crazy Bet."

"Joseph, they've got Caesar Augustus in there. Can you help me get him out?"

"You bet." Leahy stepped back. "Get away from me, you Secesh bastard!"

Harry was genuinely startled. He retreated, until the sergeant caught hold of his arm and dragged him out of the crowd of prisoners to the stairs.

"Maybe you better not come back," the sergeant said. "I think some of these Yankee boys would like to kill you."

Chapter 14

Harry took Estelle by the hand. He had an impulse to put his arm around her, for she looked so forlorn. But that would attract stares and unwelcome speculation. As it was, he heard catcalls. Not knowing whether they came from prisoners at the windows or the Confederate soldiery by the gate, he kept going, not looking back.

She tottered along behind him, as though she were still wearing shackles.

"You see Caesar Augustus?" she asked.

"Yes."

"What he say?"

"He's kind of blue."

"He say anythin' about me?"

"He said he's fond of you."

She hurried her pace to catch up with him. "Where we goin' now?" she asked.

"Away from here."

The walk back to the boarding house took him along a familiar way. He knew almost every storefront, recognized old dogs and horses tied to rails. Yet the city now seemed an altogether different and frightening place. There was a hungry look to some of the people, wariness, and the beginnings of despair. There were beggar children on Main Street, with clutching hands and dirty faces. He ignored the prostitutes, who were as numerous as the pigs in the dirty streets, but one of them simply overwhelmed him. Dressed in torn and faded finery, she must have been sixty years old.

There were many in Richmond, he knew, who yearned to see Miss Van Lew reduced to such a state.

He gave the poor woman a dollar, then took Estelle by the arm and hurried on.

THE proprietor was waiting in his parlor, reading the *Richmond Whig*. At Harry's entrance, he took out his watch.

"Is it over?" he asked.

Harry stopped, trying to redirect his mind to the question. "Is what over, sir?"

"The buryin'. They're putting Mrs. Mills in the ground. The paper says it was to be this morning."

Harry sighed. His spirits were as low as they'd been since he'd arrived in this city. "Where?"

"Hollywood Cemetery."

"Not Shockoe?"

"No, sir."

The Hollywood burying ground was down by the river just west of the city—and just upstream from Tredegar.

"I'll saddle my horse."

He was reluctant to leave Estelle in his room, fearing she'd wander away—or into some trouble.

"You'll come with me," he said. "You can ride behind me."

*   *   *

THEIR way took them by the Virginia State Penitentiary, which was too full of genuine criminals to provide room for Union soldiers. To the west, two military camps sprawled over the rolling landscape, the white tents so numerous they resembled some sort of agricultural crop in the distance.

Harry turned his stumbler of a horse another way, following a path across the grounds of the Belvidere House that led to a slight hill overlooking the cemetery grounds.

The burial service was still under way. There were few mourners. Pulling on his spectacles and standing in his stirrups, Harry thought he could recognize Palmer Mills, but none of the rest.

"You goin' down there?"

"When they're done."

"I goin' stay here."

"No, you stay with me. This city's a dangerous place for any woman now. There are drunken soldiers and criminals everywhere. You best stay with me until I figure out what to do with you."

"You goin' to give me freedom?"

"You already have that, as far as I'm concerned. But we have to get you out of the Confederacy."

"North?"

"To the Union. After I attend to Caesar Augustus."

Harry returned his attention to the burying party down the hill. He could hear singing. When it ceased, the few figures began to turn away and walk toward the carriages parked in the cemetery drive. Mills proceeded in a different direction, angling toward the river. Tredegar was not far.

When they were gone, Harry dismounted and led his horse down the slope, holding Estelle tightly by the wrist. She was far more reluctant than the animal. He saw that she was frightened.

"What is it?" he asked. "You afraid of her ghost?"

Her eyes replied in the affirmative, but she spoke no word.

Reaching the grave, he saw that there was as yet no headstone; only a mound of fresh dirt and a few paper flowers. Letting go of Estelle's arm, Harry moved close to it, shaking his head.

That macabre night in the mortuary, he had wished for nothing more than to have this poor woman safe at last beneath the ground of this gentle bower, a place of peace and endless rest by the broad river she had loved so deeply. He had thought there'd be consolation in this, and resolution. But he felt just as troubled and frustrated as before.

"You weepin', Mister Raines? You weep for her?"

He put his hand to his face. "I suppose I am. It's very sad."

"It gets sadder, Mister Raines. Here come my master."

Harry looked to see Mills striding toward him with great purpose from the direction he had gone in. He was moving fast. Unless Harry turned now and fled like a thief, or a coward in battle, there was no avoiding this confrontation.

Mills stopped about ten paces away. "You were not invited, Raines."

"I realize that. That's why I waited until you had finished."

Mills pulled out his Le Mat revolver, holding it firmly and keeping beyond Harry's reach. "I want you to go. Now."

"All right." Harry gave Arabella's grave a small salute and then started back up the hill, taking Estelle by the hand.

"Estelle," said Mills. "You come back here!"

She looked at him, and then at Harry, and then broke

into a run. Harry waited for the pistol shot, but it didn't come.

"What are you doing with her?" Mills demanded.

"Found her in the street."

"You catch her again, you send her home."

"Good-bye, Palmer."

"I warn you, Raines. You ever come back here, I'm gonna have someone shoot you down."

"You can't do your own killing?"

"I have business elsewhere."

"That's right. The ironclad. It's keeping you so busy."

"I do mean what I say, Harry. Mark me well. You stay away from this sacred ground."

CLIMBING into the saddle, Harry urged the clumsy horse into a trot, catching up with Estelle at the top of the hill.

"Estelle, stop!" he said.

She did.

He dismounted again, then led her to a nearby boulder, where he made her sit. She looked up at him apprehensively.

"Don't worry," he said. "I'm going to get you to a safe place. But you can't stay with me. Mills will come looking for you there."

He smiled. She did not.

"You say I'm free."

"You will be. I need to ask you some more questions, Estelle."

"Please Mister Raines, I don't know nothin'."

He sat down next to her. "Can you tell me exactly when Mrs. Mills left the house to come to my hotel?"

She shrugged. "I don't know. Afternoon."

"Early afternoon?"

"No. It was later. Late afternoon."

"Was the Mills's carriage at the house until then?"

"I guess. They keep it in the barn."

"Where was Mister Mills?"

"He warn't home. He go to the Ironworks. Like every day. Stay there late."

"And did Mrs. Mills tell you where she was going?"

"Nosir. She just say I can't go."

Harry studied her light brown face. "How was she dressed?"

"Like always. Like you found her."

"Estelle, when I found her, she wasn't dressed at all."

She began crying and put her hands to her face. Harry put his arm around her, then got her to her feet.

"Come on, then. We're going to find you a safe haven."

THERE was, of course, only one such place in all of Richmond that Harry knew about. He dared not go right up to the door again. Instead, he took her up the back way to Church Hill, tying his horse to a tree outside St. John's Episcopal Church.

Leading her by the hand, he took a seat in the rearmost corner. A rector at the front of the pews looked their way curiously, and for rather a long time, then shuffled off through a doorway. There was an old woman in an aisle seat several rows ahead, on her knees and bent in prayer. Harry, who'd been raised Presbyterian, knelt as well.

Taking a piece of paper from his pocket, he used the moment to scribble a quick note:

"I am liberating this poor woman, Arabella's maid. She needs swift passage to freedom. H"

"Can you read?" he whispered.

"Not much."

"No matter. There's a big house just the other side of Grace Street from this church. I want you to go to the back door and present this note. They will take care of you."

"What if they don't?"

"There is no doubt, Estelle. I'll rejoin you tonight. Now go."

He waited a few minutes after she left, then slipped out the door and went into the churchyard, using what cover its bare-limbed trees provided to observe Estelle's approach to the door. She was accepted within. A moment later, the thin, yellow-haired figure of Miss Van Lew appeared, coming out onto the steps and looking about in all directions—whether for him or Nestor Maccubbin's men, he could not say. Then she returned inside.

Harry looked down at the gravestone at his feet. "Elizabeth Arnold Poe," the beautiful Richmond actress who had so besotted his father's generation, but died young, and in near poverty.

So many such women to weep for.

And thousands of men.

H E took lunch in a small tavern, paying a reasonably honest-looking boy to hold his horse for him in back, out of view of the equine press gangs. There was a fresh copy of the *Richmond Sentinel* on the bar. He put down twice the price and took it to his table.

The news was mixed. There'd been skirmishing up along the Potomac, near Pohick Church and Mason's neck, the Confederates and the *Sentinel* proclaiming victory. Yet, over in Harpers Ferry, federal troops under General Nathaniel Banks had retaken the town for the Union.

Ominously, there was a story announcing that the Confederate Congress had voted to give President Davis the right to suspend habeas corpus. Anyone could be arrested now for anything and held without trial at the government's pleasure. This was a power Mister Lincoln had already conferred upon himself, mostly to deal with the rabid Secessionists in Baltimore, but it gave Harry a chill to read the words.

The South had likened its rebellion to the fight for independence from Britain, proclaiming its "Second American Revolution," and a blow struck for freedom and liberty. Yet, there was slavery, and now this.

Were it not for Caesar Augustus, Harry's course would be simple. Ride out of town and keep going until across the Rappahannock—perhaps never to return again. He had proved to be an inept spy—or "scout," as Pinkerton preferred to call his people. Miss Van Lew was by far his superior at the calling, and now it seemed his mission had been fulfilled by some person unknown to either of them. All he had to show for this long, unnecessary journey behind enemy lines was a dead former sweetheart and an imprisoned friend.

And if he didn't quit this place soon, he'd find himself a member of the enemy's armed forces. There was a result of this enterprise that would cheer Mr. Pinkerton all right.

He finished his beer, and then his wretched stew. Davis had declared a forthcoming National Day of Fasting to consecrate the Confederate cause. Meals like this put Harry in the mood for it.

Turning sideways in his chair, he looked out to the street. Soldiers had been marching by, in bunches, but so regularly they seemed almost a procession. There were so many army camps around Richmond the city seemed under siege by its own army.

There was disease in those camps—bad food, cold

quarters, nasty companions, lice, rats, boredom, pointless labor, and more card cheats than Harry had seen in four years as a professional gambler. He had criticized John Wilkes Booth for refusing to put on a uniform so often and reflexively, Caitlin Howard had accused him of haranguing her on the point—a just charge.

But how better was he? Booth was serving his beloved Confederacy as a smuggler, spy, and agent provocateur. His duties on behalf of the Union and Mr. Pinkerton were much the same, absent smuggling.

HE passed the afternoon—wasted was truer to the fact—roaming the city along the path of his earlier footsteps. He stopped at the Exchange Hotel, asking after the Negro boy Jimmy, only to be told to go away. Harry went out back and tried the rear door, but the boy was not to be found and the kitchen staff were uncooperative.

Walking past the capitol, and then the War Department, he could think of no useful reason to stop at either place. There was nothing further to be learned from Tredegar. The saloons yielded nothing but whiskey, and Louise, once again, was not at her boardinghouse domicile, though the servant who talked to him said she would be at the theater that night.

At the end of the day, he was seated on his own bed, persuading himself that the best thing he could do for Caesar Augustus was to stock up on sleep. Maybe then his brain would function better. As he lay there, listening to the wind rattle his window, he couldn't make it work at all. The only means of deliverance for his hapless friend that came to his mind was attempting to convince Maccubbin and his "Plug Ugly" friends that he had himself murdered his old sweetheart.

But that would be folly. Given the choice between

hanging a white man and a black, the Confederacy would go reflexively for the latter. Harry had seen it happen all too often.

He awoke to darkness. Lighting a candle, he set about washing himself, changing into cleaner clothes, arming himself with Derringer and Navy Colt, and putting on great coat, gloves, scarf, and wide-brimmed hat. Then he went out into the night.

THERE was a livery stable of some reliability but two blocks from the theater. Harry bribed the stable hand an outrageous sum to safeguard his mount from the government's thieves, instructing him to leave the animal saddled.

The streets were again acrawl with drunken soldiery and the cutpurses, confidence men, and easy women they attracted. Outside the theater, two dogs were fighting over a scrap of food. Harry warily stepped around them, just as a third hound darted into the fray and snatched the morsel away. The sneak bounded down the alley that ran along the side of the building, with the two former enemies now allies in pursuit. It would not go well for the thief. The alley was a dead end.

In a moment, there were yelps of pain. The chastened interloper came limping out a moment later. A lesson in life. The escape should be the highest priority, not the loot.

Harry leaned back and lighted a cheroot. There would be a considerable wait. The play was long, and Louise liked to linger in her dressing room until the theater was clear of its audience. Happily, he'd refilled his flask, but he'd be careful. He needed his wits about him.

*   *   *

SHE came out the stage door much earlier than he'd expected and moved so swiftly she almost caught sight of him before he ducked back into a doorway. But she was bent on her destination, whatever it was, and kept her attention straight ahead, her face largely hidden within the hood of her cloak.

Harry gave her a minute's head start, then moved out in pursuit, turning right at the corner as he saw her do.

She was climbing into a carriage. Pausing to put on his spectacles, he thought he recognized it, but wasn't entirely certain. He remained where he was until the driver flicked the reins across the backs of the team and the vehicle began to move.

At the next corner, the driver turned south, toward the river. Now Harry was certain. He ran pell mell for the stable. The door was unbarred, but the stable hand was not in evidence. Swearing silently, Harry went to the stall, dropped a half dollar onto the floor, and took his reluctant mount in hand. The animal's gait was flawed, and the dirt streets hard and a little slippery in the cold, but Harry had no choice. Moving the horse into a brisk trot, he returned to the intersection he had just left and then to the carriage's trail. Crossing the north channel of the canal and turning into Byrd Street, he accelerated to a full gallop. He'd been under fire for hours in the battles of Bull Run and Ball's Bluff, but in neither case was he as frightened as he was now. A single misplaced step on the frozen ground and this horse might kill them both.

Somehow they survived. Pausing at the edge of a small ridge behind two leafless trees, he watched the carriage proceed down the entrance drive to the bridge and the gate beyond. The driver barely halted and was waved on.

Harry waited several minutes, wanting his prey to get where they were going. Then he followed, coming up to the sentry at a gallop.

His pass again performed its mission, but Harry wasn't content with that. "I have an important message for Lieutenant Mills," he said. "Is he at the office?"

"No, sir. He's at his house."

"His house? You mean in Manchester?"

"No, sir. The house he has here. It's a little brick house just along the ridge there, right past the spike mill."

"You're sure he's there?"

"Yes, sir. Should be just arriving there. His coach just came through."

Harry moved his beast on down the lane at a good clip, but, once past the big armory rolling mill, slowed and proceeded the rest of the way with more stealth.

The carriage had stopped where the driveway ended, about fifty yards from the house. Tying his horse to the railing of a fence, Harry crept close, keeping to the shadows.

The house was tiny—no more than two rooms. A lamp was lit in one of them, but the windows in the other end stayed dark. Harry moved close to the window.

When he looked within, he found the room empty. The two from the carriage had moved into the other chamber, which remained dark. He remained there until he could stand the cold no longer. He doubted, at all events, that the two would be coming out anytime soon. That, apparently, was the whole point of the house.

After climbing into the saddle, he looked back. He thought he saw a shadow move across the glow of firelight in one of the windows, but there was nothing more. No one called out to him.

Moving across the Tredegar yard, he thought he heard a door slam shut, but the sound could have come from any of the buildings.

The sentry stopped him again before he could cross the bridge. "You find Lieutenant Mills?" he asked.

"I did," said Harry.

"How'd he receive you?"

"I decided not to disturb him."

The sentry laughed, letting Harry pass.

THE Van Lew smokehouse, frustratingly, was locked, compelling Harry to go once more to the back door of the mansion itself. He rapped gently at first, then, after a brief interval, with some vigor.

Miss Van Lew herself responded. There was anger and surprise evident in her face, but as he stepped inside, that vanished, replaced by melancholy—and some anxiousness.

She led him to the kitchen, and quickly poured him a glass of brandy.

"I've been trying to find you for hours," she said. "I feared for you. Dictator Davis has had his Congress grant him the power of arrest and imprisonment without trial. He means to use it."

"He remains my father's friend. I should be all right."

"That counts for little, as you see. We've so little time now."

"Time?" Harry said. "Time for what?"

"You've not heard? Caesar Augustus has confessed to the murder of Arabella Mills."

Chapter 15

"**A**RE you sure?" Harry asked, thinking her crazed indeed. "This could be their contrivance—a scheme to hang him before I can do anything about it."

Miss Van Lew sank back into a chair. "No, Harry. This is, lamentably, the truth. I was told it by one of the prisoners—a Union officer. You need not know his name, but he is a man to be trusted."

"A tall man, with red hair?"

Miss Van Lew remained silent. She took this business of spying far more seriously than Harry did, though she was not officially enrolled in the ranks of Mr. Pinkerton's Secret Service.

"His name is Joseph Leahy," Harry said. "We work together—or did in Washington. I had until now thought him one of the most sensible men in the Federal cause, but he has committed this folly—allowing himself to be taken prisoner in the guise of a Union officer. He says there is an abundance of military information to be had from prisoners, but getting out of prison with it is quite another. The only Yankees who come out of that place are the dead."

"We will attend to Mr. Leahy's deliverance by and by,"

she said. "Our worry now is Caesar Augustus."

"I thought he was secondary to the greater mission."

"Indeed he was—as were you and I. But that is accomplished. So now we must deal with this injustice. It represents to me every evil of this vile system."

She put her hand to her brow, closing her eyes. He could scarce imagine how exhausted she must be.

"I cannot think of any reason for Caesar Augustus to do this," Harry said.

"He must have been in great torment. They treat him badly, as you must know."

On a plantation near his father's, a Negro boy about thirteen had run away on his master's horse, breaking one of its legs in an ill-taken jump. When captured, he had been tied to a tree and then had both his legs cut off, after which he had been left to bleed to death. Harry and Caesar Augustus had gone that night to help him, but he had lasted no more than a few minutes after they cut him down.

"Caesar Augustus is a singularly brave man—far braver than I. He would not succumb to torture so easily."

"He might, if he were trying to protect somebody."

"Give up his life for a murderer's? If Caesar Augustus knew who killed Arabella, he would tell me. He would not put me through this, or put our cause at risk."

"Are you sure?"

"I have known him since we were small boys. Yes, I'm very sure."

Miss Van Lew fretted with her hands, glanced to the glowing red coals on the hearth, and then turned to look at Harry quite directly.

"Would he have reason to commit this crime?"

"Arabella told him to stay away from Estelle—the girl I sent to you today. But even if Arabella was at her worst, that would not provoke murder. Not on Caesar Augustus's part. He has an anger, as must smolder in all their hearts. But he wouldn't kill a white woman just because of the severity of her reproach. He'd simply find some other way to see Estelle. I'm sure that's what he did. He's clever, you know."

She found the fire now insufficient and rose to stir it. "Where did he say he had gone, before he came back to your rooms?"

"He didn't. And he won't say. I don't know why."

"What have you learned about Arabella Mills's death, Harry? You have been at this for some time."

"Too much time—and too little known. I can tell you that Arabella died some substantial time before Caesar Augustus says he found her, and that Mills's coach was seen outside my hotel twice that day—afternoon, and then evening. I know that she must have used the kitchen door at the rear of the hotel to reach my room, a common thing for women wishing to make discreet, unchaperoned visits to guests of the Exchange."

"I am aware of the practice. It is much talked about."

"None of the cooks or maids recalled seeing her come in, but a kitchen boy I talked to said he saw three people enter that afternoon—two men and a woman. One of the men was white. He may have been drunk, or sick."

"Was the woman Arabella Mills?"

"He said he could not tell. She wore a hooded cloak."

She poured him more brandy without being asked. "Then it could have been her."

"Yes, I suppose. But a hack driver told me he saw a woman standing by the Mills's carriage—a woman with long black hair, who wore no hat."

There are few ladies in Richmond who would go about the public streets without hat or bonnet. It would be considered brazen—behavior to be expected of a woman of the streets. Or an actress.

"Was it Louise Devereux?" she asked. "She is famous for the flagrancy of her bold comportment."

"You have a quick mind, Miss Van Lew."

"Do you know her?" she asked.

"Yes. I knew her in Washington. She is the friend of a friend."

The pale blue eyes were studying him, with swift result. "You know her better than that, I do believe."

"She is having an affair with Palmer Mills," Harry said.

"That woman is a Rebel spy, as bad as Rose Greenhow. She is lucky she was deported to the Confederacy. She might have been hanged."

"They haven't hanged a woman yet."

Miss Van Lew rubbed her throat. "Let us hope."

"Arabella was having an affair with George Broward," Harry said. "He is a very bad man. From what I know of him, he would not take rejection well. And he has treated women poorly."

"With all this talk of lovers and rejection, spies and mysterious arrivals at the Exchange Hotel, do you know what you are telling me, Harrison Raines?"

"No, Ma'am."

"You are telling me that you are not much closer to finding the truth of this than you were when you began. And now the time is half gone—near to all gone, according to our friend Mr. Leahy."

He took a sip of brandy. He wanted to light a cheroot, but would not so offend the house of Miss Van Lew.

"I fear you are right," he said, finally.

"Are you certain this girl Estelle has told you all she can?"

"All that she can that I need to know. Doubtless she is more familiar with the intimacies of Arabella's indiscretions than she has let on, but my surmise will suffice on that account. The coachman, Samuel, is quite hostile to me."

"Where is she?" he asked.

"Upstairs. In my secret room."

"Why there?"

"It would be the ruination of everything I've been able to accomplish if I were to be found harboring a slave that belonged to Arabella and Palmer Mill. If not held liable under the Fugitive Slave Act, I would be pressed to explain our connection. At the very least, it would be the undoing of 'Crazy Bet.' "

"You cannot keep her."

"I do not intend to. She says you promised her freedom."

"I did, and it's a promise I will keep when I can."

"The Underground Railroad down the peninsula to Fortress Monroe is still open, but it's very dangerous now. This young lady is not very resourceful."

"Can you keep her until we have Caesar Augustus safe?"

"I suppose I will have to. Their freedom is what this war is all about. Freedom for every one of them. It bewilders me that only these Secessionists seem to understand that."

"Mr. Lincoln understands that."

"That is my constant prayer."

"I'd better talk with her."

ESTELLE was asleep on a cot at the far end of the chamber, which was a long, low-ceilinged chamber carved out from beneath the eaves. Harry gently shook her shoulder. "Estelle?"

She opened her eyes. They were full of apprehension.

"There's bad news," Harry said. "Caesar Augustus has confessed to Mrs. Mills's murder."

Estelle sat up. "I know, Mister Raines. Miz Van Lew done tol' me."

"It becomes very hard now to save him."

"I guess it do. So why he done that?"

"I'm not sure. But we're not giving up."

"I don't expect you would."

"If we succeed . . ." he paused. "Or if we fail. I'm leaving Richmond soon. I will be taking you with me."

"You gonna keep me?"

"I'm going to free you, as I promised."

"Soon?"

"As soon as I can."

"What do I do now?"

"For the time being, you'll stay here." He looked to Miss Van Lew, who nodded.

She put her hand on his arm. "You goin' to help Caesar Augustus, too, Mister Raines? You won't let them kill him for this? He wouldn't do nothin' to Miss Arabella."

There was a commotion downstairs. Miss Van Lew rose and hurried from the room. Harry bid his goodnight and followed.

On the main staircase, they encountered Mary Elizabeth Bowser, who was in a state of high excitement and depleted breath. She must have run all the way from the presidential mansion.

"Miss Van Lew," she said, her wind returning in snatches. "At dinner tonight, Mister Davis, he said he's going to let them kill Caesar Augustus in the morning."

"He can't do that!" Harry said. "I was promised a week."

"He says he has no choice, now that Caesar Augustus has confessed. He says it's for the good of the Cause."

Chapter 16

HARRY hurried down the stairs and to the front door.

"Harrison! Not that door!"

Taking him by the hand, Miss Van Lew led him to a small breakfast room he'd not been in before. There was a many-paned door leading to the garden. She blew out her candle, then faced him. "What will you do?" she asked.

"I will go directly to the War Department and wait outside for General Lee. He's an honorable man. He will not permit this."

"But he is subordinate to Davis."

"President Davis leans heavily on his advice."

She considered matters a moment more. "After you meet with General Lee, what then?"

"I'll get word to you as soon as I can—good or bad."

"And if he refuses you?"

"Good word, bad word. You will know."

"I will be at Libby Prison."

"Then I'll contact you there."

"No. Harry, you are not thinking clearly."

"Miss Van Lew, I cannot simply wait . . ."

"But you must. I'm going to try to meet with Mr.

Leahy." She put a hand to his arm. "There may still be a way."

He stood there.

"I have a man in our service, a Mr. Lohman," Miss Van Lew continued. "He is of German birth and has a grocery store and restaurant. He deals in gold, smuggled Union greenbacks, and black market goods."

"Has he something to do with Libby Prison?"

"One of his business associates—a purveyor of pickled pork named Martin Lipscomb. He has the contract for burying the dead federal officers who are brought out of the prison every morning. I think he can be bribed."

"The object is to get Caesar Augustus out alive."

She released him. "Good luck, Harry."

GENERAL Lee was residing at the Spotswood Hotel at Eighth and Main Streets and had made a custom of walking to his War Department office. He arrived shortly after sunrise, impeccably dressed, booted, and polished, and without aide or companion. A parade of one. Even in his best clothes, Harry felt shabby in the man's presence, and Harry had often been accused of being a dandy.

Lee was not happy to see him, but, as always, was careful to avoid any discourtesy. "Good morning, Mr. Raines," he said. "You arise early today."

"It would be accurate to say I retire late this night, General Lee."

A shadow of disapproval came and went over the man's face, but he said nothing. If he wished to think Harry had been on a long carouse, Harry would not discourage him. It was preferable to his divining Harry's actual whereabouts that night.

"Have you come to see me, Mr. Raines?"

"I have, sir, on the most solemn purpose. My Negro

has confessed to the murder of Arabella Mills."

"Well, then. I suppose that concludes the matter." He turned to mount the entrance stairs. "I am sorry for your sake. A good day to you, sir."

"No, General. I've come to ask that the government be held to its promise to me. I do not think the man is telling the truth, and I fear I will need the rest of the week to prove it, the full week that was granted me."

"Do you have reason to believe that the government will renege on its word?"

Harry was groggy, but not so careless as to let slip that the Confederate president might have a domestic spy to worry about.

"Not to believe, sir, but to fear the possibility."

"However, if your man has admitted to this crime, what is the point of going on with this?"

"A point of honor, sir."

A sudden gust of wind caused the general to shiver slightly. He shook it off and resumed his ascent of the stairs.

"I had hoped you had come to talk about your place in the Army. I have discussed this with your father."

"That is why I have come, sir. But I would remind you that, in return for my promise to enter the service of my country, I was promised a week in which to rescue my manservant from an unjust fate."

"Let us continue this in my office," Lee said.

LEE'S young major was already at work. It mystified Harry how he got into the building, as no one had passed him. Perhaps he had spent the night there. The young man stood and gave a Lee a salute and a warm "Good morning, sir," took note of Harry with a cursory nod, and then resumed his labors.

Entering his own office, Lee paused before a map spread out upon a side table, studying it a full minute before finally and formally taking his seat.

"I have discussed your situation with your father, Mr. Raines. He disapproves of your conduct in the matter of Mrs. Mills, but if you wish to join his regiment, he is amenable to it. But it cannot be as aide de camp or, I am reluctant to say, as any kind of officer."

"He insists I serve as a private?" Harry's brother was a captain.

Lee nodded. "I can of course secure you a commission elsewhere in the Army. Your horsemanship and knowledge of horses would be of great value. But not in your father's regiment. I must respect his wishes."

Harry pondered the window view a moment, then reminded himself how valuable was the general's time.

"Sir, my interest lies elsewhere. I would like to join the Navy."

Lee's eyes widened slightly with otherwise restrained surprise.

"The Navy has no need of horsemen, sir. It already has a sufficiency of officers, but a scarcity of ships. Your usefulness would be limited. I would be reluctant to recommend you to Navy Secretary Mallory."

"General," said Harry, exaggerating. "I've sailed small boats on the York and James for most of my life. Let me go to Norfolk and offer my services there. Surely there is something I can do."

"And if you're required to serve as an ordinary seaman?"

"If that's required, sir, I'll do it."

Lee sighed. "Very well. I'll commend you to the officer commanding." He reached for pen and paper. "Then we'll be done with this. I do not think this will please your father, Mr. Raines."

"My concern, sir, is that it please my country."

The general gave a nod and completed his swift writing task, handing Harry the finished note.

"There you are, Mr. Raines. Now if you'll excuse me . . ."

"And the fate of my slave?"

"That is not for me to decide."

"It's certainly a matter for the president to decide. If you would intercede . . ."

"Your father is his friend, and His Excellency has made no such effort."

"General Lee, sir," said Harry, rising. "Two men and a woman were seen entering the Exchange through the rear door at the time the Mills's carriage was parked outside. Two men, sir. It may well be that my Caesar Augustus was one of them, but if so, his testimony is necessary as concerns the other."

Harry had heard people describe Lee as cold and strict, but knew he had a warm side as well, having seen him play with small children. He also had a fierce temper. It never betrayed his patrician comportment, but made itself visible nevertheless. It was beginning to then.

"General," Harry continued. "This affair is not being decided as a matter of honor or justice. It's the rule of the Plug Uglies. Ruffians and bullies have taken over the law of the city. You can't . . ."

Lee raised his hand to stop the flow of words. "Where can I find you, Mr. Raines?"

"Sir?" Harry had hoped to wait in the general's outer office.

"I will do what I can for you. Where can I send word to you?"

Hesitating a moment, Harry gave the address of his boardinghouse.

"Wait there. I will send word to you. Whichever way

it goes, Mr. Raines, I would be obliged if you would then lay this unpleasant matter behind us. We all have more worthy uses for our time."

There was a finality to his words that made them seem carved in marble.

"Yes. Thank you, sir. I am obliged to you."

As soon as he was back in his room, Harry realized his mistake. Instead of waiting here, isolated from any message save the good general's, he should have gone to some saloon near Libby Prison. The bar at the Exchange would have sufficed. Here he could do nothing. The general's promise to send word was as good as a manacle around his ankle.

He paced the floor a few minutes, then sat, turning his chair to the window. As soon as he got word from Lee, he would fly to the prison and seek another interview with Caesar Augustus. One way or another, he'd make the man explain himself. Perhaps he could secure Boston Leahy's assistance. Miss Van Lew would be seeking it, possibly at this very moment.

He dozed. The sound of someone pounding on his door stirred him abruptly to consciousness. He had not expected someone so gentlemanly as Lee to send so rude a messenger.

Opening the door, he found no messenger, but a face all too familiar, though the military uniform was not.

"George Broward," Harry said, dumbfounded.

The officer pushed past him into the room, then stood formally. He was wearing large gauntlets and removed them, holding them under one arm.

"I was looking for you," Harry said.

"Well, now I'm found. This is not a social call, Raines."

"Neither was mine. I wished to ask you some questions, about Arabella Mills."

"Were I you, sir, I would not utter that good woman's name again. Not in Richmond. You have lost that privilege. Raines, you are being called out."

"What?" Harry said.

"A duel, Raines. Tomorrow, at sunrise."

"Are you mad, George? This is 1862. Dueling was outlawed in the District of Columbia more than twenty years ago. It's against military regulations. It's ridiculous. It's passe."

"This is not the goddamned District of Columbia. This is Virginia." Broward paused to look disgustedly at Harry's rumpled civilian suit. "And you, sir, have no worry about military regulations. You are supposed to be a member of the Virginia chivalry, Raines. I find you unworthy of that honor, but you have no choice but to abide by its custom."

"Why are you doing this? I've done nothing to you."

Broward sniffed, as though the air in the room was repellent. "You have sullied my name in public rooms up and down Main Street, sir, suggesting an improper liaison between me and Mrs. Mills. I've grounds to call you out a dozen times. You are a cad and a bounder, sir."

Harry threw up his hands, then took whiskey and glasses from a shelf and set them down on his table. "Here," he said. "Refresh yourself. Come back to your senses."

Broward, his sword clanking as he leaned, filled the glass and knocked it back in three swallows, wiping his lips with the back of his hand afterwards.

"It's not me who's calling you out, Raines. It's Mills."

"Mills?"

Harry imagined the naval officer still abed, in the mys-

terious little house on the grounds of the Tredegar Ironworks.

"He has asked me to serve as his second, which I gladly
do. He demands satisfaction for the insults you have
showered upon his wife's good name and his own. And
for obstructing the justice due her foul murderer."

Harry sat down on the edge of his bed, shaking his
head. "I spoke with Mills not long ago. He seemed in no
way inclined to this nonsense."

Broward poured himself another drink. "This is Virginia, Harry. It ain't nonsense."

Reminding himself of his more important concerns,
Harry looked at his watch. It was nearly noon. "When did
you say this charade is to take place?" Harry asked.

"Tomorrow sunrise. On the Kanawha Canal the other
side of Hollywood Cemetery." He finished the whiskey.
"Who will be your second?"

There was a question that more than begged an answer.
Harry's two best friends in his current life were both behind the gates of Libby Prison.

"He really means to go through with this?"

"He does," said Broward.

"I'll find someone."

"Please do," said Broward, pulling on his gloves again.
"You be there—for the sake of your family's name. If
you skedaddle, it'll be a shame you'll bear forever. You
won't ever dare come back to Richmond again."

WHEN his unwelcome guest departed, Harry set about
washing, shaving, thoroughly cleaning his teeth, and putting on fresh clothes, hoping to look as respectable as
possible. With so much time elapsed, it was clear the general would not or could not help. He would have to go to
Davis himself.

Celerity was essential. He'd have to risk the equine press gangs and use his horse.

He was leading it, saddled and bridled, from the stable when the Confederate officer came cantering to the boardinghouse's picket fence. He saw Harry and dismounted, to Harry's surprise, coming to attention and saluting.

It was the major, Lee's principal aide. Harry was astonished that the general would allow him so far from his office duties.

"General Lee's compliments, Mr. Raines," the major said. "He regrets to inform you that we are too late."

"Too late?"

"Yes, sir. The slave Caesar Augustus is dead. His Excellency, the president, has asked that the matter of Mrs. Mills's untimely death be officially closed."

Chapter 17

"**D**EAD?" said Harry, holding on tightly to his horse's reins as a sudden dizziness struck him. "When? How?"

"I do not know, sir," said the major. "The general suggests that you inquire further at Libby Prison."

The man returned to his own mount, pulling himself swiftly into the saddle.

"The general has sent word to the Gosport Navy Yard in Norfolk to expect you, Mr. Raines. I believe he said within the week, if that's convenient."

With that he dashed away, as though a courier in time of battle with urgent orders.

THE day was warming, and the dirt of the streets had softened. In places, there was mud. Disregarding the hazard and his horse's ill-footed gait, Harry galloped downhill toward the prison, scattering pigs and the occasional pedestrian in his path.

Startling the loiterers around Libby's gated entrance, Harry kept up his reckless pace nearly all the way, pulling up violently at the last instant. It must have seemed he was about to charge the door. Two soldiers stepped before him with muskets forward and bayonets fixed. Two others joined them, along with a lieutenant. "What in hell do you want?" he said.

"I want to know what happened to my slave! Caesar Augustus. He was held in the cellars here."

The lieutenant, a gaunt and sallow-faced man who seemed near middle age, became obdurate. "Don't know what you're talking about—or who you are. Get away from here, or I'll have you locked up."

Harry once again pulled out his arsenal of official papers, including those he'd acquired from General Lee that morning. The lieutenant, unimpressed, ignored them. Instead, he took hold of the reins of Harry's horse, gesturing to one of his men to seize Harry himself.

Harry kicked at the man, then pulled the reins from the lieutenant's hands. He turned his horse around in a quick, full circle, its hindquarters clearing his adversaries from proximity. Angry now, the lieutenant pulled out a long-barreled dragoon's pistol.

"Damn you! Hold!"

The booming voice came from behind. A full colonel emerged from the building's entrance, Nestor Maccubbin beside him.

The colonel appeared to be the commandant of the prison. He didn't give his name.

"You Harrison Raines?" he said, stepping to the side of Harry's horse.

"Yes, sir. I've come about my slave—Caesar Augustus—you were holding him in . . ."

"He's dead."

Harry waved his papers with vigor. "How can this be so? I was promised by President Davis and General Lee that nothing would happen to him for a week. You were given orders to that effect."

"We had nothing to do with it, Raines," said Maccubbin, who'd been joined by two of his Plug Uglies. "Much as we wished. It was the Yankees. He was killed by one of the prisoners, a Union officer."

"That's impossible."

"Couple dozen of 'em saw it happen. A big fellow, he was. Stabbed the Negro right through the heart as we were taking him out."

"I'd like to talk to him."

"No."

"Have you charged him with murder?"

Both the colonel and Maccubbin stared at him strangely.

"What the hell for?" Maccubbin asked.

Harry's horse now turned about without being bidden to do so. With tight rein, he reasserted his control. "Damn it! He belonged to me!"

"Take it up with the War Department."

Union prisoners were looking out the windows.

"Where are the remains?" Harry asked.

Maccubbin shrugged. "Crazy Bet took the body. She and that pork peddler Lipscomb. He's got the buryin' contract on the Yankee dead. He usually takes 'em out to Oakwood Cemetery. Don't think he'd plant a Negro there, but it'd serve 'em all right if he did."

"Why did this officer kill my slave?" Harry asked.

Maccubbin shrugged. "News is out about how your man confessed to killing Mrs. Mills—how he strung her up naked like that. It's in all the Richmond papers. Somethin' like that'll rile a Yankee as much as it does a true Southerner. Right kind of Yankee. Somethin' like that'll get to any man."

"You know he didn't do that, Nestor," Harry said.

"All I know is what's in the papers," said Maccubbin. "And they say he's the murderer." He smiled amiably and stepped back, thinking Harry would now leave.

"What about his personal effects?" Harry said.

"How do slaves have personal effects?" Maccubbin asked.

"Whatever he left, it belongs to me."

"I'll let you take a look," the colonel said. "Then I want you out of here."

HARRY stayed close behind as the commandant led the group into the prison. Taking up a lantern, the colonel moved easily through the pack of prisoners to the stairs that led to the dank place below.

The smell was worse than before, perhaps to be blamed on the warming weather. Prisoners and guards made way.

"Where'd it happen?" Harry asked.

The colonel hesitated, then pointed to the stone floor, holding the lantern above dark stains.

"Right there," he said. "The Yankee came at him in a rush, soon as we had him out the cell door."

"Where were you taking him?"

"Out back. We were about to hang him."

They lowered heads to enter the small, dark chamber.

"Over there," Maccubbin said.

The colonel, holding his nose, raised the lantern. Maccubbin fetched a burlap cloth bag up from the far corner.

"Son of a bitch," he said. "That darkie had four dollars."

"I'll take that," said the colonel. "Help pay for his upkeep. You can have the rest."

He handed Harry the bag. There was nothing in it but the small, carved wooden figure Harry had found in the room at the Exchange Hotel and returned to Caesar Augustus.

Along with another small figure just like it.

*   *   *

HIS stumbling horse was not enthusiastic going up the hill, but Harry somehow managed to keep him at a trot. He went up Twenty-Third Street, pulling up by Miss Van Lew's front gate.

There'd be no suspicions about his visiting now. The lady had made off with the body of his slave.

Mary Elizabeth Bowser opened the door, quickly allowing him to enter.

"I was wonderin' if you were ever goin' to come, Mister Raines. I got to leave soon for the Gray House."

"You were expecting me?"

"Miss Van Lew said you'd be coming."

"Where is she?"

"She's gone to her farm. She's scared they may come for her and not just her horse this time."

"What about Caesar Augustus?"

"He's in good hands, Mister Raines." She looked to the windowpane beside the door. "Wait here. She left you something." She darted into the front parlor."

He heard voices. In a moment, Miss Bowser appeared with Estelle, who seemed weary and frightened. Perhaps that had become her natural condition.

"Are you all right?" he asked.

"I'se tolerable, Mister Raines." Estelle wiped at her eye.

"Miss Van Lew left you a letter," Miss Bowser said. She produced it from a pocket in her dress.

There was neither salutation or signature, lest these prove compromising. The message was brief:

You will be content when you discover where he rests. I wish you well in the swift completion of your journey.

The first sentence confused him. The second was an instruction to leave Richmond as soon as possible. Indeed, there was no reason to stay, but one—the ridiculous duel.

"That's all?"

"You have enough money?"

He nodded. Impoverishment was not a familiar complaint.

"Wait again." She went down the main hall this time, turning into a room at the end. This time she returned with two revolvers. One a small, short-barreled, four-shot Sharps pocket pistol; the other a long-barreled Remington Navy revolver of .44 caliber. Both were loaded. These were excellent weapons, but he already had a Derringer and a Navy Colt.

"Why does she think I'll need these?" he asked.

"She wanted to give you them as presents. And if the Plug Uglies come through the house, they'd just take them."

As he was carrying his Colt in his belt, he stuck the Remington and the Sharps in the side pockets of his coat. The weight of iron he was carrying now was mighty noticeable.

"When does she return?"

"When things are quiet. After you're gone, Mister Raines."

He was being asked to leave.

"Did she say where I was to go?"

"Fortress Monroe is as near as the Union Army has got to. You know the way?"

"I certainly do."

"She hopes you get there quick."

"I'll have to pass through Confederate lines."

"Miss Van Lew, she wishes you luck."

"Thank her for me," Harry said.

"President Davis, he's powerful irritated with you over

Caesar Augustus. This is a bad time for him to be that."

"I understand. Thank you."

"You goin' to go now?"

"Yes."

She pushed Estelle forward. "Safe journey."

He recalled the road to Oakwood Cemetery, though he'd never visited the place. When he reached the burying ground, it was deserted. There were fresh wagon tracks and several fresh graves, all unmarked. If one now contained Caesar Augustus, there was no way of telling which one it was.

Dismounting, he walked among the mounds of turned earth, to no useful end. Finally, he sat down on the ground and took out his flask. Its contents were providing the only available answer to his nagging questions.

"They bury him here?" said Estelle, seating herself near him.

"That's what I was told."

"Black man in dis cemetery?"

"It apparently was Miss Van Lew's wish."

"But you don' know where?"

Harry said nothing. He sank back upon the grass, supporting himself on one elbow and drank until the flask was empty. Then he rolled over to lie fully on his back, staring up at the pale blue sky visible in the rifts between clouds. He could not imagine anyone making a greater wreck of his affairs.

"What we goin' to do, Mister Raines?"

"Leave Richmond," Harry said, closing his eyes. "Tomorrow."

"We goin' north?"

"Don't know."

* * *

BOTH Estelle and his horse were still there when he awoke. The woman sat as Indian women did in paintings Harry had seen and admired of the West, cross-legged, her back perfectly straight, her gaze on the distant horizon.

"Are you sad, Estelle?"

She didn't speak, or move.

"About Caesar Augustus," he said.

"I'se sad about all of us."

He heard voices. Raising himself, he saw a small group on the opposite side of the cemetery, a few gray uniforms visible near a four-wheeled cart. It was a burial party, as ubiquitous these days as trash collectors or peddlers.

Harry got stiffly to his feet, then slowly walked over to them, asking a corporal who seemed to be in charge whether they knew anything of another burial there earlier in the day.

"We been buryin' here since sunup. They had a bad night at Chimborazo."

"You'd remember this one. A Negro man from Libby Prison."

"A Negro? Here?"

"Have to be a crazy person, try to put one of them in here," said another soldier.

The burial party included two black grave diggers. All of them looked at Harry now as if he might be such a crazy person—or possibly something more dangerous.

"Sorry," he said, smiling. "Must have made a mistake. That darky has something of mine. Just trying to find him."

"Well, sir, you sure ain't goin' to find him in this dirt."

Harry walked slowly away, though he felt like running. "Estelle," he said. "We're leaving."

Her head turned slowly. "Goin' North?"

"Back to Richmond."

"Why?"

"Unfinished business."

"I'se hungry."

"I'll attend to it."

THEY stopped at a country grocery and bar, where Harry refilled his flask and had a drink on the side. Despite the National Day of Fasting, he was able to buy some pork and cornbread and a sweet potato. The bill was outrageous. Soon they'd be having Days of Fasting every day.

Coming to a patch of woods near a meandering creek, he divided the food and served Estelle her share. She devoured everything quickly. He ate a small amount himself, but soon had lost his hunger. He gave his ample remains to her, and then found his flask again.

"We never goin' to get anywhere we keep stoppin', Mister Raines."

He took another drink. "Be quiet, Estelle."

HARRY stopped his unhappy horse behind the Exchange, letting Estelle down to the ground.

"What you want me to do, Mister Raines?"

"Find a small boy named Jimmy and bring him out here to me. They might be more cooperative with you."

"Kitchen boy?"

"Yes."

She moved slowly toward the door. Once she was inside, he began to wonder if she might seize the opportunity to go out the front door and run off once again.

But she apparently had tired of that.

"He ain't in there," she said, returning. "Ain't there no more."

"No more?"

"That's what they say. He's dead. He was braggin' he had a silver dollar, and somebody killed him for it."

Harry felt so very weary. "Very well. Let's go."

HE left her at his boarding house, instructing the land-lord to feed her if she got hungry. The man was much less hospitable and demanded extra money, saying he feared he might get arrested if caught doing such a thing. Harry gave him the sum without protest and added a little more.

He went to the Swan Tavern on Broad Street, ordering a beer with an egg in it as his own sustenance. There were copies of both the *Richmond Whig* and the *Enquirer*. The news was glum from the Southern point of view. General Sterling Price was retreating through Southwest Missouri toward Arkansas. Union troops were moving on Charleston, in the western mountains of Virginia.

How long would Davis tolerate so free a press? How soon would retreats be ordered transformed into victories?

Harry looked about in search of a poker game, but there was none. The other patrons seemed as gloomy as the newspapers. It was as though conviviality had been suspended by act of the Confederate Congress as well.

He'd been given an extraordinary opportunity to serve the Union here, and squandered it. He might as well have not come.

Turning a page of the newspaper, he wished he had not come. There was a story in the *Whig* about the execution of a spy over at Monroe Square at the west end of the city.

A pleasanter prospect occurred to him. There was a

chance Louise had returned to her residence—or her theater. Neither was far, and the night had not yet turned cold.

Still, he wondered how much he could trust her. He had sorely displeased the president of this rump nation and numerous others in authority. She might find advantage in that for her designs and purposes, whatever in the hell they were.

He would keep his appointment on the morrow and then go, as everyone—friend and foe—seemed to wish.

In the meantime, he would drink. He drained his beer, set the glass aside, and ordered whiskey.

He recalled having several drinks at the Swan, and buying many for others. Eventually, though, the bonhomie faded. Everything faded. The bartender settled his bill without his asking and then strongly suggested he take his custom over to the Powhatan House.

Harry did so, glad for the fresh air. The Swan had had few customers, but the streets were full of people. He smiled at them, bumping into a few who did not smile back. He tripped once, his knees striking the dirt of the street hard, but he managed to stand erect and keep on.

He had forgotten that the Powhatan, located just across the street from the Capitol, was a hostelry beholden to the temperance principle. Finding this vastly amusing, he stumbled back outside and went forth to find an establishment less principled.

Harry found several. The New Market Hotel, over at Sixth and Marshall, was one. There was a private party in its central hall, called "the saloon," and the guests were mostly politicians. Harry pondered the why of a hotel across from the Capitol forbidding spirits, but another, full of legislators, keeping its guests awash in them.

Their generosity extended even to him—for a time. Then he was asked again to move along.

The name of the last bar he entered eluded him. He knew only that it was near the canal and that the sinks in the alley behind it smelled awful. He made use of them nevertheless. Then, reeling with fatigue and an incredible sorrow, he sat down in the alley and fell asleep.

HE awoke to find himself with friends—gentlemen so affectionate they were running their hands all over him. Displeased, he started to rise, when he of a sudden realized they were going through his pockets. One already had his wallet out. Harry went clumsily for his Colt, but it was missing from his belt. He then tried reaching for the knife he carried in his right boot, but this produced oaths of a foul sort from one of his new companions. Then came two blows of a pistol butt.

Harry pitched forward, covering his head with his arms. His assailants then turned to kicking him. He lost count of how many blows he received by the time oblivion blissfully returned.

Chapter 1 8

A patter of rain was falling—on his face. Harry blinked, painfully, and slowly opened his eyes. He was still in the alley, curled up on his side. It was still night, the only light coming from a streetlamp. A scrawny dog was licking at a puddle a few feet away. Otherwise, he was entirely alone.

Slowly, he stretched out his limbs, barely able to keep himself from crying out. It was impossible to tell which of his many discomforts came from the night's carouse or the beating he'd received at the hands of thieves. At all events, they quickly blended into a single, all-encompassing agony.

Sitting up, he began to take inventory. Amazingly, his arms and legs seemed to function. No bones were broken, though his head felt as though someone had emptied a pistol into it.

As might soon prove to be the case.

He reached inside his coat. His Navy Colt was missing. His Derringer was still in its hiding place, however. His assailants had also somehow overlooked the two pistols Miss Van Lew had given him. They'd been much more attentive as concerned his wallet, which he found lying in another puddle. He'd been carrying a mix of United States and Confederate money. The thieves, demonstrating a sagacity that few in President Davis's circle seemed to possess, had left the Confederate dollars.

They'd also failed to examine his belt, which had five twenty-dollar gold pieces sewn into it.

All in all, he supposed he'd been fortunate. He hoped he hadn't used up too much luck. He'd soon be needing a great deal more.

THE door to his boardinghouse stood open, a warning he ignored. Entering, looking about the first floor rooms, Harry found no one present but Estelle, who was in the kitchen, gnawing a ham bone. She gave him only a glance—nothing more, no greeting—returning to meal.

"Breakfasting early?" said Harry.

"Where you been, Mister Raines? I been waitin' for you to come back."

"I was busy being robbed and beaten. Where is our friend the landlord?"

"They come for him."

"What do you mean?"

"They come for him, and they took him. That Nestor Maccubbin and his Plug Uglies. They say he was a Union man."

"They took him to Castle Godwin?"

"Don't know."

She set the ham bone down very carefully on the kitchen table as though it were a fragile object, then wiped her hands on her dress.

"Where we goin' now? We ain't stayin' here?"

He slumped into a wooden chair and took out his flask, taking a generous swig. It didn't help.

"We're leaving," he said. "I have an appointment down

the river, and then we're leaving this fair city. I hope."

"Down the river?"

"Up the river, actually. Up by Belle Isle." He took another swig, then put the flask away. "I fear I am tardy."

"They took your horse, too, Mister Raines. They said it was for the army."

"Then we'll have to walk."

At the door, he paused, taking out the four-barreled pocket pistol Miss Van Lew had given him. He placed it in Estelle's hands. "The appointment I'm going to keep is a duel, Estelle. Do you know what that is?"

"Yessir. White man's way of settlin' quarrels."

It was time to face facts. "If I don't survive this encounter, I want you to run away. Not just to some place in Richmond, but out of the city. Any place in the country where you think you can find friends."

"What if you live?"

"I don't think we'll have to worry about that." He wrapped her hands around the pistol. "If you find yourself in grave danger, use this. But only in extremis."

"What that mean, Mister Raines?"

"Only if you think someone is about to kill you."

THEY were standing in a small group by a coach at the end of the small field, all much the same drab color in the lingering morning mist. As Harry approached, one of them detached himself from the others and came forward. It was George Broward, in uniform, his pocket watch in hand.

"You are forty-two minutes late, sir," he said, pompously. "If you did not arrive by the stroke of the hour, we would have left the field. Your reputation would be in ruins."

"Better the reputation than the mortal coil."

Broward frowned, in brief puzzlement, then sneered. "You come without a second, Mister Raines."

"I'll be my second. I would have chosen my manservant, Caesar Augustus, but he has been murdered."

"Surely you have friends . . ."

"I suspect that what friends I still have in Richmond have been run off or rounded up by the Plug Uglies."

"I was your friend."

"No you weren't, Broward. Mills was, but now, demonstrably, he is not."

"You understand what this means?"

"I understand the rules of the Code Duello. Accept this as one of the shortages of war. Now let's get on with it. Here I am, prepared for the complete pageant."

The other stood uneasily a moment, then bade Harry to stay where he was and walked swiftly to the group by the carriage. They were all in uniform. They conferred a moment, then Broward returned.

"All right, we'll proceed."

"What weapons?"

"Pistols. Are you armed?"

Harry took out the .44 Remington, checking the cylinder. It was fully loaded. "Yes."

"I'll show you your mark."

Harry stood on it, unhappy, waiting for Mills to take his position at his back. Realizing he had forgotten something of no little importance, he reached into his pocket and pulled forth his spectacles.

Both lenses were smashed from the previous night's encounter. A piece of glass stuck in his finger. He pulled it out, jamming his ruined eyeglasses back into a pocket.

"Are you all right, Raines?"

It was Mills, no more than a few inches behind him. "Yes."

"Are you ready?"

"Yes." It was a lie.

Broward called out instructions. Each man was to step off ten paces at Broward's count, then turn and fire. Each would have one shot.

Harry cocked the revolver. He had, of course, never fired it and had no idea how true its aim. But, without his spectacles, it wouldn't much matter.

"One," said Broward.

The command took Harry by surprise. He took a faltering step, but made it a long one. Without his spectacles, he had small chance of hitting Mills, even if he wished to, which he did not. All he could do was put as much distance between himself and the offended Mills as possible.

He tried to remember: Was Mills a good shot?

Broward, a little unevenly, continued the count. At "five," Harry took a quick look to the right, at the river. The James had been an important part of his life. It was a depressingly appropriate place to be taking his leave of it.

"Seven."

Harry stumbled a bit on that one, but quickly regained his balance.

"Eight."

He was holding the pistol straight ahead of him, the barrel pointing down slightly. This would not do. He bent his arm fully, aiming the revolver straight up. He practiced in his mind how he might turn, aim, and fire. There would be no time to aim.

"Nine."

This was absurd. Everything that had happened to him since he had returned to this hard city of his youth had been out of the Theater of the Absurd.

Now this, from the Grand Guignol.

"Ten."

There was only one thing to do.

With a sharp report that startled him, his pistol discharged straight into the air. Sneezing from the smoke and powder that came into his nose, Harry turned slowly to face his adversary.

Mills made his own turn as deliberately, aiming his pistol with great care. Harry saw him take a deep breath, then exhale only slightly, holding perfectly still. He meant this shot to be perfect and true.

Harry shifted his gaze to the river, remembering his interludes there with the young Arabella, especially the last one. If the situation weren't so darkly comic, someone might make a grand romance of all this.

There was only the tiniest instant between the gunshot and the sudden, ripping pain and blow that spun Harry to the ground.

Chapter 19

THE echoes of the gunshot dissipated in the misty air, and then there was an eerie silence. As it continued, Harry wondered if he was dying in pieces, his hearing the first of him to go. But then at last he heard a crow calling, and some chirpier birds. Listening with more care, he could discern the distant thump and grumble that was the Tredegar Ironworks beginning to busy itself.

Mills and Broward were standing over him, Mills's smoking pistol still in his hand.

"He's alive," Broward said.

"Of course he is," Mills said. He leaned close. "How are you, Raines?"

Harry's left arm stung as though swarmed by a thousand bees, all of them seeking the same spot. He looked to it, and saw the cloth of his coat stained red above the elbow.

"Tolerable," said Harry. "Why didn't you kill me?"

"Why did you discharge your weapon before you turned? Why didn't you take a shot?"

"I wished you no harm."

"That was a very brave thing to do, for I sure as hell wish you harm." Mills stepped back, placing his revolver in its holster.

"Put him in my coach," he said.

Two army officers Harry did not know came to either side of him and reached to lift him to his feet. As they pulled, his left arm felt as though it was about to come off, but he somehow refrained from crying out.

Erect at last, he leaned heavily on the man to his right.

Samuel, glowering, sat on the driver's seat, making no move to assist Harry. It was Mills who helped lift him inside. Wincing, Harry slumped back against the rearward facing seat, clenching his teeth and closing his eyes against the pain.

"You promised you would not hurt him."

At the sound of this very feminine, Louisiana-accented voice, Harry opened his eyes wide.

"I didn't promise that," Mills said, seating himself next to Louise and closing and fastening the door. "I said I wouldn't kill him."

"A man of his word," Harry said, grimacing. Runnels of blood had reached his wrist. "Why are you here, Louise?"

She gave him a scant glance; nothing more.

"I'm taking him to Chimborazo," she said, to Mills.

"Do as you will," Mills said. "After I get to the Navy wharf at Rocketts' Landing. They're holding the boat for me, and I am late."

"You'd be on time if you'd avoided this foolishness."

"Miss Devereux, ma'am," Mills said, removing his hat. "You do not understand the ways of Virginia."

"I come from a place where men kill each other this way all the time," she said. "It's just as stupid back in Louisiana as it is in your 'Old Virginia.' "

Mills made no reply. They seemed so displeased with each other they resembled more a long-married couple than lovers fresh from a dalliance.

Harry shut his eyes again. It would be a short ride to Rocketts'.

MILLS hopped down to the ground but lingered by the open door, waiting as though hopeful of a farewell kiss. After a moment's hesitation, Louise leaned forward and gave it to him, showing affection, but not exactly ardor.

He took her hand afterward. "I'll write to you when I can."

"How long will you be gone?" Louise asked.

"You keep asking that. I cannot say."

"But it could be weeks."

"If we succeed, and replenish coal stocks and munitions, it could be a long time, yes."

"But you're not even a member of the crew?"

"I represent Tredegar. Things may go wrong. It's essential I be aboard."

"While I sit here and wait—and wilt—with no word."

"No worry, Ma'am. You will shortly learn that we are invincible and master of the seas."

He brought her hand to his lips, then stepped back and saluted her. As he walked away, Harry leaned to watch him descend to the quay, where a small, side-wheeled gunboat stood waiting, steam up.

"He's off to Gosport," Harry said.

Louise put a finger to his lips.

"Harry," she said, "I told you to flee. Now look at you."

He shrugged, instantly wishing he hadn't. "I'm fine."

She patted his knee. "I do hope so, but you do not look it." She then rapped twice on the coach's padded side. There was a slap of reins and then the jangle of harness as the carriage began to move.

"Chimborazo Hospital," she commanded.

"Yes'm." The black man said it almost in a grunt.

"We'll tend to your wound," she said. "If you are well enough to travel, then truly you must go. President Davis this morning is ordering more arrests."

"The Plug Uglies have already begun that work."

" 'It is the part of men to fear and tremble,' " she recited, " 'when the most mighty gods by tokens send such dreadful heralds to astonish us.' "

"Shakespeare aside, Davis is no Caesar."

She smiled, then continued her recitation. " 'And why should Caesar be a tyrant then? Poor man! I know he would not be a wolf, but that he sees the Romans are but sheep. He were no lion, were not Romans hinds. Those that with haste will make a mighty fire, begin it with weak straws.' "

Harry pushed himself up in the seat. His pain was easing—or at the least, in her presence, he was better able to ignore it.

"These are strange words to hear from the lips of a Confederate spy and assassin," he said.

Her countenance darkened. "Be still, Harry. Talk no more of this."

"I will think upon it."

"Do so elsewhere. Not in Richmond. I think this now the most dangerous place on earth."

"Then why do you linger?"

She shook her head, sadly. "You trespass, sir."

"Tell me one thing, before you leave me," he said. "The day Arabella Mills was killed, you were seen on the street outside my hotel, stopping by the Mills's coach."

"Yes."

"Was Arabella in it?"

"No."

"Who was?"

"Palmer was."

"What were you doing there? A public rendezvous?"

"I had come by to see you, to explain the invitation to the president's. With Palmer there, it was best I did not come calling."

He studied her, trying not to be distracted by her loveliness. "I wonder which side you serve," he said.

"If you wonder, then I am succeeding."

"Just one question more. When I helped you escape from Washington, you showed me a paper—a document testifying to the purchased freedom of a New Orleans mulatto woman. A creased and worn piece of paper some three decades old."

"Please, Harry."

He wondered why he was asking this. Her answer would likely prove nothing. "Was that woman your mother?"

She gazed at him, looking wonderfully and terribly beautiful. "I thought you were my friend."

"I am your friend, as you have seen."

"Then you will know the answer to your question."

The coach rolled along briskly. The street here was cobbled, to support the heavy freight wagons from the wharf. The rumbly bumping brought back his pain.

"Why Mills?" he asked.

"He's not really such a bad fellow."

"I fear he may have killed his wife."

"Many a good man has done that." She leaned forward. "Harry, he was with me—in that little house at Tredegar where you have subsequently discovered us. His coachman took us there from the Exchange, and he stayed with me until I left for our dinner."

"Where did he go then?"

"To his office. It's just down the hill."

"So he could say he was doing work for the ironclad."

"He was with me until past dark, Harry."

"How did you get to President Davis's house?"

"Samuel drove me to the hotel and I hired a hack."

He winced. "This doesn't ring true."

"Then you are a poor detective."

"Well, you are right on that. I've made a mess of the whole thing and got my best friend killed."

"These are terrible times, Harry. This is a terrible place."

The coach crossed the stream called Bloody Run and followed the street named for it, clattering over the tracks of the York River Railroad. They were soon across the city limits. Ahead, Harry could see the sprawling complex of Chimborazo.

Louise took note of it as well. She moved herself to sit beside him, taking his hand.

"I can tell you this much, Harry," she said, almost in a whisper. "There was a child mixed up in this."

"A child?"

"It was to be sold down the river."

"A slave child?"

"I do not know anything for certain, but Palmer was sorely vexed about this child. Arabella, too. There was trouble about it."

"Whose child?"

They had stopped.

"I've told you all I know."

Her hand came to his face, and she pulled him close, kissing him gently on the lips. He wished he were far more presentable.

"Thank you," he said, as she sat back.

"I wish you well, Harry. I always will." She reached across him and opened the coach door. "Go now. Take care. And do leave this city. I do believe your name is on a list."

He got out with great reluctance. "Louise . . ."

Samuel abruptly slapped the reins, and the coach jolted

into motion. Louise kept back, out of view.

Harry's arm was beginning to feel numb.

THE Union Hospital in Georgetown, run by Harry's friend the Army surgeon Colonel Phineas Gregg, was considered an exemplary institution, but hardly compared to Chimborazo. It was an immense establishment of one hundred fifty separate buildings sprawling over forty acres. Someone at the Davis's dinner party had told him the establishment could handle three thousand patients.

Six month's before, it would have been hard to imagine such a need. Now, with all the death and sickness in the military camps, it was doing a brisk business.

Most of the structures were wooden, but Louise had deposited him before a brick building of imposing size. Fighting back dizziness, he stumbled into its foyer, startling a clerical type who sat behind a small desk.

"I need to see a doctor," Harry said, indicating his arm.

"Sir, this is a military hospital."

Harry pulled out the letter from General Lee, holding it aloft.

"I'm enroute to Gosport for naval service," he said. "I'm Colonel Raines's son. I've been attacked by robbers."

He must have seemed about to pitch over, for the clerk suddenly rose and came around to take hold of Harry's good arm. "Come with me," he said.

Harry was led down a corridor to a large waiting room, where a half dozen sickly looking soldiers were seated, one of them asleep or unconscious and lolling back against the wall. Harry was given a wooden chair with arms, and was grateful for it. The clerk wrote down his name in a small ledger book, then departed.

Not only was this hospital cleaner than Colonel

Gregg's; it was the neatest and tidiest place he had ever seen. His family's own plantation house had not been this well scrubbed when readied for one of his mother's dancing parties.

The physician, when Harry was finally brought to him, seemed amiable and competent enough. He was also greatly curious about Harry's wound.

It was less serious than both had feared. Once his coat had been removed, his shirt sleeve rolled up, and the flesh of his upper arm washed, he could see that it amounted to a deep score across the skin just below the shoulder, a gouge that could have been made as easily by saber slash as bullet. The bleeding had mostly stopped. The cut was a thick red channel, welling at the edges.

"Gunshot, you say?" said the doctor, peering close.

"Yes, I was set upon by thieves in an alley."

"Too much of that now."

The doctor stuck a probe into the cut, in two places, each strike sending lightning bolts of pain up Harry's neck and skull. Taken by surprise, he called out at the first, but held steady at the second.

Then the physician took to squeezing the muscles around the wound, pressing thumbs hard against the bone. Harry clenched his teeth so tightly together he feared they would break.

"Some torn muscle tissue," the doctor said. "The bone's intact. You are lucky your assailants were such bad shots. An inch to the left would have smashed the bone, and I would have had to take the arm off. Robbers, you say?"

"Yes."

"There are no powder burns. Did they rob you from afar?"

"The gunshot came later. First, they beat me up a bit."

The doctor shifted his attention to Harry's head, sticking his thumb and fingers in a variety of places, all pain-ful.

"Hmmm," he said, then pulled back. "I'll sew up the arm." He went to a tray that sat on a table, taking from it needle and thread.

"One moment, sir," Harry asked. "Have you whiskey?"

"The sewing won't take long."

"Please."

The doctor frowned, then went to a cabinet, removing a bottle of inexpensive spirits and a glass. He poured it full, then handed it to Harry, sitting back impatiently.

Harry nodded his thanks, then raised his injured arm and poured half the whiskey in the glass into the cut. It took all of his dwindling self-control to keep himself quiet.

"What are you doing?" the doctor asked.

"Something I learned. It's supposed to have a salubri-ous effect."

He drank the rest of the liquor, as the doctor com-menced his seamstress work. When done, having wrapped Harry's arm in a clean dressing, he rose, and then yawned.

"I would say you are not fit for naval service, or any kind of service," he said. "Not for a while."

"You said the arm was not serious."

"It's not—at least yet. No, it's your head. Two bad contusions there. I'm amazed you're on your feet."

"Me, too."

"Go home now. Take some rest. The Navy can wait. With the Yankee army still up by Washington, they won't have need of you just yet."

He poured himself a glass of whiskey, then called to his orderly for the next patient.

* * *

THE words "go home" came languorously upon his spirit. Over the last several years, he had both yearned to return to Belle Haven and despised the idea. Now, it occurred to him, going there was exactly what he should do.

But he wasn't through with Richmond yet.

Harry's dizziness hadn't abandoned him, but it hadn't incapacitated him, either. He could walk, slowly, though he feared his endurance might flag, as he had much ground to cover.

As he had done at General Hooker's Union Army military encampment in Washington so many weeks before, Harry moved along innocently through the Chimborazo compound until he came to a string of saddled officers' horses tied to a long rope. There were soldiers about, however, and one of them took note of him as he stepped near a large and healthy-looking bay gelding. Moving away, Harry at last came to a low building he took to be a stable, and so it proved to be. The only occupant was a black groom.

The South's perverse insistence on suppressing Negro literacy was, with luck, going to cost it one saddle horse.

Harry went up to the man as boldly as his infirmity allowed, thrusting General Lee's letter at him and demanding that he saddle a mount.

"I'm on a mission for General Lee at the War Department," he said.

The man looked uncertain, if not dubious.

"I was waylaid by Yankee sympathizers, which is why I've come here. I've been attended to by a physician but now I must complete my mission." He jabbed his finger at Lee's signature three times. "General Lee's orders. Now get me a horse."

The man did so, but reluctantly, and with no dispatch. It was an uncomfortably long time before he reappeared from the back stalls with white-stockinged chestnut mare

with a sickly eye. The cinch appeared to be loose and
Harry stepped close to tighten it himself, wondering if he
was dealing with negligence or sabotage. He couldn't really blame the man either way.

"You got to sign the book," the groom said.

"Where is it?"

The black man led him slowly toward the main door,
where a cloth-bound ledger lay on a wall shelf. He handed
Harry a stubby pencil.

There were surprisingly few entries. Harry signed himself, "Captain Harrison Raines," which was true enough,
though the Confederates wouldn't be aware of that fact.

He hoped.

Climbing clumsily into the saddle, Harry hesitated before putting heels to the mare's flanks. The soldier who
had eyed him suspiciously back by the officers' mounts
was now standing just outside the door.

Giving him a swift, dark, and disdainful look as a riposte, Harry left the stable at a brisk trot. He passed
through the gate with no one in pursuit.

$\mathbf{H}$E was not far from Miss Van Lew's house, but there
was too much folly and too little promise in that. Instead,
he headed for the Mayo Bridge that led to Manchester.

$\mathbf{T}$HE coach was in the drive, the horses standing calmly
in their traces. Harry presumed that Louise had alighted
somewhere in the city, but there was no way of telling.
If she had come to Mills's house, he would be happy to
find her. He was in need of allies, and she had shown him
she was that, no matter where her other loyalties lay.

Tying the mare to the porch railing, he went up to the
door. He was about to knock, but thought upon it, and

did not, turning the knob instead. As he guessed, it was unlatched. He stepped inside and stood a moment, listening, hearing nothing. He remained there for several minutes. There was only the ticking of a clock.

Mills had an office in the house, just off the central hall. Harry went to it, seating himself at the rolltop desk, which had been left open. The cubbyholes were full of papers, but they all seemed to be tradesmen's bills or had to do with nautical matters beyond Harry's ken. A locked drawer quickly yielded to his pocketknife but contained little he thought of interest, until he came to an affectionate letter written in an elegant feminine hand, but unsigned. Reading through it, he decided it was not from Louise. There was not a single Shakespearean allusion. He guessed it was a quite different lady, perhaps a married one, well born, and possibly from one of the James River plantations.

He was wasting time. Poking here and there one last time, he decided to move on, heading upstairs.

Palmer and Arabella Mills had not shared the same bedroom. His was a shambles, smelling of whiskey. Hers looked as though she had just left it. Her hairbrush and other oddments were still in place on the dressing table by the window. Some pieces of jewelry and a small miniature had been left on a night table beside the bed.

Looking through a clothing chest, he found only neatly folded dresses. Hatboxes produced hats. A chest of drawers contained stockings, camisoles, and corsets. He began to feel disgusted with himself.

More quickly now, he went through the rest of the house. He returned to Mills's office, at last finding one of the items he had sought: an inventory of Mills's slaves. There were three belonging to this house—Samuel, Estelle, and another named Eben. A total of twenty-seven were listed as attached to the main Mills holding down-river.

There was no reference to a child attached to either Estelle's name or Samuel's. He wondered if it could be Eben.

Unsatisfied, Harry went to the kitchen at the rear of the house, and then out back. There were more dependencies to this house than he'd expected—a coach house and stable, a large shed, and two small cabins he took to be slave quarters.

One clearly was Estelle's, a neatly but cheaply furnished one-room abode with a fireplace but no stove. It backed up to the woods at the edge of the property and would have been amenable to "discreet" visits, if Caesar Augustus had been of such a mind. There should have been no need of a clash with Arabella, unless she'd come upon them by accident.

The other cabin was of the same dimensions, but quite dirty. It contained of all things a rusty and tarnished spittoon. There was a small slab of chewing tobacco on its central table.

Harry started for the stable, and the living quarters he judged to be in the loft above it. Crossing the yard, however, passing a brick, open-air fire stand obviously used as a forge, he caught sight of something and turned to it.

In the ashes was a small, half burned piece of rope and a fragment of cloth that, on closer inspection, proved to be a portion of a coat or jacket, scorched and frazzled on the edges. It had a lining of now grimy silk and two tarnished but intact brass buttons. He could tell by the way they were placed on the coat that it was a man's garment, and that another button that should have been there was missing.

Pondering this find, he heard a crunch of heavy feet in motion. Turning, he looked up to see the coachman Samuel coming at him, an axe held high over his head.

Chapter 20

HARRY had time only to do one thing, and he had no idea what that thing might be. But through some strange alchemy born of the wedding of anger to fear, his brain was induced to function. As the onrushing man raised the axe higher for the intended blow, Harry threw himself down to the ground, his motion toward his attacker. This put him within the arc of the axe's swing, and caused him to roll with some violence against Samuel's legs. The coachman, off balance, tumbled forward and down, his axe sliding from his hands.

Though his injured arm stung with renewed pain, Harry was able to rise to his knees and reach for his pistol. Unfortunately, he was not able to bring it into play. Instead of going for his axe, Samuel flung himself upon Harry, bringing to bear a decided advantage in weight, strength, and malice. A knife had somehow come into his hand. The blade flashed past as Harry rolled once more.

The black man came upon him again, but this time Harry was able to arrest the knife-wielding arm, though it took both his hands to hold the weapon off. With his free hand, his assailant gripped Harry's throat. The light of the day began to fade. All he could hear was the fierce strain of his own breathing and the loud thumping of his heart. He gathered what strength he had, attempting first to kick Samuel in a painful place, then twisting the arm with the knife.

This failed to loosen the weapon, but the big man fell sideways and let go of Harry's throat. He lunged back, half righting himself, just as the sharp and sudden explosive snap of a gunshot crackled through the air. For a moment, Harry feared that the pistol in his belt had discharged, but, if so, he sensed no injury.

Going for the knife again, Harry found his attacker much less resistant. He'd been grunting, but now there were groans.

There was another gunshot, and a third, both striking the earth. In panic, Harry thrust himself free, pointlessly putting both hands protectively before his face. A fourth shot zinged close, then the full great weight of the coachman collapsed upon him.

Harry lay there a long moment, then, taking a deep breath and clenching his teeth, hauled himself free.

Estelle knelt on the ground not ten feet away. The four-barreled pocket pistol he'd given her still in hand, she was sobbing.

"Damnation, Estelle," he said. "You could have killed me."

"I'se sorry, Mister Raines. I didn't mean to hurt nobody."

"You have surely killed him."

"I'se sorry. He was makin' like . . ."

"It's all right, Estelle. I'm grateful."

With great effort, Harry got to his feet. Samuel was sprawled face down, still gripping his knife. There were two dark circles visible in the dust of the back of his coat.

"I don't understand," Harry said. "How could a black man be so loyal to a household such as this?"

"Don' know what to say, Mister Raines."

Harry began brushing off his own coat, then wondered at the good of that, and stopped. He went over to Estelle, placing his hand on her shoulder. Her crying had eased, but she was trembling.

"The time has come to leave this place, and to do so swiftly."

"Yessir, Mr. Raines."

"I do thank you. But for you, I would have been slain."

"Yessir." She started to rise. He helped her to her feet.

"Do you know anything about this?" he asked, picking up the burned piece of cloth with two brass buttons.

"Nossir."

"Why burn a coat? There's a shortage, what with this war on."

"I don' know, Mister Raines."

"Gather your things," he said. "We must go now."

She stared down at Samuel's motionless body.

"We must leave his burial to others, Estelle. There's no time for it."

She nodded, sadly, then turned toward the house.

SHE found bread and a chunk of smoked ham in the pantry, adding it to her bundle. Harry paused to return briefly to Palmer Mills's bedchamber, going to the dressing room. He found two shirts, a waistcoat, a pair of torn riding breeches, and a spare Confederate naval officer's coat and drum-shaped cap.

He had suffered much because of the Mills family. He was due a little compensation. He took one of the shirts and the cap and coat.

Passing Arabella's room, he stopped, then went within. There was a small, jeweled pin on her bed table, one he remembered from their youth. He felt a bit ghoulish, but he picked it up. Thinking a moment, he then put it in his pocket. Should he flag in what he'd promised, it would be there to remind him.

He sat a moment on her bed, touching the pillow, and then running his hand over the blanket.

Something sharp struck his finger. He picked it up. A piece of straw.

Estelle waited by the mare, who was browsing the dried winter grass, unconcerned.

"We're not taking the horse, Estelle," he said.

"How come?"

"They'll be looking for me on a horse. We're going to walk—along the river."

"Where we goin'?"

"To a better place."

As they started down the short lane that led to the road, Harry looked back and was startled to see an old black man in a wide-brimmed, beat-up hat standing over Samuel's body, staring after them.

Estelle kept going.

"Who is that?" Harry asked.

"That's Eben."

Stealing a boat proved easier than stealing horses. Wearing his approximation of a Navy officer's uniform, Harry led the way upriver, following the tracks of the Richmond and Danville Railroad around a curve of the James to where a wide channel separated the southern shore from Belle Isle, on which stood the Old Dominion Iron and Nail works. As Harry remembered, there was an assortment of boats moored or pulled up on the bank. He chose a small skiff, as it would have a low profile on the water.

They were not far from the fall line and its rapids, and the current was swift. Harry took to the oars but used them only to steer and alter their course as they floated past the capital and under its three bridges. They had to round the sharp bend of the James opposite Chimborazo Hospital and proceed another three or four miles of the river's long southerly stretch before they came upon what Harry sought—a trim-looking, small sailboat tied to a dock with sails reefed.

Coming up to it obliquely, and seeing no human figures on the lawn of the great house on the hill above, Harry quickly had Estelle and himself aboard. Keeping the skiff's oars, he cast the sailboat off, paddling canoe fashion at the bow to gain the middle of the river. Then he freed the sails and had the little craft under canvas within minutes.

"They goin' to kill us if they catch us," Estelle said.

"Don't worry about that just yet."

"You know how to work these things, Mister Raines?"

"I do," he said, settling at the tiller. "Caesar Augustus and I grew up on this river. I was afloat as much as I was in the saddle."

"Won't they catch us with one of them big gunboats?"

"They might try, but once we get south of Drewry's Bluff, there'll be swamps and creeks to either side all the way to City Point. We can get where they can't go. The water will be too shallow for anything with a boiler."

THEY sought the refuge of such backwaters only twice during their journey, once to avoid a small Confederate naval vessel and then again to pass the night. The most dangerous moment came in passing Fort Hoke and Battery

IV, where the Confederates were working at putting obstacles into the river. A rifleman perched on some piling far out from the shore hailed Harry, asking who he was and where bound. Harry said he was Lieutenant Mills, taking a runaway slave down to Bermuda Hundred. The soldier asked if naval officers were working as bounty hunters. Harry replied he was doing a favor for a friend.

They ate the last of their food, washed down with river water, just below Bermuda Hundred and the Shirley Plantation. Harry was in his home country now. The fields and bluffs and woods that stretched away from either bank were familiar. Even without his spectacles, he recognized old tree stumps sticking up from the swampy shore.

"You say you go here with Caesar Augustus?" Estelle asked.

"For years and years. When we were boys, and later. We fished and swam and fooled with boats all along here."

"Your house near here?"

"Around the next bend, where the river widens. It was my home for twenty-one years. Caesar Augustus's, too. Both of us were born there. Weren't for slavery, we'd both be there still."

"Not Caesar Augustus."

"No, I guess not."

She huddled further in her shawl, though the day was warmer. Noting a shift in the wind, he let out the main sheet further. It was a pleasant little boat. Harry wished he'd been able to buy rather than steal it. He began to wish he had not been so willing to burn bridges behind him. If he somehow managed to get out of the Virginia tidewater alive, he knew he could only return in the train of a Union army. With McClellan in command, that could be a long time coming.

"You sad about Caesar Augustus?" Estelle asked.

"Very sad. It was all my fault."

She said nothing, her eyes turning to the murky water.

"Estelle, I was told there was a child involved in this."

"I don't know of no child."

"I think I'm talking about a slave child."

"Ain't no child at the Mills house at Manchester. All the children at the plantation down in Charles City County."

"Estelle, was Mrs. Mills about to sell one of them down the river?"

"I don' know. She don' talk to me about things like that."

"You were her housemaid, Estelle."

"She weren't my friend. You know how she be about black folks."

A crane lifted from a stump and, with a shrill call and a flap of long wings, climbed high, turning in a slow circle.

"Did you have such a child, Estelle? Did you have a child by Caesar Augustus, that she was going to sell?"

"Nosuh."

"By Samuel, then?"

She wasn't looking at him. "Nosir. I ain't got no child by no one."

He took out the piece of cloth he'd rescued from the ashes of Samuel's forge fire.

"This is a man's coat—see where the buttons lie? An expensive one, by the look of them. Why would Samuel burn it?"

"That's not Samuel's coat. He only got one coat."

"But it was in his forge fire."

She shrugged. She seemed as sad and somber now as she'd been the day Caesar Augustus had perished in Libby Prison.

"Do you know where Caesar Augustus went that day—the day Arabella died?" Harry asked.

"Nosir. He not come to see me that day."

"What about Samuel?"

"He drive the coach. I don' know where he go."

The wind stiffened, then shifted to off the port quarter. Harry drew in the mainsail, and the boat began to heel. Ahead, past a long point extending from the right, he could see the masts of two small vessels far downriver.

"Estelle, before we part, you're going to have to tell me the truth."

"I tell you the truth, Mister Raines, but why you keep on with this? Mrs. Mills dead. Caesar Augustus dead."

"That, Estelle, is why I keep on with this."

Chapter 21

REACHING Belle Haven's dock, Harry maneuvered the little craft between two boats already tied to it, holding on to one of them but making no mooring. After helping Estelle out, he rigged the tiller with a loop of the mainsheet, using one hand to spare his injured arm. Then, getting out, he shoved the sailboat at an angle out into the current. There were some small islands ahead, but if the little craft missed them and the wind didn't get too flighty, it might yet travel miles before it was recovered.

He knew very well that, if General Winder were to send men after him, they likely would head for his family's plantation sooner or later. But he didn't intend to stay long.

The path up the bluff to the house was bordered by flowers in the warm seasons, and he was pleased to see an emerging bud here and there. Estelle followed him dutifully, as she had followed so many masters.

There was a long gallery at the rear of the house, leading to a vegetable garden at one end and a formal English one at the other. Stepping up onto it, he saw a woman in a pale green dress seated at the latter place, reading a book. She took note of his approach when he was still a few paces shy, turning tentatively, her mind still on the words she'd been reading. When she saw who it was, she dropped the book, with no care to keeping her place.

Then she was rising, flinging herself into his arms. He held her tightly, so closely they rocked back and forth. After a long moment like this, they finally eased their hold upon each other. He stepped back so he could see her face. They bore a strong resemblance to each other, yet she was by far the handsomer. Her hair was much lighter in color, almost blonde; her eyes amber, while his were simply a soft shade of brown.

"Elizabeth." It gave him such a happy feeling to say her name.

She smiled, seemingly as happy. "I had feared this war would have to be over before I set eyes on you again."

"After today, that may well be true. I'll not be here long."

She stepped back further, her eyes examining his over-sized naval officer's coat.

"Harry? That's Confederate. You haven't . . . ?"

"No, this is just a convenience. I hope to regain Union lines. I doubt I'll be able to come back."

Her happiness faded at the edges, then altogether vanished.

"That is sad news."

She was nearly twenty-six, and still unmarried. Her views on slavery were almost as hostile as his own, and not much shared by the Tidewater beaux. She said she could not bear to become a plantation wife like her mother, yet her only alternative had been continued residence here, where a hundred human beings labored for their father without reward.

And now, a hundred and one.

"This is Estelle," he said, turning to the black woman. "I have brought her with me, and I mean to set her free."

His sister drew the black woman close. "I think I do know you. Do you work for the Mills family?"

"They's my masters. Least they was."

Elizabeth's countenance now darkened. "Arabella . . ."

"We'll talk about that later," Harry said. He put his arm around Elizabeth's shoulders. "Is there food?"

THEY ate at a table on the gallery, two kitchen maids attending to the serving. There was lemonade, biscuits and jam, some roast pork, and custard. Harry insisted that Estelle sit with them at the table, causing some wide-eyed consternation with the servant girls. When the meal was done, Elizabeth summoned the majordomo of the household—a large black man who might have been an older relation of the deceased Samuel—and instructed him to find Estelle quarters. She followed him meekly, looking a little fearful.

"The war will put an end to this," Harry said.

"But who will put an end to the war?"

He fought the impulse to explain himself—to pour out everything to her as he had done when they were children, Allen Pinkerton, Mr. Lincoln, the Secret Service, and all. But it was unfair to make her share that burden, to endanger her with such knowledge.

In effect, he had taken up arms against their state, their father, their brother. Despite her Abolitionist sentiments, he wasn't sure she would understand that.

"I was surprised to see you come upon our porch, Harry, but, in truth, I've been wondering if that might actually happen. The Richmond papers come in the mail pretty regular. Last one I read said that Arabella Mills had been killed by a Negro named Caesar Augustus. Was that our Caesar Augustus?"

"Yes."

"Did he do that thing?"

A minute before, he would immediately have said "No." Now, something stayed him.

"I've spent the past many days trying to prove the contrary—if only to myself."

She simply stared at him, her eyes full of her question.

"But it no longer matters," Harry said. "I was told he was killed—in Libby Prison, where they'd been keeping him. They said it was a Union officer."

"Can that be true?"

"I don't know. There's a severe shortage of truth in Richmond these days, as there is of everything else."

Elizabeth shook her head sadly. "Poor Arabella. She was always so romantic, a lady out of Walter Scott."

"Life is not a novel."

"Oh, yes it is. A very sad novel." She smiled again, wanly. "I once feared I would end up having to marry Palmer Mills. He was so jealous over you and Arabella. I was afraid he'd demand me as compensation—put a stick into you with that—and that father would go along."

"I suppose he might have."

"No. He disapproved of Palmer. Thought him a drunkard."

"Father's in Richmond," Harry said. "Or he was. I saw him, but only for an instant." He hesitated. His father had doted on Elizabeth. "He was not friendly."

"No."

"Has he come here?"

"No. His whole life is the army now. We get the occasional letter."

Harry wanted to change the subject. He pointed to his arm. "Palmer Mills shot me yesterday. I suppose he could have killed me, if he wished."

"Shot you? How? Why?"

"A sort of duel. Over Arabella."

"Oh Harry." She went to his side and helped him remove his coat. Ripping open his blood-hardened sleeve,
she slowly unwound his bandage. "This needs changing."
She peered closely at his wound. Though not to the same
degree, her eyes had the same failing as his own.

"Am I well?"

"There is no proud flesh. But I am no doctor."

He sniffed. "I need a bath."

She wrinkled her nose. "Yes you do." She stood up,
preparatory to summoning more servants. "Then we'll attend to your wound."

"I need a change of clothes. Would there be anything
of mine left?"

Elizabeth took his hand, leading him inside. "Everything is left. After you walked out of here, father never
went into your room again."

His most useful find was a pair of old spectacles, the
focus nearly as good as that of the pair that had been
smashed by his alley assailants. Once bathed and shaved
and freshly dressed, he lingered in his room, looking
through old books and framed daguerreotypes of himself
and his family that still sat atop his dresser. In one, he
stood stiffly with his older brother, Robert, in front of the
house. It was striking how much the brother resembled
their father and he, their mother.

Elizabeth looked exactly like their mother.

"You look much restored," she said, when he'd returned to her. "You are your old self."

None of them were that.

He looked at his watch. "Are there still horses here? I
think I'd like to pay a visit to the Mills's place."

"You won't be back by supper."

"Probably not. But it's something I'd better do while I'm here."

"Could you not go tomorrow?"

"Tomorrow I must go—for good."

They stood together on the front veranda while a groom saddled him a mount. In the distant fields, farmhands had begun some early plowing. Harry could see a mounted overseer moving along with them.

"If the Union prevails and this rebellion is put down," he said. "All this will end."

"I suppose you're right. I think about that a lot. Perhaps if we paid them—but father would never do that."

"I suspect he would consider that dishonorable." Harry shook his head.

The groom brought the horse—a fine looking animal.

"Father will no doubt think me a thief if I don't bring back this one."

She made no reply. He took the reins, nodding his thanks and dismissal to the groom, who ambled lazily away.

COMING down the Mills's plantation drive at a fast trot, Harry went by the main house and continued on to the slave quarters, hoping to avoid the overseer but find a black who might hold some responsibility. Pulling up by the barn, he found several slaves at work, none of them showing much enthusiasm for their labor or his arrival.

"I'm here about the slave that's for sale," Harry said, dropping from the saddle.

"Ain't no slave for sale," said a field hand. "Anyway, you go see the people in the big house."

"I did," Harry lied. "Could find no one in authority. I heard there was a child for sale."

"Ain't no slave child for sale," said the field hand.

Harry looked around the yard. There were two children visible, standing by a large black woman. One was a boy about seven; the other younger, and a girl. Both were ill dressed, virtually in rags.

"Not for sale?"

"Nosuh. But you go ask at the house."

Harry remounted. "Was there a child sold? Has one been taken away?"

The black people only looked at him.

"You there! What do you want?"

Harry turned his horse with a slight touch of rein, finding himself facing a white man in a duster coat and broad-brimmed hat. He was obviously the overseer, but no one Harry had seen before.

"I'm Harrison Raines, from the Belle Haven Plantation down the river. I am looking to buy a house servant, and I heard you had one for sale."

The man looked fit, and a prime candidate for military service. But his lot would probably be exempt from conscription. The system had to be maintained.

"You heard wrong, mister. Got none for sale. Need every hand."

"This was a child I heard about. We need someone for the kitchen." He paused, then gestured at the boy and girl. "What about one of these two?"

"Not for sale. We're shorthanded here."

"Did you sell one recently? Maybe I can catch up with the buyer and make a better offer."

The man took a step forward, coming near enough to lay hold of Harry's bridle.

"I said, Mister, we've got none of them for sale. Now if that's your business, it's done. Move on."

Harry backed his horse away a few steps. "Is Mr. Mills on the premises?"

"Mr. Mills is dead."

"I don't mean the father. I mean the son. Lieutenant Palmer Mills."

"He's not been here for weeks. Don't expect him soon. Now, sir. Please move on."

Harry pressed heels to flank and trotted out of the yard, passing a great many sullen, silent faces.

IT was full night when he returned to Belle Haven. Elizabeth had saved supper for him and sat with him while he ate it. She had opened a bottle of wine for him and took a glass herself.

"This is very good," he said.

"It's one of father's best. There aren't many left. The blockade."

"He will be angry."

"The prodigal returns. That should be occasion enough."

Harry sipped, and sighed. "You have no idea how much I wish I did not have to move on."

"It can be no more than my wish for you to stay." Her voice was sweet, but quavered. "Still, you are going North again, so I can only be glad for you."

"I wish you could come with me."

"I've thought of that. There have been opportunities. But who would look after all our people? Our new overseer—Nicholas—he is a hard man. I caught him skinning a girl with a grain flail last week. Said she was impudent—and we can well guess what he meant by that. Were I a man, I would have taken it to him."

"Caesar Augustus bore such scars."

"Yes. Poor man."

He refrained from lighting a cigar, knowing her dislike of them. "Do you get out much in society, such as there is any in this war?"

"Here in Tidewater, yes. I stay away from Richmond."

"I am happy to hear that," he said, pouring more wine.

"The city has become such a hellish place."

"With worse to come." He sat back, physically content, but bothered in spirit.

"Has there been gossip about Palmer Mills? Gossip about a slave child?"

She seemed embarrassed. "Well, there's always that kind of gossip going around Tidewater. No one is spared."

"There's said to be a child, a child who might have been sold off the plantation. But I could find no record. And they denied it at the Mills's place."

"Then perhaps there is none."

Harry stared down at his now empty plate. "The Mills's coachman, a man named Samuel. He's dead. Killed in a fight."

"I believe he was a friend of Caesar Augustus. Now they're both gone."

"He was defending the Mills's house in Manchester against intruders. Could a black slave be that loyal to white masters?"

She made her reply softly. "It has been my hope that our people will prove so—when the day comes for their freedom."

Harry rose and walked to the windows that looked out onto the rear gallery. "That day could come soon, if General McClellan would ever get off his behind and bring his army down here."

He could see a lantern light out on the river, moving slowly. "But then," he added, "there is the 'Monster' at Norfolk to contend with. It could put an end to the blockade very quickly."

" 'Monster?' Do you mean that iron-sided ship?" She did not like talking about war.

"Yes. It's built. It's almost ready. Could be any day."

"Harry, are you here because of that vessel? Is that why you've come?"

"What do you mean?" It offended him to lie to his sister, but he did not want her knowing of such things.

"I know you, Harry. Better than you . . ."

She appeared of a sudden stricken, as though by some paralytic force. He turned to follow the direction of her gaze. In the doorway stood a figure as tall as he, an imperial figure, in gray coat and gold epaulets and braid.

Colonel Raines looked to them both, but otherwise did not move an inch. "You have disgraced this house," he said finally to Harry. "You know what you have done, and soon so shall all Virginia. General Lee is much aggrieved by your behavior, but told me he kept his word to you. It is more than you deserve."

He took one step into the dining room, but advanced no farther.

"Father . . ."

"Be quiet, Elizabeth!" The older man turned away from her, his attention fixed malevolently on Harry.

"I will give you fifteen minutes to gather your belongings and leave this house," he said. "You are not to come back, sir. Not as long as I live."

"Father!"

He swung about and walked somberly out of the room and back down the hall. A moment later, Harry heard a door being slammed shut.

ELIZABETH hung on to his stirrup.

"I'm so sorry, Harry."

"Nothing's changed."

"I keep hoping."

"It's a small matter, compared to everything else." He

leaned down and touched her hair. She took his hand and kissed it. Tears were in her eyes.

"Damned war," he said.

"Damned war."

If his father was listening, he was not visible.

"Elizabeth, I must ask a favor. The woman Estelle, I promised her her freedom."

"Yes, you told me."

"I fear I must ask you to see to it."

"Ask me?"

"I can't take her with me. The Union holds Fortress Monroe, and Hampton and Newport News besides. If she could be brought near enough. It's something you have done before . . ."

"I will try."

"The Confederate force down here on the Peninsula is said to be very small, but . . ."

"I am a Virginia lady, sir. I should come to no harm."

"I am grateful for today."

"I, too."

"I won't say good-bye."

"No. Do not. I will see you again."

He smiled, then gently moved his horse forward at a walk. He could not bring himself to look back.

Chapter 22

From the next morning on, a cold, driving rain accompanied him every mile of the road down the peninsula, turning it to a thick, soupy mud that slowed his horse to a struggling walk. He cut into woods and across fields, but they improved his progress very little. At times he'd wait for the rain to pass, but each time it slackened only long enough to lure him out onto the soggy highway, then fell upon him again.

Finally, reaching the old colonial capital of Williamsburg, he realized he had to find a faster means of travel or give up all hope of his goal. He'd become very fond of this strong and steady animal he'd taken from his father, but nevertheless left it at a local stable with a week's board paid for.

He anticipated a long, miserable walk from Williamsburg to the banks of the James, but he was spared a large part of that trudge when he found a flatboat pulled up on the shore of a now rain-swollen creek, leading south to the river. It had no oars, and he had to use a broken tree limb as a sort of pole to steer it, but it sufficed to get him to the river.

* * *

In the end, he had to steal two more boats, grateful each time for the cover provided by the heavy rains and hanging mists. Shortly after abandoning the flatboat, he found a small farm barge that he cut loose and steered into the main river current, using the rudder as a scull to increase his speed. When he finally reached the confluence of the James and the Nansemond River, he hauled up on the shore and went looking for a more seaworthy vessel, discovering a small, gaff-rigged skiff with a reefed sail moored in a creek a short distance from a fishing dock.

He waited until just before dark to take it. There was a Confederate battery across the Nansemond on Pig Point—the Richmond papers had written of it firing on the Yankee blockade fleet—and he wanted to avoid the gun crews' curiosity.

The rain came on hard, but with generous wind. Once around Pig Point, he was able to hold course steering by the light at Wise's Point, though it kept disappearing in the murk.

The first pale light of dawn found him hauled up at the mouth of the Elizabeth River. The wind had fallen, and he feared he'd make no headway against its current. The Gosport Navy Yard was several miles upstream, adjoining Portsmouth and across the river from Norfolk with its well-armed and white-washed little fort.

The brightening sky brightened his hopes. It showed clear in the northwest. In a few minutes, the wind breeze shifted to that direction, and he headed into the Elizabeth on a broad reach. The sail was much patched, but held.

There were Confederate pickets along the shore, and several called out to him, getting no response. One, angered at his refusal to reply, fired his musket at him, but the ball struck the water far short, and he didn't fire another. The Southern warships Harry passed—a two-masted steam frigate and three armed sloops—paid him no mind, perhaps because his little boat was so small and he was sailing it along with such nonchalance.

IT was mid-morning when the narrowing river yielded his first view of Norfolk, and then the busy Navy Yard across the river on the right.

The Union Navy supposedly had burned the place upon abandoning it, but much of it seemed to have survived. There were masts, smokestacks, and buildings visible in great profusion, and many small boats moving on the water. The establishment looked to be as busy a works as Tredegar.

He steered closer to shore. The wind had been a friend back at the mouth of the Elizabeth but had declined the farther upriver he advanced. When he looked up again, it was with a chilling realization. One of the buildings he had noted, a long, barnlike structure with a high smokestack, was actually in the water. He had finally come upon the Monster, waiting in its lair.

HARRY was accosted almost immediately upon docking his boat—seized by two burly sailors and half dragged to a quayside shed and an elderly senior enlisted man who seemed to be functioning as harbor master.

He explained his arrival by saying he'd come from the War Department in Richmond and had traded his horse for a boat because of the muddy roads. Beyond that, he offered only the letter from Lee endorsing Harry's enlistment in the Confederate Navy. Much of the ink was smeared, but the general's signature was still legible, as was a reference to Navy Secretary Mallory.

It sufficed. Harry now owed the good general considerable in this war, though he doubted that the old gentleman was much delighted with the obligation.

One of the sailors escorted Harry down a muddy lane that wound between some large buildings, emerging finally near the yard's enormous dry dock and a slightly smaller wharf to which the ironclad was moored. A military band was playing, and there was a crowd of sorts on the dock, a mix of black-coated civilians and both Navy and Army uniforms. Harry quickly got the idea he was presumed to be one of a number of dignitaries gathering here, presumably for the Monster's maiden voyage. He expected it would be a sea trial to determine whether the fiendish contraption could actually function as a warship.

The sailor took him to a Confederate marine posted at the top of the steps leading down to the dock, vouching for him. The man saluted, letting Harry pass. He simply nodded in reply. Wishing he were more presentable, and hoping none of these worthies would recognize him, he moved to the edge of the group, fixing his attention on the huge, fantastic vessel.

She was easily two hundred fifty feet long, with her dark, forbidding above-deck casement taking up some two-thirds of that length. It had sloping sides, reached a height of two stories, and resembled a sort of malevolent, floating barn. It appeared to be heavily covered with iron plating—as was the low, flat deck extending fore and aft. The plates were so thickly applied it was indeed a wonder the ship did not sink at her mooring, as they had joked in the Richmond bar. As it was, recurring swells from the wakes of passing vessels were spreading water over the deck flooring in intersecting circles. Heavy seas might well cause the craft to founder.

It was a prospect mightily to be wished. The ship had four, fearsome-looking gunports on the sides, plus another at the stern end, and presumably at the bow as well.

If the armor proved as impregnable as it looked, there'd

be little left useful for Union gunners to shoot at—a single smokestack, two ventilators, a high central mast, and a shorter one from which a Confederate stars and bars now hung limply, for the wind had died completely. There were also two ship's boats on each side hanging from davits.

Shooting all that away would likely be no more than a trifling irritant to her captain and crew. There was no way of telling how well this vessel could fight. She looked to have all the maneuvering ability of a giant brick. But she also looked able to withstand anything the North might fire at her. If she were a fort on dry land, she might be impossible to take by assault.

But every weapon had its flaws and drawbacks.

Harry moved along the edge of the group, nodding to anyone who looked his way and then turning elsewhere. He caught snatches of conversation. There were complaints that the design had been faulty, leaving the ship so high in the water that, despite the overhanging iron plating, its unprotected wooden hull was exposed at the waterline. To bring it down again, crewmen had labored through the night loading the vessel with a pig iron ballast. The draught of the vessel was deep, and so there were contrary worries about its ability to breast the underwater sandbar where the Elizabeth joined the James at Hampton Roads.

Workmen were swarming about the sides of the casement, some of them standing on ladders. They appeared to be painting it—which was peculiar, so close to its sailing.

A few of the dignitaries in the crowd voiced criticism of the choice of captain for the *Virginia,* as the Monster was now named. Because of seniority—a system as rigid in the Confederate Navy as the Union's—Secretary Mallory had picked the sixty-one-year-old Franklin Buchanan, who had been the first superintendent of the U.S. Naval Academy and now commanded the Confederates' Chesapeake Bay squadron. The younger Catesby ap Jones, who had served on the ironclad when she was the U.S. Navy steam frigate *Merrimack*, had been relegated to second in command.

"There's the whole damned Yankee blockading squadron out there," said a man standing next to Harry, a baldheaded civilian in a frock coat who looked about carefully before speaking. "We're putting all our eggs in this one basket."

Secretary Mallory was not fifteen paces away.

"She looks invincible to me," said Harry.

The civilian introduced himself as a Confederate congressman, squinting as he took in Harry's weatherdamaged appearance.

"I had a rough trip," Harry said. "Rotten weather."

"You didn't take the train?"

"Horse and boat."

The squint became sharper.

"Who are you, sir?"

The telegraph traffic between Richmond and Norfolk was fairly constant, and there was clearly a danger that it might contain warnings about a fugitive named Harrison Raines. The charges General Winder could bring to bear were numerous and even capital.

"Harrison Raines," he said, forthrightly. "Colonel Raines's son."

"I don't know him," said the congressman, who added he was from Alabama.

"Owns the Belle Haven Plantation up the James."

"You come from there?"

Harry shook his head. "From Richmond, the War Department. General Lee."

The congressman appeared satisfied. "Does the good general think we'll win the war with this?"

"I don't think so."

"Maybe he's as smart as they say."

Harry nodded, his eyes on the ironclad. "Why are they painting it?" he asked.

"They're not."

"But those buckets and brushes?"

"That's grease. They're covering the slanting sides of that thing with grease. Make the Union balls fly off all the easier."

"Won't that stuff catch fire?"

"Let us hope not."

"If it did, the poor souls inside would have a hard time getting out of there."

"Unless they're near the gunports."

The congressman moved on. Harry went in the opposite direction, asking after Lieutenant Mills. No one seemed to have heard of the man. He was about to give up, for a number of eyes were on him now, but then a young naval officer, standing near a gangplank leading to the vessel, said Mills had gone aboard the ship.

"He's going to sail aboard her?" Harry asked.

The officer started to reply, then looked away from him. Many heads were turning in that direction. Secretary Mallory had climbed aboard a wooden crate and was beginning to speak. With everyone's attention distracted, Harry began to edge closer to the ship.

Mechanics were coming out from the *Virginia*'s interior, stepping out on the ship's deck, their labors within the huge ironclad complete. Sailors began taking up the mooring lines. High above everyone, a wisp of oily smoke curled up from the top of the smokestack.

Harry moved closer still, halting at the edge of the dock. When Mallory finished, the assembled dignitaries applauded, then began to shift about. Suddenly, there came the boom of a cannon from across the river over by Fort Norfolk. Captain Buchanan's red ensign, marking his ranks as a flag officer, went up the rear mast, just as a great, boiling cloud of dark smoke erupted from the stack.

The spectators were cheering. The men with the grease buckets began to peel away from their work and return to the dock, causing the dignitaries to back up. The full complement of mechanics drew together, then began jumping to the dock as the deckhands slipped the moorings. As they jumped off, Harry quickly jumped on.

He heard someone shouting behind him, but wasn't certain the words were directed at him. Ignoring them in any case, he kept moving. Just as he was about to step through the main hatch, he heard someone on the dock call out: "Go on with your metallic coffin! She'll never amount to anything else!"

Harry looked back. The remark seemed to come from an old man standing to the side of the crowd. Harry couldn't tell for certain, but the man appeared to be vastly amused by the ship and the occasion.

A sailor bumped against him, but raised no objections to Harry's presence. He stepped through the iron-framed doorway, entering the noisy, crowded, fume-laden, and forbidding interior.

A marine holding a musket stood just within, but did not challenge him, perhaps taking him for someone important. Despite hanging lanterns, it was oppressively dark. Harry had only gone a few steps when he began to feel the heat. Moving along past gun crews, he saw that they were preparing for battle. He held out hope that this was all merely part of a drill.

An officer came by, accidentally colliding with Harry and then giving him a hard look.

"Who tell hell are you?" he said.

The man had a full, well-trimmed beard and moustache, intelligent eyes, and an agreeable if somewhat weathered face. He appeared to be in his forties, which was old for his lieutenant's rank. But the Confederate Navy was small, and rank was limited.

The officer had a bluff manner and a decided air of command. Harry realized he was talking to Catesby ap Jones.

"Raines, sir. From the War Department. I was seeking a Lieutenant Palmer Mills."

"Why in hell are you looking for him now?" he said, speaking over the engine din. "We're under way! This is not a river cruise. How did you get aboard?"

"Just came aboard, sir. I promise you I will not interfere with the operation of this vessel in any way, but I must talk to Mills. Here, I have this letter from General Robert E. Lee."

Jones raised his hand to object. "Mills is up forward, with Captain Buchanan. But, damn you, stay out of the way."

Harry gave his thanks, moving back to get out of Jones's way and striking his head on a metal overhang. He was already slightly dizzy from the heat and noxious, acrid fumes that were everywhere in the interior. There was noise, too—of crushing loudness.

Proceeding on, he encountered pyramids of cannonballs set in their deck monkeys. Stepping around them, he saw what looked to be a small forge fire, then realized unhappily what it really was. The Confederates were preparing to ready hot shot. They meant to do battle in the nastiest fashion.

The gun ports were open. Ducking down as he went

along, Harry stole glances of the shore, surprised at how slowly they were moving. The Union squadron would be ready. They had been warned. But what could they do?

He found himself in a narrow passageway, repeatedly having to flatten himself against its walls as crew came through from both directions. Finally, he grabbed hold of one young seaman and asked where Buchanan could be found. The youth pointed out the way and Harry pressed on. Inexplicably, his injured arm now began to hurt, sharply at first, then with a duller, throbbing pain.

He lurched through the hatchway indicated, emerging into a remarkably crowded space. Buchanan, a beaky, older man, was in the midst of a crowd of uniforms, standing near the helm and complaining to an engineering officer about leaks. A river pilot was standing just to the side of him, looking steadily through an open, forward-facing hatch and calling out the course to the helmsman.

Harry moved along the wall to gain a better view of the other officers. He finally saw Mills off to the left, conferring with another man in uniform over a map or some engineering plan.

When Mills failed to notice Harry standing before him, Harry touched the lieutenant's shoulder, an inconsequential act among old acquaintances but an impertinent one aboard a warship. Mills looked up, ready to snap, then froze, his mouth hanging open slightly. "Raines? You?"

"Hello, Palmer."

"What in damnation are you doing on my ship? You're supposed to be in Chimborazo. Damn all, I shot you, Raines!"

"Not well enough, Palmer. Just tore out a little skin, though it hurts, I will say."

"I could have killed you—should have. If it weren't for this fool regulation against dueling . . ."

"Lieutenant Mills!"

It was Buchanan, his hawk-like face flushed with color. "Sir?"

"What is this altercation? Who is this man?"

Mills stammered. "No altercation, sir. He's from Richmond."

Harry waved his faithful letter. "From General Lee, sir."

Buchanan's complexion darkened further. "I've not authorized you to be aboard this ship. All civilians were to go ashore. We're under way, damn it! Remove yourself from this deck!"

Obedient, Harry started for the exit. Mills, highly agitated, followed close behind.

"What is it you want, Harry?" he said, when they reached the companionway beyond. "Haven't you plagued my life enough?"

"I need a question answered."

"You came all this way to ask me a question? For God's sake, man. Arabella's dead. Your man Caesar Augustus is dead. You and I have fought a goddamned duel. Can you not now drop this thing? Has it made you crazy?"

"Just one question. Can you tell me of a slave child, one that Arabella was going to have sold down the river?"

Mills furrowed his brow. "A slave child?"

"Yes. Marked for sale."

"There may have been such a child," Mills said, finally. "But I think it ran off."

"Was it Estelle's child?"

"I don't keep close watch on the domestic lives of those people. What have you done with that woman?"

A seaman hurried by, carrying a leather-handled metal box.

"I took her to Belle Haven."

"That's theft."

"No, she came on her own. Who was the father of this child?" Harry asked.

"Damnation, Raines, with these darkies, you never know."

That was hardly true. Harry's father kept track of the bloodlines of his slaves as dilligently as he did his horseflesh—to Harry's immense disgust—for the very same reason.

"Was it your coachman, Samuel?"

"Could have been."

"How about my man Caesar Augustus?"

"You'd know that before I."

Someone was calling out Mills's name.

"Palmer," Harry said. "Your Samuel is dead."

"How can that be?" Mills stared at him. "You kill him?"

"Estelle did."

"Estelle?"

"He was coming at me with an axe, and she shot him."

Mills grabbed Harry by the shoulders and thrust him back against the bulkhead.

"What more you goin' to cost me, Raines?" He shoved him again with even more vehemence. "What else? Am I goin' to lose my commission now, 'cause you took a mind to follow me onto this ship?"

A sailor was at Mills's elbow. "Captain Buchanan wants to see you right away, sir."

Harry shook himself loose from Mills's grip, then reached into his pocket, removing the two carved African figures he'd retrieved.

"A moment more, Palmer," he said, extending them in his hand. "Have you ever seen these things before?"

Puzzled, Mills took one, holding it up to whatever light was in the corridor. He returned it, shaking his head.

"No. Damned slave nonsense." He took a step, then

halted. "I'm going to have you put ashore at the first con-venience, Raines. Then I don't want you to come near me—ever again! I swear, you come back to Richmond, you're dead!"

He stalked off, the sailor following. Not a minute later, two marines appeared, each taking Harry by an arm.

"This way," said one.

They took him a deck below, to a small officer's cabin containing a table, chair, closet, and bunk.

"You're to wait here," the marine said. "Lieutenant Mills's orders."

"What is this?"

"His cabin."

There was a small, hanging lantern, but it was not lit. When they closed the door, he was left in darkness. Harry heard the click of a lock.

H E struck a match, and retrieved the lantern. Striking another, he touched it to the lantern wick.

One of Mills's uniforms hung on the back of the door. It would be folly to put it on. There weren't but a dozen officers on the ship, and they'd all be well known. His next stop would be the brig, if this peculiar vessel pos-sessed one. After that, the gallows.

Leaving the uniform unmolested, he set about a search of the tiny cabin. The most interesting thing he found was a bound packet of letters, which he quickly perused. They were florid and dramatic, in places quite passionate, and quoting Shakespeare's sonnets. All were unsigned—though he knew the hand to be Louise's.

Inside a drawer, he discovered a photographic *carte de visite* portrait of Louise, along with a framed, formally posed daguerreotype of Arabella and a little girl, along with another photographic plate of Bella when she was younger, possibly about the time she and Harry were trothed.

He pondered it sadly, then returned it to the drawer. The one of Louise, however, he pocketed.

For a while, he lay back on Mills's bunk, listening to the noisy throb of the *Virginia*'s gigantic steam engine and the wash of water just the other side of the hull. They were not traveling very fast. Whatever her virtues as a warship, they did not seem to include speed, and her deep draught could be dangerous in bodies of water as full of shoals as Chesapeake Bay and Hampton Roads.

If only he had some means of informing the Union forces across the water of these facts.

Harry took out the two figurines. He hadn't examined them very carefully, assuming them to be nothing more than little totems from Caesar Augustus's interest in the dreadful Voudon that had been more his mother's religion than slave camp Christianity. Harry remembered that Caesar Augustus had kept one of them on his person. Now two.

He took off his spectacles and held one of the objects close. As he had not realized before, it was highly detailed—a miniature work of advanced craftsmanship. The head was much like the African masks he had seen his father's slaves sometimes making, and was clearly male. Placing it now gently down on the mattress, he raised the other to his eye.

Just as clearly, it was of a woman.

Harry sat up, rubbing his chin. Then he stood up. Taking out a now very soiled handkerchief, he wrapped the two figures with great care and placed them deep in a pants pocket. He put his wallet and his pocket pistol in the other.

He had to get off this boat.

Chapter 23

FROM time to time, Harry heard running footsteps in the companionway outside, and once, voices just outside his door. But no one disturbed him. He doubted he'd been forgotten. More likely, he'd been put out of mind until Buchanan's more pressing concerns were dealt with. If there was to be a battle, he'd be left here. The cabin was below the waterline, and presumably safe.

Unless, of course, the *Virginia* sank.

Crouching by the keyhole, he got out his penknife—thankful that they'd not bothered to search him for weapons—and worked Boston Leahy's magic on the lock. Opening the door just enough to steal quick peeks both ways down the corridor, he listened. He could hear a noisy mingle of sounds, including men shouting, but nothing near. Overall was the rhythmic thump of the engine. He closed the door, then extinguished the lantern. He'd wait.

A very long time passed—easily an hour, possibly more. The ship's passage was so regular Harry found himself lulled almost to sleep. Then came the sudden sound of a cannon shot. It was loud, and apparently near, but not from this ship.

Reopening the door, then closing it as several sailors trotted by, he stood back against the wall, just as the cannon, wherever it was, fired again.

Harry could stay in this confinement no longer, but he knew he'd be spotted the moment he went outside. If Mills's officer's coat was too dangerous and useless a disguise, there were at least a hundred and maybe two hundred crew aboard. Being taken for one of them would be much easier.

After thinking a moment in the dark, he removed his coat, waistcoat, and shirt and made a bundle of the garments, which he set carefully by the cabin door. Off came his boots and socks next, placed beside the bundle. The ship's interior was hot. If there weren't sailors dressed in this informal fashion yet, there would be once the engagement truly got under way. Harry doubted he'd have to wait for very long.

The cannon fired again, sounding a bit closer. Harry heard a concussive whang against the hull, and then the splash of water. It was time.

Putting his spectacles carefully in place, he stepped out into the corridor. The shouting, apparently coming from the *Virginia*'s gun deck, was vociferous now—generated more by excitement than command.

There were several wooden buckets under the stairs leading to the main deck. Harry took one and started up the steps. There was dirt and oil aplenty. He stopped to smear some over his face and shoulders, then, head down, made for the guns, trotting quickly along the raised gangway that ran between the twin lines of cannon.

No one stopped him. He didn't halt until he had reached the far end, where a Parrot rifled cannon pointed through the forward gun port over the bow. Crouching by a support beam, he was able to see forward, though his view was only of open, empty water, with a thin line of land at the horizon. Moving to the other side, he found a better vantage point. He could see the source of the cannon fire, a Union steam tug apparently armed with a Parrot rifled gun of its own. It fired two more shots, then turned, heading toward what appeared to be Newport News.

"You, sailor!"

He'd been discovered. He rose, turning toward the voice, hoping it wasn't an officer.

It was, but he had found no fault with Harry greater than malingering.

"Why are you larking about there, you lazy son of a bitch?"

"Sir?"

"Get down to the magazine. We're going to need more powder. Forward."

"Yes, sir!"

Harry was uncertain just where the magazine might be, but guessed amidships, not far from the wide main staircase. That proved near enough. He told an enlisted man he encountered he'd been sent for powder but had gone to the wrong place. The man gave him a curious look, but then provided directions. It occurred to Harry the fellow was in fact malingering himself, having perhaps a reluctance to be on the gun deck as the *Virginia* chuffed on toward battle.

The crew stationed in the powder hold were happy to oblige him with enough to be toted but much heavier than Harry had expected. Shouldering it, he started to trudge away, when he was halted by a sailor's voice.

"Where's your station?" the man asked.

"Forward gun," Harry said.

"You're supposed to tell me that."

"Aye, aye."

He managed to get his load to the gun without stumbling, whereupon the officer commanded, "More!"

Other crewmembers were performing the same chore. Harry got in line with them. Every time he returned to the forward Parrot, he stole a look through the ports.

There were now two high-masted frigates in view, the tug heading for the one at the left. The alarm had been given in the Union fleet and black smoke was pouring from the funnels of smaller vessels anchored nearby as they got steam up.

As Harry thunked down the sixth package of explosive, the wound on his left arm hurting badly, the officer told him to leave off his fetching and stand by.

"Yes, sir."

Harry retreated to the nearest beam, crouching down again to look through the gun port. The *Virginia* was turning, but with dismaying slowness—another flaw in the supposedly invulnerable Monster. This was indeed to be a sea trial—of the most hazardous kind imaginable.

Rising slightly, Harry squinted for a view of the *Virginia*'s bow. There was no wind at all now, and nothing at all in the way of waves, yet water was coming over the foredeck.

Of a sudden came the sound of more explosions. They'd drawn nearer the point of land and Harry could see puffs of smoke rising from the Union batteries. One of the high-masted frigates then unleashed a rolling broadside. All the shots fell short.

The steam tug had taken the other frigate, on the left, under tow, bringing it around so that all of its guns would bear. As soon as it had done so, the ship's beam side flamed with cannon fire. Harry heard splashes and then more accurate thumps and bangs of a rain from hell, as cannonballs and shells struck the *Virginia*'s forward deck and casement. Struck and bounced. Harry was some forty feet from that iron plating and, except for the hideous noise, could discern no effect.

Buchanan was holding his fire. The ironclad continued its lethargic turn, an inexorable, malevolent force ignoring the defense fire as a mastadon might flies. This sangfroid was perhaps too bold. When the range closed more, the enemy shot might prove the master.

The "enemy?" Harry had been in the Confederacy too long. He belonged on one of those Yankee ships lying off the bow—or, more preferably, on the land beyond.

The *Virginia*'s guns were now all loaded and primed, the gun crews standing by in taut anticipation. Both the Union frigates had the range now and were whipping the ironclad with solid shot and explosive shell.

Again no effect, though a few sparks and metal fragments spattered through the forward gun port when a shell exploded just below it.

The *Virginia* still made no reply. The officer was shouting at him, but Harry couldn't hear any of the words. Not knowing what the man wanted, he ran again for more powder, wondering when the *Virginia* would fire its first shot.

When he returned, the officer had gone. He set down the powder package and sat on it.

Whang!!! Solid shot hit the *Virginia*'s upper plating just a few feet from Harry's head, showering him with a sooty dust. He moved behind the support beam. It was difficult to discern much out the gun port now, as the Union guns had laid so much smoke.

Mills and another officer entered the area, examining the walls and ceiling for damage. He stood for a moment just inches from Harry, looking up at the beam, then he moved on, as though Harry was not there.

More fusilades. More crashes and banging. More sooty dust. Here at least was open ventilation, though sweat continued to run down Harry's back. He wondered how hard this must be on the men below the waterline.

A gunner officer barked an order loudly enough for Harry to hear—a command to spread sand on the decking around the guns. Harry knew enough about naval matters to understand the point of that. The sand would soak up blood.

The *Virginia* had completed its turn and now was heading straight for the high-masted frigate on the left. As the Federal fire continued to strike, cannons bellowed on either side of the *Virginia*. She had picked up escorts Harry hadn't noticed before, and they were announcing their presence and intent.

An officer descended from the upper deck and rushed to the lieutenant in command of the gun deck. It was difficult to make out everything he said, but Harry picked up "captain" and "signal for close action." Then came, "Run out your guns!"

The well-trained crews leapt to the task. Harry's view forward was obstructed by some of their efforts, but he could see they were steaming steadily toward the left frigate, the progress grudging, but inexorable. All the while came the maddening thuds of the cannonball rain, interspersed with exploding shells.

One member of the Parrot crew was proving too enthusiastic for his own good, in his haste knocking loose several heavy round shot from their stack, one of them rolling over his foot. Hopping on one leg, howling from pain, he brought operations to a halt until the gunnery officer intervened.

"Get yourself to the surgeon," he hollered. Looking about, he took happy note of Harry. "You, take this man's place."

"Never worked a gun crew before, sir."

"What? What's your duty station?"

Harry tried to think. "Haven't been assigned one yet, sir. I came on as a last minute replacement."

An exploding shell struck near the gun port, causing one sailor to jump back as flying embers spattered around him.

"They'll tell you what to do. Step lively!"

He was given the job of fetching powder. He decided on the spot that, if the time ever came for him to put on a uniform in defense of his country, it would not be a Navy one. There were advantages to the Secret Service, and one of them was the luxury of sitting out naval engagements in the comfort of a hotel bar.

Another solid shot kabanged against the outside casement wall near him, showering Harry with more sooty dust. Then a shell exploded in almost the same spot, its smoke drawn in through the ventilator and darkening the deck.

Harry coughed like all the others.

They were now very near the frigate, which was firing every weapon it had at the *Virginia*, in concert with its sister frigate to the right.

One of his crew grabbed his arm and pulled him back. Harry looked at him strangely, then heard the shouted word, "Fire!" From the corner of his eye, he saw someone pull the lanyard, and then the Parrot let loose, its great weight snapping back along its wood and metal slide as though it were a child's toy. The report was so deafening, Harry thought at first something had gone wrong and the cannon had burst. But it was intact. Harry looked through the port again, just in time to see the shot strike the Yankee frigate's starboard quarter rail, sending up a shower of broken wood and dismembered men.

He had contributed to those deaths. His own people. His country. He recalled General Lee saying that he had declined the command of all Union forces because he could not possibly bring himself to raise his sword against Virginia. Harry had helped strike such a blow, against his country. He felt ill—and angry.

He would get off this vessel—somehow. In the meantime, he had to change onboard occupations, fast. He went to the stack of shot and pretended to better arrange it, very deliberately causing one ball to come loose.

It struck the deck, not his foot, as he intended, but then proceeded to roll over two of his toes anyway, which had not been his plan. He howled as loudly as his erstwhile comrade had done, though the man had been much worse injured.

The gunnery officer succumbed to a daft mix of rage and bewilderment. The former gained the upper hand and for a moment Harry thought the man was going to strike him with his sword—or shoot him.

Instead, he just shoved Harry backward, then returned to his duties. Several of the *Virginia*'s guns were now in play. Already deafened, Harry could hear their reports only as muffled sounds, but the shudders of the deck came close to toppling him.

He careened backward, seizing upon the upright beam. There was so much smoke and confusion now the gunnery officer seemed to have forgotten him. The Union ship was looming large now, orange flares appearing along its hull, smaller, sparklike flashes showing along its rail.

If those meant bullets, Harry could not hear the ping of their hits.

His two injured toes had turned nearly crimson, the nails dark, doubtless from blood. The pain had been replaced with numbness, which Harry did not take as a good sign.

"Go to the surgeon!" Someone shouted close by him.

Limping, he started aft, glad to escape.

He did not get far. Returning to the main gun deck,

whose crews as yet had nothing to do, he asked after the doctor's whereabouts. He'd taken no more than two steps in the indicated direction when he was grabbed by the shoulder from behind and spun around.

"Raines! What are you doing?"

Harry gave Mills an honest, disgusted answer. "Helping the Southern cause."

"What do you mean?"

"I'm on a gun crew." He looked down at his partially disfigured foot. "Anyway, I was."

Mills took his arm, hard.

"Have you lost your mind?" His face came nearer, as though Harry's held some secret he was only just divining. "Why are you here on the *Virginia*?"

Harry had another question.

"The child, Palmer—is it yours?"

"What in hell are you talking about?"

"Did you father a child by the slave woman Estelle?"

Three or four Union cannon shots hit the thick, iron-plated wall beside them nearly simultaneously, jostling them where they stood. Mills looked an insane man. He turned around, completely, looking first to the helm, where Buchanan was barking out a stream of orders; then to the inside of the battered bulkhead, and then back to Harry.

"What hold do you have on her?" Mills demanded. "What magic spell have you cast?"

"On Estelle?"

"On Louise!" He stepped forward again, taking Harry by the shoulders. "Why wouldn't she let me kill you?"

Harry had no answer. He never knew what he should believe about Louise Devereux.

"I'm going to leave this ship, Palmer. Now. But I must know this. Whose child was Arabella going to sell down the river? Was it yours, or Samuel's?"

Mills turned away, looking to two nervous marines who held muskets at order arms. He pointed to Harry.

"Arrest this man! He's a Yankee agent!"

Startled at first, then seemingly glad to have something useful to do with the sea battle raging all around them, the two marines stepped forward. Harry hobbled backward, then bent low and shoved his way past them, his foot hurting horribly as he banged the injured toes on an iron bar.

He headed straight for Buchanan, who looked at him now with some alarm. A moment later, the *Virginia* crashed to a halt. Harry was knocked to his knees and sent rolling forward. As he painfully got to his feet, finding both of the pursuing marines also down, a great cheer went up within the ship.

Harry looked past the fierce-countenanced Buchanan, eyes fixed on the viewing port just beyond the man. It appeared just wide enough. It would have to be.

With only two scrapes of sharp metal against his right side, he shoved his way through, gulping marvelously fresh air and sliding down the sloping casement to the iron deck. The sea water cascading over it was cold. Harry lifted his eyes. No wonder the otherwise sluggish *Virginia* had so suddenly stopped. She'd rammed the Union frigate near her bow. The two ships were jammed tight together, nearly prow to prow. Union marines on the deck of the sailing ship were laying down a compelling small arms fire. It seemed almost that Harry could dance on the bouncing bullets.

Ignoring the pain in his foot, as well as that in his arm, back, and skull, he ran across the deck to the left, hurling himself into the water.

Chapter 24

HARRY could not tell which side was shooting at him. For a time, it seemed to be both. He kept underwater as much as he could, swimming alongside the federal vessel but not toward it, not until he reached the stern and swung himself behind it grabbing hold of the rudder chain—for the time being, out of the musket fire.

The name of the ship was writ large just above him. The *Cumberland*.

It looked to be a hard climb up to the deck, but he wasn't sure he wanted to be up there just yet. The *Virginia*'s fire was devastating, each shot striking true and throwing up clouds of smoke, debris, and men. The Confederate gunners had cleared the fore and after decks and were now going after the federal cannon.

The Union vessel made no effort to escape this punishment. Harry at first thought it might have run aground on a shoal, for it had full sail up and hadn't budged an inch. But another look found the sails hanging slack. The ship was becalmed. Its fate would be shared by all the other sailing vessels in the Yankee fleet, if the wind would only stir.

Peering around the side of hull, he watched as the *Cum-*

berland kept up its fire despite the slaughter progressing along its own deck. From here, he could observe the magical phenomenon. Every ball bounced straight up or to the side, denting the *Virginia*'s plating, but causing the ironclad little bother. The exploding shells, though spectacular to see, damaged nothing.

Buchanan had stopped his return fire, concentrating on a more pressing matter. Under the waterline, the *Virginia*'s mighty ram had gored the *Cumberland* mortally, but it was stuck fast.

Among the cries of pain and anger above him, Harry heard a new burst of shouting. The wooden-sided *Cumberland* was sinking. But in her death throes, she was performing a noble service for her sister ships. The *Virginia* was straining, black smoke pouring from her stack, but she could not pull herself free of her victim. Harry had no idea of the depth of water here, but if it was enough to put the federal frigate completely under, she could take the Monster to a watery grave with her. He felt like cheering, but refrained. The desperate *Cumberland* crew would misunderstand.

The *Virginia* shuddered, then paused in her labors, as if to catch breath. Oddly, her prow still impaling the side of the *Cumberland,* she began to drift sideways. There was no wind, but the tides were strong in these waters, and the incoming current was pushing the ironclad back onto the beam of the sailing ship, making an opportunity for broadsides.

The Confederates quickly took advantage. The four cannons began a rapid fire, smashing great holes into the frigate's hull and blasting showers of wreckage into the air. Somehow, the Union gunners kept up a return fire. The space between them began to fill with smoke, weirdly illuminated from within by the orange flame from the cannon barrels.

Harry swam back to the rudder chain of the frigate, hooking an arm over it. Sailors from the *Cumberland* were beginning to jump into the water. Some simply fell, splashing into the sea and then floating there, not moving.

There were two fierce explosions and then a pattering rain of wood and metal fragments over the surface. Looking to his right, Harry saw a Union sailor floundering along.

"Over here!" Harry shouted. "Grab the chain!"

The man heard him, and with a clumsy, ineffectual stroke came nearer. Harry feared he'd not make it and so let loose of the chain and went to him, pulling him to the rudder.

"If she goes down," said the man, who seemed to be of some high enlisted rank, "this is a bad place to be."

"Is she sinking?" Harry asked.

"Yes."

"Can you swim far?"

"Yes, but I got a big sliver in my leg. Can't get it out."

There was another broadside from the *Virginia*, which was swinging yet nearer, almost parallel to the *Cumberland*. Harry wondered if Buchanan meant to take advantage of this proximity and send a boarding party.

But there was no need. The *Virginia* of a sudden broke free, throwing up water over her stern deck as she lurched backward. It occurred to Harry, that with the sideways pressure, the ram must have broken off inside the dying frigate, as Harry once saw happen with a bayonet thrust into a Confederate soldier.

If gone, the ram had certainly done its work. Without the ironclad's prow in it, the hole in the *Cumberland*'s side was now a gaping intake of seawater. The ship began to heel as rapidly as it was settling at the bow.

Harry looked about, spotting a flat piece of deck wood floating some twenty yards distant.

"Can you get to there?" he said to his companion.

The man winced. "Guess I got to."

They released the rudder chain and struck out. Harry found himself too weak with fatigue to haul the other man and keep afloat. As he moved along, he kept looking back, fearing the fellow would slip beneath, but somehow the sailor labored on. When they got to the planking, he helped the man shove himself upon it. The splinter he'd talked about was sticking out of both sides of his thigh.

Holding on to their makeshift raft, Harry began to kick. They were much too close to the *Cumberland* and it was going down fast. Harry's hopes that it might simply settle on the bottom with decks above the waterline were quickly dashed. The swirling seas curled over her. In the end, only her masts protruded. The sailors who clung to them were lucky they'd not been shot away.

Content with its victory, the *Virginia* began to move away, commencing a slow turn toward the other Union frigate, which had commenced a fight with three small wooden-sided Confederate vessels.

Harry's injured sailor friend began cursing, an amazing, seemingly unending stream of words.

"We're done for," the man said.

Turning to see what had prompted this, Harry realized he was quite right. The Union tugboat he had seen hours earlier was bearing down on them, spewing smoke. On its bow was the name *Zouave*.

AT the last instant, the tug steered to avoid them, turning nimbly, then hove to just shy of the mizzen mast of the sunken frigate, its crew going to the rails and into the sea to haul aboard what they could of the *Cumberland*'s crew.

Harry and his raft companion were seen to quickly and placed side by side on the tug's aft deck. The wounded sailor, so stoic in the water, began to cry out from pain. Harry, shivering now, ripped open the man's trouser leg, jarring the jagged splinter and causing more grief. The injury was nasty, and blood was still oozing from both sides of the thigh, but the fellow could count himself lucky. If it had been a musket ball, it doubtless would have smashed the bone and cost him the leg, if not his life.

Harry snatched at a member of the tug's crew as he came by.

"This man needs a surgeon," Harry said.

"They all do, mate."

"Are we headed for Fortress Monroe?"

"Not very damn soon. Got to help the *Congress*."

"The what?"

The crewman gave him a hard squint. "Your sister ship. The *Congress*." He pointed forward.

"Right you are."

When the man had moved on, Harry knelt again by the injured sailor, who gave him a forlorn look.

"They'll have no surgeon aboard," Harry said. "Do you want me to pull out that wood splinter?"

"It's hurtin' worse."

The wound was oozing more blood, but not in great volume.

"No whiskey," Harry said.

"Just do it."

Harry tore of a strip of cloth from the pants leg, rolled it into a thickness, then handed it to the man to bite down upon. When he had it in place, Harry quickly put his foot on the man's leg, took hold of the offending wood projectile, and yanked.

It came out with ease, though blood spattered on Harry's foot and began to flow from the puncture. The sailor cried out only once, though his hands kept clenching at the air.

Using what remained of the torn cloth, he made a sort of bandage, winding and tying it tight.

"That's the best I can do."

"You're not off the *Cumberland*," the man said.

"No."

"What ship then?"

Harry hesitated. "The one that sank you."

"You son of a bitch."

"I'm not one of their crew."

Lies, lies. The gun crew he had assisted may well have fired the shot that injured this man.

The man's face had blanched white. In a moment, he lapsed into sleep—or unconsciousness. Rising, Harry went forward, A crewman who took note of his shirtless state reached into a bag and gave him a sailor's blouse. He was grateful, but it didn't stop the shivering.

Finding a place finally at the bow, he sat down on a coil of heavy rope, wishing for a country not so insanely bent on destroying itself. He yearned for Louise's bed as though it was some impossibly distant paradise.

It was easy to divine the tugboat captain's intent. The other frigate, presumably the *Congress,* was under fire from the three smaller Confederate vessels, all wooden hulled. The frigate, still becalmed and lacking steam power, was taking a pounding from these inferiors. If the *Virginia* joined the contest, it would be as doomed as the *Cumberland.*

The *Virginia* was slow, the tug much faster. If it reached the *Congress* in time, it might be able to take the frigate under tow and move it to safer waters.

*   *   *

For a time, it seemed that the *Zouave* might succeed. Reaching the *Congress* well ahead of the *Virginia*, the tug took a hawser off the frigate's bow and began chugging shoreward. The orders came from the *Congress*'s captain. Neither Fortress Monroe nor the federal batteries on Newport News Point were near enough, but if they could get the vessel into shoal waters, she could at least be kept from sinking. With her guns above water, she could still fight.

All went as hoped. Drawing the frigate into the shallows obliquely, the tug was able to put her aground with her hull turned broadside to the open water and her pursuer. But Buchanan was highly sensible to his ironclad's peril out of its depth and halted her some two hundred yards off—a cat contemplating its mouse.

The *Congress* began firing its guns, but, stuck in the mud, could only traverse them so far. Buchanan, blessed with an incoming tide, shifted his ship until the Union weapons could no longer bear.

Then he proceeded to murder the *Congress*. An initial broadside took off the figurehead and bowsprit forward and the pilot house aft. Those that followed chewed off bit and parts, the exploding shells starting several fires.

As the ship was being savaged, so was the crew. Crouched down in the bow of the tug, looking up at the frigate, Harry saw a human head go sailing into the air like a ball in a game, then plummet into the sea. The *Zouave* worked to take aboard the injured, but came under fire also, a shell whizzing not six feet above the bow and Harry's own head. Small boats came out from shore intent on rescue, but the *Virginia* punished them for their good deed with some long-distance fire.

But she hadn't forgotten the *Congress*. After intimidating the rescue boats, her guns returned to the stricken frigate. Another shot came across the bow of the *Zouave*.

A second, following closely, hit the *Congress* forward, the explosion setting off a fireworks of huge sparks and fiery trails. Two men appeared at the ship's rail, both aflame. One rolled over the side and into the sea. The other fell back.

Harry stood up, driven to this exposure by an uncontrollable anger. The malevolent form of the ironclad lay off at some distance, but he felt as though its regard was directed at him. Its menace took on a human form as he imagined Mills standing at one of the gun ports, contemplating Harry the target as he had in their encounter with pistols.

More exploding shells. The air was full of a snow of bits of flame and burning debris. The *Zouave* had not been hit, but there was a lot of blood on her deck. Harry shook his fist at the *Virginia* and began shouting at it, at Mills, at all of them, at Jeff Davis back in Richmond. The words he used would have caused his sister to blanche.

Someone pulled him down. He returned to his rope coil, wrapping his arms around his knees and closing his eyes.

The din at once evaporated. There was still some firing, but not near. The *Virginia* had halted its attack again. Harry looked up. The *Congress* had struck her colors.

Its deck now crowded with men from the two frigates, the *Zouave* bore off, as though making room for two boats that now set out from the idled southern ironclad. Harry assumed that they'd been sent to secure the formal surrender of the ship—and to scuttle it.

A boat from the *Congress,* amazingly still intact, came forth to meet the others. The ensuing colloquy could only be imagined, but appeared unsuccessful. Instead of taking the *Congress*'s officer prisoner, the *Virginia*'s boats sat where they were as the officer was rowed back to his dying vessel. He scurried back onto his burning deck, then disappeared below.

Looking to the ironclad, Harry saw that it was continuing to receive hits. Sporadically, heavy shot still struck its plating. The fire was not coming from the helpless *Congress*, but from soldiers on the shore.

Abruptly, the *Virginia* let loose a broadside in angry retaliation. The shells roared across the intervening space of water and seemed to strike the *Congress* everywhere. There were more explosions, more leaping wounded and hurled bodies.

Harry heard shouting from the *Zouave*'s wheelhouse. The tug's engine coughed and chuffed, and the craft began pulling away, lest it, too, become a victim of this barbarity.

"Bastards," someone said.

The tug headed northeast, toward a line of other Union warships. Harry kept his eyes on the *Virginia,* surprised that it did not pursue. Making another of its slow circles, it disdainfully put its stern to them, making for Norfolk across Hampton Roads.

As Harry had not noticed, it was growing dark.

THE *Zouave* took them to a wharf just shoreward of the line of Union warships. The injured were debarked first. One *Zouave* crewman, seeing the blood on Harry's leg, helped him to his feet.

"No," said Harry. "I'm all right. But I need to speak to an officer."

"What?"

"Your captain. I have information about the *Virginia*."

"Wait here."

He remained where he was as the last of the crews of the *Cumberland* and the *Congress* were taken off. Finally, an ensign and two armed sailors came up to him.

"You wanted to talk to an officer?" the ensign said.

"Yes, sir. I have . . ."

He was yanked to his feet.

"You'll get to see plenty," the ensign said. "They're taking you to Fortress Monroe, Reb—with all the other prisoners."

Chapter 25

THERE were only five other prisoners. Two from a smaller Confederate vessel named the *Teaser* that had been bested in a fight with one of the Union gunboats and three cavalry troopers who had strayed too close to the federal lines west of Newport News. Tied together, they were marched from the wharf along a rough dirt road that led along the river toward Hampton and the Union Army post called Camp Hamilton. It was a long and hard trek. Harry's bare feet suffered more than a little and when they reached their destination he asked again to see an officer.

There was no immediate response to his request. He and the others were put in a shed with straw on the floor, but no other comfort. Everyone but Harry went immediately to sleep. Instead, he found a place near the drafty door that the others shunned, somehow keeping awake as he waited.

His patience was rewarded, though it took a very long time. A sentry with a lantern opened the door, peered within, then summoned Harry.

"I need shoes," Harry said to his erstwhile companion.

"All you Rebels need shoes," was the reply.

The officer he was brought to was only a lieutenant,

and a young one at that. Harry worried that the man might well ignore what he had to tell him for fear of annoying a superior.

He listened, politely. "You claim you're with the intelligence section?"

"I am with the Secret Service. A scout. If you want to verify this, telegraph Washington. A Major A. E. Allen. Telegraph him at either the War Department, the President's House, or General McClellan's headquarters on H Street. Tell him you have Harrison Raines in custody. That I am off the Confederate ironclad *Virginia* and have information."

At the mention of McClellan, the captain had made a notation on a piece of paper. When Harry spoke the name of the *Virginia*, he made another. Then he sat back.

"You were on the *Merrimack*?"

"Now styled the *Virginia* by the Rebels. Yes, sir."

"How'd you get aboard her?"

"I slipped aboard when she was leaving her mooring at Portsmouth."

"How'd they let you get into the Gosport Navy Yard?"

"Sir, if you will just telegraph Major Allen, then I'm sure everything will be explained to your satisfaction."

"Why not explain now?"

"I'm not sure how much Major Allen wants me to say."

The lieutenant pondered that, then nodded, as though in approval.

"I have things I need to report about the *Virginia*—er, the *Merrimack*," Harry added.

"She killed a lot of our boys today."

"Yes. Sadly, she did."

The lieutenant called to the soldier who had brought Harry to him, then scribbled a note.

"I want you to take this prisoner up to Fortress Monroe," he said, when done. "And get him a coat and some shoes."

"Yes, sir. Should he be manacled?"

The lieutenant pondered this as well.

"Yes," he said.

He was provided with a pair of too-large boots, a private's rough wool jacket, and a cavalry trooper's breeches with yellow stripes on the side of the legs. Harry wondered if the trooper's garb had been prompted by his telling them he was a scout. No matter, he was greatly appreciative.

Bound at the wrists, he was put in the back of a small supply wagon, so crowded with boxes to make the ride extremely uncomfortable. The route ran along the shore to Hampton, and then down the long peninsula that led to Point Comfort. Two mounted soldiers, bored with their duty and unhappy in the cold, rode escort to either side of the wagon. There was no need for them. Given the opportunity to escape, Harry would only have looked for a place to sleep.

He managed somehow to doze as they bumped along, until jolted awake by the sudden thunder of an enormous explosion and a flare of brilliant light out on the water. Harry thought at first that the ironclad had returned to finish the bloody work it had begun that morning, but quickly realized they would not dare take it out in the darkness, with so many shoals waiting to trap it.

"It's the *Congress*," said one of the soldiers to the other. "It's the end of her."

The captain had thought to save the ship from sinking by running her aground, but that failed to halt the spread of the fires to its powder magazines. Harry was amazed she hadn't blown up earlier.

Two of the Union's finest warships were now just debris, yet the *Virginia* had steamed blithely away, dented, singed, but essentially unscathed. What havoc might she wreak on the morrow? On all the morrows? The panic she had generated in the North wasn't so unreasonable after all.

The flames illuminated the entirety of Hampton Roads with an eerie orange glow. Off to the south, lying in waters not far from the hulking walls of the fort, was a strange, low shape. For a moment, Harry took it for the bottom of some foundered, capsized vessel. But then he noted the high, dark cylindrical silhouette that rose from its deck.

"You see that?" Harry asked one of the soldiers, pointing toward the apparition.

"Looks like something broke loose from someplace," was the reply.

"What do you suppose it is?"

The man shrugged. "Dunno. Maybe one of those floating batteries."

He turned his horse. The wagon driver resumed their progress. Harry sat back unhappily. Shakespeare had written no tragedy as sad as this.

THEY gave him a room within the fort's casement walls. It had a small shuttered window, a decent cot with two blankets, and a lantern hanging from a hook on the stone wall. Harry was provided with a meal of cold beef, bread, and excellent coffee.

When he was done, he lay back on the bunk, abruptly recoiling from a sharp prick of pain below his hip. Standing, he reached into his pocket. His captors had taken his wallet and other possessions, but left him the two little African figures. Lying back again and pulling the blanket over him, he held them up to the light, admiring once more their remarkable craftsmanship.

Squinting, he brought the female figure very close, studying something he had not noticed before.

She had a large, round, protruding belly.

THE door slammed open. Raising his head, Harry saw two soldiers stride in and come right to his bunk.

"You're to come with us, at the double quick."

They were serious. With one of the men ahead of him and the other just behind, they hurried as best Harry could manage through the stone and brick passageways of the fort, coming to a halt in a large interior court. Harry was made to wait while one of the men went to a door and knocked. It opened, and in a moment, Harry was beckoned forth.

It was the commandant's quarters, and it was full of officers, Army and Navy. Harry noted two brigadier generals, a colonel, and a Navy lieutenant. They were in the midst of a meal, though it was in the middle of the night.

Harry was told no one's name and was not invited to share in the feast, but was given a chair, which they turned toward the officers' table. He felt very much like a criminal in the dock, as perhaps had been the intention.

He was harshly queried about his escape from the *Virginia*; his explanation was received skeptically. There were several pointed questions about the Secret Service and operations in Richmond, but Harry refused to give any details. Oddly, that seemed to diminish some of the skepticism.

Odder still, when he told them everything he knew about the *Virginia*—its slow speed, its clumsy turning ability, its dangerously deep draught, its poor ventilation— they seemed little interested. Only the naval lieutenant, a handsome man with full moustache and beard and slicked down hair, asked a question, and it appeared more a schoolmaster's test of Harry's knowledge than a request for information.

"You say deep draught. How deep?"

"Two decks below the waterline, sir."

"You sure? How many feet?"

Harry shrugged. "Two dozen."

"Twenty-two feet?"

"Could be."

"Twelve guns?"

"No, sir. Ten. Two Parrots—one fore and one aft. And four smooth bore cannons each side."

"Is Buchanan still its captain?"

"He was when I ran past him to jump off the ship, sir."

"Not Catesby ap Jones?"

"No, sir."

"And the steering's sluggish?"

"A half hour to turn one hundred eighty degrees, sir."

The officer nodded. Harry had passed the test. His inquisitors hadn't learned very much from him, but they didn't much seem to care.

A few of them lighted cigars. Harry looked at them hungrily. His own smokes had been ruined by the rain, and it had been days since he'd had one.

The brigadier took note of this, but shook his head, as though disapprovingly. Soldiers appeared to either side of Harry again, and he was returned to his stone-walled chamber.

THE next time, it was a clank of keys that disturbed his sleep. It was hard to see his caller, as the lantern had gone out and the shuttered window admitted only a few thin shafts of light from what appeared to be a newly rising sun.

"You're Harrison Raines?" a man asked.

Harry squinted, then reached for his spectacles. His uninvited guest was in uniform—and an officer. Harry had given his name freely and repeatedly to his captors. Why didn't the fellow know that?

"Yes. I'm Raines. Who are you?"

Without reply, the officer turned on his heel and walked out again. A moment later, another, much taller, very muscular man entered, dressed in civilian clothes that fit him too tightly.

"In the nick once again, eh Harry?"

Harry was suddenly terribly confused. He was certain he was in Fortress Monroe and that he hadn't succumbed to visions.

"Joseph?" He sat up.

Leahy looked to the officer. "Open that shutter and then leave us be, if you would, sir." He thought further. "If there's some coffee, and biscuits, I'd be obliged."

"Yes, Mr. Leahy."

When they were alone, the light of day slowly filling the room, Leahy pulled up its only chair close to Harry's cot.

"They told me there was a man here asking after a Major A. E. Allen," he said. "I figured it might be you, probably had to be you. But I thought you'd be leaving Richmond the way you went in—west, along the mountains. Not down the peninsula."

Leahy sat very erect, as always, but was at the same time entirely relaxed. He was the fittest man Harry ever knew. Thrown into a prison, he'd be the last man standing.

"How did you get out of Libby?" Harry asked. "No one gets out of Libby."

"Only two ways I know of," said Leahy. "In an exchange for Rebel prisoners, or feet first dead."

"You're not dead."

"They sent me out on the very next prisoner exchange to Monroe—that very day. My reward for what they must have considered services rendered. I suppose they also feared my brother federal officers would take unkindly to me."

"Reward for what services?"

Leahy grinned. "Murderin' that vexatious darky."

Harry could not believe a single word. He wished mightily he was hallucinating.

"You killed Caesar Augustus? It was you?"

Leahy kept grinning.

"Damn it, man! Answer me!" He was gripping the edge of the cot so tightly he suddenly realized the sharp edge of the iron frame was cutting into his fingers.

"It was the only way he was going to get out, laddy buck. Feet first. The poor devil was doomed as soon as he stepped inside that infernal place."

"You killed him to spare him execution?"

Leahy leaned forward, remonstrating with Harry as he might a child. "Harry. The man's alive. I only wounded him—and not badly. The rest was play acting. He's got a way with it, that fellow. A regular John Wilkes Booth."

"Mr. Leahy, I was informed by General Robert E. Lee himself that Caesar Augustus was slain—and by a Union officer."

"Aye, that was me." He rose and came over to Harry, reaching to put his finger to Harry's bare, grimy chest. He drew an invisible line just below the collar bone and then down to the armpit.

"I cut him like that," he said. "Lightly, then deeper where the chest and shoulder muscles come together. Nasty wound. Looked like hell. Bled all over the place.

Sure looked mortal. Must have hurt like damnation. But he survived. And he stayed perfectly still. Doubt I could have done that. You, either."

"And he's still alive?"

Leahy frowned, as though something had been misunderstood. "Did not Miss Van Lew tell you, then?"

"Miss Van Lew? I was told she took his body. I didn't meet with her again."

"She made everything possible. Raised such a ruckus over your Caesar Augustus that no one much bothered the 'remains.' She lit into me like some banshee. That was a great performance, too. 'Crazy Bet.' "

"She didn't tell me."

"Sorry, laddybuck. Didn't mean to leave you in such doubt. Happened fast. He's on the mend, your fellow. Miss Van Lew and her people got him through the lines, such as they are on this boggy peninsula. He's here— safe—in the contraband camp over by Hampton."

Harry stood up, his joints aching. "I want to see him."

"Not just yet, boyo. Is it true you got aboard the ironclad?"

"Got aboard. Got off—in the wrong place."

"If it got you here, you picked the right place, though I think Major Allen would have been a bloody lot happier if you had remained in Richmond. Did you know that Edgar Allan Poe once stayed here at Fortress Monroe?"

"As a prisoner?"

"No, as a sergeant. Must have been much the same thing, as he left the Army shortly after."

"Why does Pinkerton want me in Richmond?"

Leahy went to the door, opened it, looked up and down the corridor, then closed it again.

"First thing, he was pleased to learn about the Confederate Congress and conscription. That was fair useful news."

"But I wasn't able to get it out of the city."

"Yes you were. You may not know the how of it, but it got out."

"Through Miss Van Lew?"

"As I say, you may not know the how of it."

"Well, I no longer hold the confidence of Mr. Davis, that is for certain."

"That may not matter, boyo. In a few weeks, Mr. Davis may not matter, either."

"What fantasy is this?"

"True, it's hard to believe. But it's happening at last. McClellan is finally going to move. He's coming down here, and he's bringing his army with him."

"Here where?"

"Here! Fortress Monroe. They're going to land a hundred thousand men or more here and march up the peninsula all the way to Richmond. Then the war is over. Or so he's told Mr. Lincoln."

Harry sank back on his cot, sighing. "I'm afraid I haven't contributed much to the cause of Union arms. I tried, but . . ."

"We all do our bit, mate. And it would seem you've done yours. But the war is far from over, and we've got a terrible lot more to do. Mr. Pinkerton now wants us out of here—as soon as possible. He fears we may have made ourselves too famous."

"Wants us to go to Washington City?"

"I'm supposed to go west. Far west. New Mexico Territory."

"Why? The war's not there."

"Will be soon. Your friend Jeff Davis is supposed to have designs on it. Something about a railroad, a Reb invasion from Texas, grabbing California.

"And me?"

The room echoed with the ringing reverberation of a cannon shot. Another swiftly followed.

"The *Virginia*'s out," Harry said. "It's begun again."

Leahy crossed to the window, peering out of it.

"It's a poor view," he said. "Let's find a better one."

THEY were allowed up on the fort's parapet, though a sergeant looked askance at Harry's peculiarly mismatched uniform, for he was still wearing a sailor's blouse beneath the soldier's jacket. Nearly all the garrison seemed to be lining the walls, as though preparing to repel an assault, though they were simply spectators to one. Along the shoreline to the right, there were more—mostly civilians. Harry was reminded of the battle at Bull Run the summer before. He hoped this one would end better.

A second cannon shot led his eyes to a large puff of smoke in the middle of Hampton Roads. As the breeze blew it clear, he saw two vessels—the hulking *Virginia,* and the flat little ship with the huge turret on it he had noticed in the night. The Confederate ironclad was on a course straight for the fort and the Yankee ships moored below it. The mysterious Union craft was moving swiftly toward the larger Rebel ship to intervene, firing as it went, though at slow intervals, two or three minutes between each pair of shots.

Leahy had borrowed a pair of field glasses from a junior officer and let Harry use them. He could see more clearly through the expanding veil of smoke. Though both combatants moved slowly, the smaller Union ironclad appeared almost to dance around the clumsy *Virginia,* a slow and graceful waltz to the other's plod. Many of the Confederate ship's shots missed, whizzing aft. Those that struck, bounced off the Union vessel as the *Cumberland*'s had off the *Virginia.*

"I don't understand how the federal ship works," Harry asked. "How do they turn that huge turret? If it's covered with iron plating, it must weigh many tons."

"More than a hundred tons, they say. I don't know much else about it, but it takes two steam engines to make it go around. The whole contraption rests on a shaft, like a pencil. That man Ericsson designed it, the fellow who invented the screw propeller. They've been building it up in New York the last three months. They named it the *Monitor*."

"Then they knew about the Confederate ironclad. They didn't need us at all."

"Harry. They made haste because of you people in Richmond. The *Monitor* only got here last night. Think if they had dawdled with more sea trials in New York. That damned Rebel boat would be sitting right off the shore there, blasting this fort—with the Union fleet a shambles."

An orderly came up bearing a large plate with two tin cups of coffee and a pile of decent biscuits. Harry was impressed by Leahy's standing with the military. He must have reported directly to the commanding general here.

The *Virginia* had been making for a new victim—a two-masted Union frigate Leahy said was the *Minnesota,* lying in shallow waters not far off the western ramparts of the fort. It sat so motionless Harry decided it must have run aground much like the unfortunate *Congress* the day before. If the *Monitor* proved unable to stop the *Virginia,* the frigate would be as doomed as its sister warships.

The ironclads continued to make their circles around one another, the *Monitor*'s agile, the *Virginia*'s not. But the circles were moving them back toward the *Minnesota,* and the rest of the Federal squadron.

"The damned British thought up these monstrosities," Leahy said. "Used them in the Crimean War as floating batteries. Now they and the Frenchies each have an ironclad ship, though neither's said to be much good. They're just sailing ships with a lot of iron nailed onto them. But these two—they're the first of their kind. No sails. Wholly steam powered. Armored everywhere. Armed to the teeth."

"The Union ship, it has only two cannon I can see."

He lowered the binoculars.

"Eleven-inch Dahlgrens," Leahy said. "They're enough to handle the Reb boat—as we can plainly see. And that turret lets them fire from any angle."

"But to no effect."

"Aye, not yet."

Drawing quite close, the two ships suddenly fired fusilades at each other almost simultaneously, so much in unison Harry wondered if their cannonballs might strike each other in mid-air. The *Monitor* appeared to stagger, though that was hard to tell at such distance. It drew off, then maneuvered itself onto the *Virginia*'s bow quarter, denying the Confederate ship a shot. The closest Rebel gun was the Parrot Harry had worked on.

The *Virginia*, billowing forth smoke, strained to maneuver yet closer, bringing port guns to bear. Two of them fired, then a third. The *Monitor* backed off and turned to starboard, its turret swiveling in the other direction, but too fast, failing to stop in time for the gunners' next shot. Both Dahlgrens fired, the balls splashing astern of the *Virginia*.

All four port guns on the Confederate ship responded, all four shells screaming over the *Monitor*'s low after deck and proceeding on, two of them striking the helpless *Minnesota*. For the first time, Harry began to feel nervous on this perch. He sipped his coffee, calming himself. He needed to get his brain working.

Now the *Virginia* began a slow turn in the opposite direction, trying to steer a course that would bring its bow to bear on the Union ship. Harry figured Buchanan was going to try to ram his adversary, as proved so fatal for the *Cumberland*. Whoever was commanding the *Monitor* apparently read the maneuver and countered with one of his own, attempting to get at the *Virginia*'s stern. He'd be aiming at the rudder. If he could smash the Rebel's steering, she'd be helpless. They could board her, or push her until her bottom foundered in the mud.

But, somehow, she evaded the Union ramming gambit, the *Monitor* sliding close, but then on by. Receiving a broadside from the *Virginia* as its reward.

"They may be the mightiest warships on earth," Harry said. "But they seem so feckless. It's like watching a chess game in which both players have only a king."

"This could be the war, Harry," Leahy said. "Right there, those two ships. If that Rebel ironclad can't be stopped, she'll tear apart our blockading squadron—all our blockading squadrons."

Harry had seen firsthand the truth of that. He reminded himself of the actual size of the *Virginia* and the heavy caliber of its guns.

"She draws too much water to make it all the way up the Potomac to Washington City," he said. "Mr. Lincoln has nothing to worry about."

"Maybe so, but she could get near enough to Baltimore, or Philadelphia, or New York. She'd sure as hell be able to knock down any house in Boston she chose to. Victory here, it changes the whole war. McClellan might change his mind, all his plans. Call off the invasion."

"That's the only ironclad they've got."

"For now. Us, too."

"I'm sorry," Harry said. "I tried. I found out what I could. I passed everything on to Miss Van Lew. I'd no idea they'd be putting to sea so soon."

Leahy hesitated, but spoke his mind anyway. "Like I

said, you did your bit, Harry. But you didn't do yourself or us any favors, getting all caught up in that woman's murder. That nasty business was something you could have foregone."

"Now how could I do that, Joseph? They took Caesar Augustus. And that woman, as you refer to her, for all her Southern notions—well, she was once important to me."

"But a slaver."

"George and Martha Washington kept slaves."

"They let them go. Were you still in love with that . . . with Mrs. Mills?"

"She was my first love. You never get over that. No matter what."

"Well, you can leave it be now. She's asleep in her grave. Caesar Augustus is safe. It's over."

"No, Joseph. It's not over."

The ironclads were coming at each other once again, but on parallel courses, fixing for broadsides.

Again, the *Virginia*'s shots missed, but the *Monitor*'s double blast ripped apart the Confederate's funnel, leaving it dangling a tattered mass of metal over the casement. Smoke and sparks spewed out of the gaping hole left in its place. If there was a way to drop shells through it, the *Virginia* could be sent to the bottom.

"I got off that ship too soon," Harry said.

"You ask me, you got off just in time."

"No. Palmer Mills was on the *Virginia*. He may be aboard today. He never answered a question I asked him—an answer I need to know. And he has a picture. A photograph. I should have looked at it carefully. I just glanced at it."

"Palmer Mills. From the Tredegar Ironworks?"

"You're familiar with him?"

"Very."

"I could have killed him. I had a chance to."

"Murder's not our trade, Harry."

"Not murder. A duel."

Leahy glanced at Harry's arm. "That how you got your wing clipped?"

"It was."

"And you missed him?"

"I didn't aim at him. I fired into the air."

"That's fortunate."

"Why? He helped create that terrible weapon we see down there."

"It's fortunate for you because, as memory serves, you're about as good a shot as General McClellan is a battler. Fortunate for us, Mills is still among the living— unless he chanced to get hit by one of the *Monitor*'s cannonballs."

"Not much chance of that. They all bounce off, as you can plainly see."

"Well, that's fortunate like I say."

"Damn it, explain yourself, Joseph."

"Mr. Pinkerton likes all of us to know as little about each other as possible, but you should know this about Mills. He's working for us."

"What? That's impossible."

"I didn't say he knows he's working for us, but he is. We have learned a lot these past weeks, thanks to him."

Harry nodded, not to Leahy, but to himself. Louise had made him more than a little nervous by pressing him to tell her if he was a Yankee spy. He suspected she had come to believe he was, and that had made him very nervous. Little had he realized she'd take comfort in the fact, being a Yankee spy herself. Or so it seemed.

"You mean thanks to Miss Devereux," he said to Leahy.

Leahy's index finger went to his lips. "That's all we ought to say about the matter, Harry. Even here. She's in a lot more danger now than we are."

Harry finished his coffee and stood up.

"I'm going to go find Caesar Augustus," he said.

"If this sea battle goes wrong, Mr. Lincoln's going to need both of us. He'll need everyone."

"Whichever way it goes, it looks to take a long time getting there. I'm going to that contraband camp." Harry nodded toward the headquarters building across the fort's central parade ground. "How much influence do you have with these people?"

"A fair bit. The name of Major Allen works quite a lot of magic."

"I need a horse. I can't walk very well." He held out the arm of his private's jacket, which was too short. "Is there somewhere I can acquire some civilian clothes?"

"Not on these premises. Maybe in town."

"How about something with a higher rank, then? In this, I'm afraid I'm going to be set to digging latrines."

"All right, boyo. I'll see to it." Leahy took a step, then halted, as did Harry.

The two ironclads were very close now. From this distance, it looked as though they had collided, though they were still moving, the *Monitor* steaming the fastest. It backed up, turning its stern away, a maneuver that brought its bow right under the *Virginia*'s guns.

The *Monitor* had one disadvantage. Its steering was in a small, armored pilot house set far forward on the deck, almost at the bow. It stuck up like a thumb, and now the *Virginia*'s gunners took aim at it.

When the smoke cleared from their blasts, the structure was still standing. But some sort of damage had been done. The ship began to pull away, back toward Fortress Monroe.

"I need to go," Harry said.

"Surely not now?" Leahy admonished.

"Now."

Chapter 26

THE officer's jacket Leahy procured for him had captain's bars on the shoulder straps. The foraging cap that went with it made Harry feel foolish, but with it and the rest of his now complete uniform in place, no one bothered him. He rode his borrowed horse right through the gates of Camp Hamilton and down its dirt main street unimpeded. A sergeant readily answered his request for directions to the contraband encampment, which lay just to the north of the military establishment.

Union batteries were firing further along the shore—at what, Harry could not tell, but he paid them no mind, remaining fixed on his destination.

He was amazed at the size of the Negroes' jury-rigged settlement. There seemed as many Sibley tents in this muddy enclave as there were in the Union Army post, and they were far more crowded.

There were a few soldiers about; none of them helpful. The Army had been so overwhelmed by black refugees from the Confederacy that it had long before ceased keeping count. It had never given much thought to taking names.

But Caesar Augustus would have a unique distinction—

the chest wound given him by Boston Leahy. He described this to a corporal who was in charge of a small Negro working party. The soldier thought a moment, then sent Harry over to a collection of smaller tents near a meandering stream that wound by the camp.

The moist ground sucked at Harry's large boots, slowing his progress. Small children ran about him, splashing into the water and then bounding back again from its cold. A few walked along behind him. Women with wide bands of cloth wound around their heads stood here and there, eyeing him solemnly, some a little fearfully. They would have no idea who he was. Slavery was still legal in the U.S., and for all they knew, Harry was someone's old master, come to retrieve his property—though that would of course now be impossible.

One woman appeared friendlier than the others.

"I'm looking for a man," said Harry. "He's hurt. He has a wound here." He pointed to his shoulder. "A big man, named Caesar Augustus."

She smiled, broadly, but the expression faded.

"Why you want him, Massuh?"

"I'm his friend." He hoped that was still the truth.

"You say friend?"

"I want him to do some work for me," Harry said. "I want to hire him. Pay him money."

She grinned again, then pointed to a tent down the line. "They down in there."

"They?"

The woman pointed again. "They down there."

HARRY hesitated outside the tent. The flap was closed, but untied. If he called out, he might spook whoever was inside.

He pulled back the flap, and stepped within. Estelle

looked up from a pallet at the side, where she was seated repairing garments in the light of a small lantern. At her side was a child, a little girl of five or six. When she noticed Harry, she drew back a little, the lantern illuminating her pretty face.

In that moment, nearly all Harry's questions were answered, as they might have been had he thought to more closely examine the photograph Mills had aboard the *Virginia*.

The tent roof was too low for his six feet of height. He sat down cross-legged on the other side of the clothing Estelle was mending. Her eyes stayed upon him. Otherwise, she did not move.

"You join de Yankee army, Mister Raines?"

He shook his head. "I'm just borrowing these. I had to leave most of my own clothes behind."

The child came up to him, fingering the gold on his shoulder straps. He smiled at her, but it wasn't returned. Only curiosity showed in her face.

"Did my sister get you through the lines?" he asked.

"Nosuh. Not her."

"Why not?"

"She didn't think it be very safe. She say to wait 'till later, but I'se afraid of your father. I don' know what he be fixin' to do."

"How did you get here then?"

"I go to the preacher man, like Miss Van Lew says."

"What preacher man?"

"Reverend Haynes. He got a church in Ruthville. Miss Van Lew say to go to him if I get down here and got no place else to go. So I go to him, and he bring me here in a wagon—me and Evangeline."

"Evangeline."

She put her hand on the little girl's shoulder. "This be

Evangeline. Reverend Haynes been keepin' her 'till I come."

"How was that?"

"Miss Van Lew and Caesar Augustus, they got her to him—so she not be sold down the river."

"This was on the day Mrs. Mills was killed?"

Now her eyes fell away. The child turned and darted out of the tent. Harry rose, painfully, and went out after her.

Estelle made no move to follow, until Harry commanded her to.

He stood and watched the girl skip down the muddy tent street. She was easily the best dressed person in the camp. Her silk dress was torn and dirty in places, but very expensive. She wore several petticoats, and finely made leather shoes. Blue shoes.

"She is not your child, is she, Estelle?"

"Nosuh. I done tol' you that."

He put his arm around the woman, intending it to be a comforting, reassuring gesture, but also a restraining one.

"Estelle, you are free now. No one's going to put irons on you or whip you or sell you down the river. You're not going to get in any trouble because of what happened to Mrs. Mills. In Richmond, maybe. But not here, not with me."

"Yessuh, Mister Raines." She was trembling.

He kept his arm around her shoulders. "Estelle, I know it was you and Samuel who brought Arabella to my room that day. You brought her to the hotel the way she'd come in before—through the back, dressed as a man, carrying her female clothes in a carpet bag. Only she was already dead, wasn't she. You held her up between you. Isn't that so?"

Estelle bit down on her lip.

"Isn't that so?" Harry said.

The child was on her way back, skipping some more, pausing to pick up something from the dirt that had fallen from her pocket. She studied it, then continued on.

"Yessuh," said Estelle, softly. "I didn't harm her none. Samuel didn't neither. Like you say, she already dead."

"Dead where?"

"At the house in Manchester. Mister Mills tell us to bring her to the hotel, like we done before, and put her in your room. He was powerful mad at you, Mister Raines. He say you kill Mrs. Mills. He say you should pay for your crime."

"But I didn't commit any crime. I wasn't there. You know that."

"Yessuh. I know that now."

"Did Samuel kill Arabella?"

"She could be mean sometimes, but not so mean as he do that. Samuel no fool. He know what happen to him if he hurt that lady in any way. They hunt him down with dogs an' shoot him right off, like they were fixin' to do to Caesar Augustus."

"Why did Samuel attack me?"

"You was trouble, Mister Raines. Big trouble. Samuel, he hung Mrs. Mills's body up in yo' room, so's the Plug Uglies come for you. But they let you go and then you turn up at our place. He musta figured you comin' after him. He afeared you goin' to kill him, or take him off to the hangman. I don't think he mean you no harm, otherwise. Except maybe he might be doin' Mister Mills a favor. He and Mister Mills, they good friends. Mister Mills paid him money for what he do."

"Why did you shoot Samuel? You fired four times."

"Save your life."

"Be honest, Estelle."

"I is. He was fixin' to kill you. He do that, the both of us get strung up. Samuel get killed, nobody goin' to care much, 'cept Mister Mills. Mister Mills and Samuel, they friends."

"Why didn't you tell me what happened before?"

"Mister Mills say he sell us both off as field hands down to the cotton plantations if we talk to anybody about anythin'. He say it only be right you hang for Mrs. Mills death 'cause everything is all your fault."

The little girl had rejoined them and stood peering up at Harry.

"Are you a soldier?" she asked.

"No," he said. "I'm just a friend of theirs."

She reached into her pocket and showed him the object that had fallen—a soldier's brass button.

"You want it?" she asked.

"Thank you, Evangeline. But I already have many buttons." He smiled, then on impulse took the Confederate button from his pocket. "Here, now you have two."

The girl held them both in one hand. They matched, both from a Confederate uniform.

He studied the delicacy of her small, gentle face. Her skin was the color of café au lait; her curly hair a dark red, like old copper, with tiny golden glints. Her lips were full, very grown up for a little girl's—and her eyes were green.

"Can you read?" he asked.

"A little."

"Do you have a doll?"

"I have lots and lots of dolls. Pretty dolls."

Harry patted her on the head, then looked around the camp. There were very few men in sight—the better part of them Union soldiers.

"Where's Caesar Augustus?" he said to Estelle.

"Down by the water, doin' carpentry work. The army's buildin' things."

"But he's badly injured—a stab wound."

"He's mendin'. And he say he don' mind. They pays him money—lot more'n Mister Mills pay Samuel—help us to get up north."

"Are you going to take care of Evangeline?"

"Yessuh."

"I mean, hereafter."

"Yessuh. That's what I done back home. When she lived in the big house. Least until this war over, and everythin' get sorted out."

"But where will you go?"

"I don' know. I'se free now."

He put his hand on her shoulder. "Estelle, I want to help you—you and Evangeline."

"What you mean?"

"You can't stay here. I don't want you to stay here."

"You ain't goin' to send us back to yo' sister? Not back to that plantation?"

"No, Estelle. Not that. Never that."

"You a nice man, Mister Raines."

Harry sighed. "Sometimes I could be nicer."

Harry started to walk away, but something nagged him to a halt.

"Estelle," he said. "Miss Van Lew. Did you talk with her while you were at her house?"

"Yessuh. She come up and talk to me when I was in the secret room."

"Did she say anything about me? Tell you not to talk to me about all this."

"She say I should be careful around you—not tell you anythin'."

"Did she say why?"

"She say you weren't very good at what you do. She say she afraid you let slip somethin' to Jeff Davis or that general and we all get put in Castle Godwin."

* * *

HE found Caesar Augustus working a long, cross-cut saw with another black man, using only his right arm. His left sleeve was torn off, and a large, dirty dressing was wound around that shoulder, but otherwise he seemed not much affected by his wound.

Harry waited until they had finished cutting their plank, stepping forward as they reached to pick up the slab of wood.

"Let me help you," Harry said.

Caesar Augustus stood up straight, saying nothing, eyes hard, his expression empty.

Harry looked for someone in authority, settling on a fat sergeant dozing on a pile of lumber a few yards distant.

"You, Sergeant!" he called.

The man sat up, then stood up. "Sir!"

"I need this man for a while."

"Yes, sir!"

They walked along the muddy shore, keeping to the dry brown and yellow grass.

"They told me you'd abandoned me, Marse Harry."

"Miss Van Lew did?"

"No. The Rebel officers at Libby Prison. Man named Maccubbin."

"Well, they lied."

Harry had no destination in mind. He only wanted to get away from the labor party.

"Boston Leahy," said Caesar Augustus, "he saved my life."

"Yes he did. He's a very brave and resourceful fellow."

There was an old weathered rowboat lying upside down just ahead. Harry gestured toward it. Caesar Augustus sat down on its stern, glad of the respite, if not necessarily the company.

"I was trying to prove you innocent," Harry said, seating himself as well. He wished he'd remembered to ask Leahy to find him some cigars.

"Why try to do that in a place like Richmond?"

"I might have succeeded if you'd been a little more forthcoming."

Caesar Augustus broke off a piece of wood from the boat's transom, then took out a pocketknife and started whittling.

"That woulda done nobody no good but me, Marse Harry. And maybe it wouldn't even do that."

Harry lifted his head, gazing out over the water. They were by a small cove that opened onto the wide one that ran north to the town of Hampton. The sun was high, and the breeze was warm. Listening for it now, he could hear the distant cannon fire of the still continuing sea battle.

Reaching into his pocket, he took out the two carved figures, holding them out in his palm to Caesar Augustus. The black man pondered the little sculptures, then quickly picked them up, setting them aside out of view.

"The female figure represents who?" Harry asked.

Caesar Augustus sighed. "I gave it to Estelle, Marse Harry. Long time ago."

"Not to Arabella Mills."

"No. Where you find it?"

"In my hotel room. On the floor. Why did you give it to Estelle?"

"She want to have a baby. It's supposed to be magic. She thought that, anyway."

"A baby by you."

"Yes. But it didn't work."

"Estelle is not the mother of that child."

"What child you mean?"

"The one who's here. The one you helped escape."

"No, Marse Harry. Evangeline is not her daughter."

"She's Arabella's daughter."

"Why do you think that?"

"I looked upon her face, Caesar Augustus. Her parentage is writ large."

The black man's knife dug too deep into the slice of wood, causing a chunk to break off. He stared at it, then resumed whittling.

"And you are the father," Harry said.

It was not a question.

Caesar Augustus frowned. "Miss Arabella told Mister Mills you were her father when Evangeline was born— after you and me went north to Washington."

"He accepted that?"

"Guess he did. He must a' hated it, but he accepted it— back then, when he and Miss Arabella got married, and all these years after. Only way he was goin' to marry her, acceptin' that child. Only way he was goin' to keep Miss Arabella."

"But you lay with her?"

"Why do you say that?"

"I said, her parentage was writ large. Her skin has such color."

Silence.

"I am not aggrieved by it, Caesar Augustus."

A sigh.

"When you went to the Mills house after we got into Richmond, it was to see her, wasn't it?" Harry went on. "Not Estelle. That's why Arabella was so agitated when she came to my hotel. Over you."

More whittling. The piece of wood was almost a chip itself.

"Only once, Marse Harry. I lay with her just once."

"You could have been strung up for doing that."

"I know that well. But I had become a free man then. I was mighty angry at all you white folks. It was a way of feeling free, of being free. And she wanted me. She was powerful mad at you."

It was growing late. Harry couldn't tarry much longer.

"I know there's not much point to my pressing on with this anymore," Harry said. "Even in a legitimate court of law, I'd have no proof. And it wouldn't do much good for anyone now for these things to be out in public. But, Caesar Augustus, I think I know what happened."

"Well, you're a smart man, Marse Harry, but I don't think you understand."

"Mills found out about your visit to his house. He's got a terrible temper. Arabella must have told him you were Evangeline's father, and he flew into a rage."

"So you think Mills killed Miss Arabella?" There was an edge of sarcasm to the man's words.

"No, I don't. A man that angry wouldn't murder his wife that way. Not by hanging her. He might beat her, shoot her, strangle her with his own hands. But not go to the trouble of a hangman's noose. Those were rope burns on her neck. Maybe not from the rope they found at the hotel, but rope burns nonetheless."

The muscles in Caesar Augustus's face were very taut.

"I think Mills found another way to get at her," Harry continued. "To hurt her, very badly. He threatened to sell the little girl into slavery. She'd been brought up white, but he was going to commit her to a life of bondage, just for spite, because she was your child."

"You got it wrong, Marse Harry."

"With your help, and Miss Van Lew's, Arabella was able to get the child to safety. But the sadness for her must have been overwhelming. She just couldn't go on as Mills's wife and suffer having her daughter gone. She went into the stable, fixed up a rope, and hanged herself. There was straw on her dress and stocking, Caesar Augustus. I found what was left of the rope."

He paused, thinking.

"Mills had Estelle and Samuel take her body to my hotel. I don't know if he wanted vengeance on me or was just afraid that he'd be accused of murder—like Othello and Desdemona. Perhaps it was both. But they did his bidding. Were it not for you, the blame would have fallen on me."

"Marse Harry, I don' truly know how Miss Arabella died. Your explanation sounds sensible, but you got to understand something."

"What I don't understand is why you confessed to it."

An actual smile. "They were going to kill me anyway. Would a' done it were it not for Mister Leahy. I thought she ought to be remembered better than was likely otherwise. And I wanted you to stop what you were doing, stop frettin' over me—and her. Get on with what we came for."

"In the end, I'm not sure how much what I did mattered."

"Everything we do against this goddam Confederacy matters to me, Marse Harry. Every gun. Every bullet. Every one of 'em that falls."

Out on the water, the cannon fire was continuing.

Caesar Augustus ceased his whittling. He looked at what he had carved, then tossed it into the water. He kept the knife in his hand.

"Miss Arabella didn't like her husband much, Marse Harry. She married him only because she was with child, and she had nowhere else to turn after we left for the North. But they did not love each other in any way. Always fightin'. Always trouble. She come to hate her life, like you say. After a while, she tried to get a divorce from him from the state legislature, like that actress Fanny Kemble got from that slaver Butler from the Sea Islands down in Georgia. There was adultery enough in the Mills family for such a writ on both sides, as we saw ridin' into town."

Harry had put the *carte de visite* photograph of Louise in his wallet. He wondered how well it had survived his swim from the *Virginia.*

"Only weapon Mills had to stop her," Caesar Augustus continued, "was he wouldn't let her take Evangeline if she left him. That's his right under law. A wife's no better than black folks in some respects."

"Where was she going to go?"

"To wherever you were, Marse Harry. To make him let go of the girl, she told him Evangeline was a black baby, and that I was her father. She thought maybe then Mills wouldn't want the little girl no more."

"That's when he threatened to sell the girl down the river."

"Yes sir. Miss Arabella, she got real unhappy, as miserable as any of the widows of this war."

"And so she hanged herself."

"Not then, Marse Harry. When you came back to town, she thought she was saved. That you had come back for her. She thought you would take her away. But when she came to the hotel, you just threw her out. It was like you threw her away. Once again."

Harry remembered. He wished he could not.

"She asked me to take Evangeline away to someplace safe," the black man said. "Once I was gone, I guess it was then she hanged herself, like you say."

The Negro workers back up the shore were singing now. They seemed almost happy.

Harry wiped at his eye with the back of his hand.

"Well then," he said. "I don't think we need to say any more."

"Somethin' you still don't understand, Marse Harry . . . I don't think Evangeline is my child."

"You said you lay with her."

"Well, that happened, that once. But, like I say, I was angry. And I was scared, too. Mighty scared. I saw the way that boy Lucien over at the Pembertons got whipped to death for kissin' their daughter. Your daddy made us watch that. Miss Arabella, I think she go with me only to get back at you, for leaving her. What I'm trying to say, Marse Harry, is that it didn't go very well. I don't think any child could have come out of that. And Estelle and me, mind we got no children, either, after all those times."

"And so?"

"I think Evangeline came from someone else."

Harry thought upon it. "Who?"

"Back then, when we was all so young, couldn't of been many had that opportunity, Marse Harry. Not out in Tidewater."

A cool summer night in the soft grass by the canal. The moon rising over the trees on Belle Isle. Their first time. Their last time. Because he was leaving, and not even her giving herself to him was enough to keep him in such a hateful place as the South.

Harry took a very deep breath. "I think perhaps you are wrong, Caesar Augustus. The Raines are a fair-skinned family." He held out his hand. "My sister Elizabeth is as fair as there is. Evangeline, she's a darker hue."

Caesar Augustus put his own large black hand next to Harry's. "That may be. But that little girl is as white as snow compared to me."

They both sat without speaking. The singing had stopped, and all was quiet. It occurred to Harry that the cannon fire out in Hampton Roads had stopped as well.

"I'm not sayin' you got Negro blood," said Caesar Augustus, finally. "That ain't the way in your family. But remember how you used to tell me about a granny you had, woman who grew up in the Indian country up in the mountains around Will's Creek. Dark-haired witchy woman, wild as they come. You used to tell me about her when we talked about Voudon, how she knew all kinds of Injun magic."

Harry made no reply, not for the longest time.

"What're you thinkin', Marse Harry?" Caesar Augustus said finally.

"I was wondering what might have happened if I had married her," Harry said.

"I think then we both still be on the wrong side of the river."

Harry stood up. He needed to leave.

"You want to leave this place, Caesar Augustus?"

"Next minute'd be too long."

"Go back to Washington?"

"Anyplace North."

"How about my farm?"

"That's in Virginia, Marse Harry."

"It's way upriver on the Potomac. So far north it's almost in Pennsylvania. You won't see many Rebel armies there."

"What do you want me to do?"

"Take care of things."

"You mean your horses?"

"Everything." He hesitated. "I'm sending Estelle there."

"Why are you doing that?"

"She has no other place to go."

Harry scuffed at his boot. He wanted desperately to be out of this uniform.

"Marse Harry, she's takin' care of the little girl."

"I'm sending her to the farm, too."

Caesar Augustus got to his feet as well. "Me, Estelle, and Evangeline, livin' like a happy little family."

"I'm not suggesting that. I'm sending them there to be

out of harm's way, and I'd appreciate it if you'd look after them."

"Like a father."

Harry said nothing.

"Marse Harry, how do you want that little girl brought up?"

Harry started walking back to the camp. Caesar Augustus lingered a moment, then came up following.

"Marse Harry, do you want Evangeline brought up white?"

"Caesar Augustus, I want her brought up the way Arabella would have wanted."

LEAHY and Harry stood at the port rail of the steamer as it plowed north up Chesapeake Bay. They were just passing the wide estuary of the Potomac—some fifteen miles across at this point.

"You still don't think the Monster could run up this river?" Leahy asked.

"Not near enough to Washington to do any damage, not drawing twenty-two feet. There are shoals all across the Potomac just north of Alexandria. She'd have foundered for sure."

"Well, it doesn't much matter now. That *Monitor* of ours sent her packing up the James. If she comes out again, she won't get far. The blockade holds. And all this big beautiful bay is Union water."

"She could still wreak havoc with General McClellan's march on Richmond, if he goes that way."

"I fear he knows that," the Irishman said. "He'll march slow. Probably go along the York River instead."

They had passed at least fifty southbound ships and boats. Looking now up the Potomac, they could see more craft dotting the hazy horizon.

"At least the campaign is under way," Harry said.

"Mr. Lincoln has got to be a happy man." Leahy grinned. "Did I tell you what he's supposed to have said when they showed him Ericsson's plan for the *Monitor*?"

Harry shook his head.

"He said, 'All I can say is what the girl said when she put her foot in a stocking: "I think there's something in it." ' "

The remark was worth at least a smile.

"You're taking a ship to Texas from Baltimore?" Harry asked.

"Yes I am. Under the damned British flag. But she's a fast steam packet. Get me to Galveston quick."

Harry looked toward the bow, where bunches of passengers were grouped on the foredeck, Caesar Augustus, Estelle, and Evangeline among them. The little girl was skipping around the two adults, still in her pretty blue shoes. She looked to Harry and smiled. He waved. Of a sudden, he wondered if he was about to make a mistake.

But he really hadn't any choice.

"We'll be at Point Lookout directly," Leahy said. "Then I guess it's good-bye to you for a while."

Harry reached into the pocket of the fine frock coat he had purchased in Hampton and withdrew a flask of whiskey, taking a draught. Leahy, a temperance man, watched unhappily, though not so unhappily as when Harry went to another pocket for a cigar.

"If it's all the same to you, Joseph, I'd like to accompany you to New Mexico."

"Truly?"

"Yes."

"I'd be right glad of it—if you'd try to curtail your vile and evil personal habits. In fact, Mr. Pinkerton suggested you come. I just didn't think you'd be of a mind to."

"Well, I am of a mind to."

"And why is that, laddybuck?"

Harry turned to look south along the green-gray Virginia shoreline, to where it disappeared into the haze. On the nearer water, the sun was sparkling.

"I've come to see what this war is all about. I know now what it's going to take to bring it to an end. I want to do whatever I can."

"It's going to take the destruction of the South."

"Yes. I'm afraid it is."

"But you're a Southerner."

"So is Abraham Lincoln."